PRAISE FOR HELENA HUNTING'S NOVELS

"Perfect for fans of Helen Hoang's *The Kiss Quotient*. A fun and steamy love story with high stakes and plenty of emotion."

—*Kirkus Reviews* on *Meet Cute*

"Bestselling Hunting's latest humorous and heartfelt love story . . . is another smartly plotted and perfectly executed rom-com with a spot-on sense of snarky wit and a generous helping of smoldering sexual chemistry."

—*Booklist* on *Meet Cute*

"Entertaining, funny, and emotional."

—*Harlequin Junkie* on *Meet Cute*

"Hunting is quickly making her way as one of the top voices in romance!"

—*RT Reviews*

"Sexy. Funny. Emotional. Steamy and tender and so much more than just a book. *Hooking Up* reminds me why I love reading romance."

—*USA Today* bestselling author L. J. Shen

"Heartfelt, hilarious, hot, and so much sexiness!"

—*New York Times* bestselling author Tijan on *Shacking Up*

"Helena writes irresistible men. I loved this sexy, funny, and deliciously naughty story!"

—*USA Today* bestselling author Liv Morris on *Shacking Up*

"Characters that will touch your heart and a romance that will leave you breathless."

—*New York Times* bestselling author Tara Sue Me on *Clipped Wings*

"Gut wrenching, sexy, twisted, dark, incredibly erotic, and a love story like no other. On my all-time favorites list."

—Alice Clayton, *New York Times* bestselling author of *Wallbanger* and the Redhead series on *Clipped Wings*

A
FAVOR
FOR A
FAVOR

OTHER TITLES BY HELENA HUNTING

PUCKED SERIES

THE CLIPPED WINGS SERIES

SHACKING UP SERIES

Shacking Up
Getting Down (novella)
Hooking Up
I Flipping Love You
Making Up
Handle with Care

STAND-ALONE NOVELS

The Librarian Principle
The Good Luck Charm
Meet Cute

A
FAVOR
FOR A
FAVOR

HELENA HUNTING

Montlake

Published by Montlake, Seattle

www.apub.com

Amazon, the Amazon logo, and Montlake are trademarks of Amazon.com, Inc., or its affiliates.

ISBN-13: 9781542015202
ISBN-10: 1542015200

Cover design by Eileen Carey

Cover photography by Regina Wamba of MaeIDesign.com

Printed in the United States of America

For anyone who's ever stayed in the shadows so someone else's light could have a chance to shine.

CHAPTER 1

BAD DAY

Stevie

As far as bad days go, this is one of the worst I've had in a very long time. I can get over the four-hour flight delay from LA to Seattle and sitting beside a man who smelled like old cheese and three-day-old underwear on the plane. But add in one of my suitcases taking a detour to Alaska—or maybe it's Nunavut; who the hell knows?—and the fact that my remaining suitcase now has a broken handle and is missing a wheel, and this day just keeps getting worse.

The icing on this crap cake? Less than an hour ago I walked in on my boyfriend, Joey—now my ex—plowing into someone who wasn't me on our brand-new living room couch. The one my brother bought for us as a housewarming gift. I guess that's what I get for surprising Joey by arriving two days earlier than expected. On my birthday.

"Are you sure you don't want me to come to Seattle and beat this douche down? I can leave first thing in the morning." My brother RJ is at his in-laws' house for the weekend, which is an hour and a half outside the city. That he's this fired up on my behalf makes me feel marginally better about the whole thing.

However, my brother is an NHL player, and a father and a husband. Allowing him to beat up my ex for being a douche and a cheater may assuage my decimated ego and help heal my broken heart, but it's not a great idea. For one, if RJ lays a beatdown, there's a good chance he'll wind up charged with assault. Then his face will be splashed all over the media, Joey will make a spectacle, and I'll get dragged into it. The last thing I want is *my* face on social media in connection with my famous brother and my slimy ex. So as much as Joey might deserve a broken nose and black eye, I'll say no thanks to the potential fallout. "I sincerely appreciate your willingness to engage in violence on my behalf, but I don't think it's worth the assault and battery charge."

"I hate that you're dealing with this on your own, and on your birthday, Stevie. If I'd known you were coming early, I would've planned for us to be around this weekend. What if I come get you and bring you back to Lainey's parents' for a few days?"

"It was a last-minute change of plans." And obviously not a great one. "And it's nice of you to offer, but the fact that you're setting me up with a place to crash is more than enough." I sincerely love my brother, but I am definitely not interested in hanging out with his in-laws during my postbreakup moping phase. "Besides, I start work at the clinic on Monday, so that would be a lot of back-and-forth for no reason. I promise I'll be fine." I watch the numbers flip by as the elevator ascends. Soon I'll be able to have a nice little meltdown after my craparific day. "I'm almost at the apartment. Why don't I call you in the morning?"

"Okay. I'll be up for a while longer, so if you run into any problems getting in, send me a message. The lock system is tricky until you get the hang of it."

"I'm sure it'll be fine; thanks again, RJ."

"Anytime, Stevie. You know that. I'm really sorry. Happy birthday, kiddo. We'll have dinner, and I'll get your favorite cake when we're back in town, okay?"

"Sure, sounds good. Thanks again. Love you, bro." I end the call and tip my chin up to keep the tears from falling.

The elevator chimes its arrival at the penthouse floor. I suppose the one plus to finding out my now ex-boyfriend is a cheater is that I get to stay in a much nicer place. At least until I can find a new apartment.

I adjust the broken handle of my suitcase as the doors slide open and roll-drag it and myself out of the elevator. I'm exhausted times a million and looking forward to a cathartic snot sob session. A pint or five of ice cream would also be nice.

I wish I could adequately appreciate the splendor of the open foyer, but my morose mood does not allow me that indulgence. As I step onto the soft, luxurious carpet, the broken wheel of my suitcase gets caught in that two-inch gap where the doors open.

"Seriously?" I yank on it, struggling to dislodge the broken wheel while the doors start to close, bumping against my bag before they slide open again. I toss my purse on the floor so I can wrestle it free, but it's jammed in there good and tight. The elevator beeps loudly, signaling that the doors have been open too long.

It's late, almost midnight, and I'm hoping these walls are sound-proof because I'm causing quite a ruckus. My suitcase finally pulls free, and I stumble back, tripping over my purse and landing on my ass. At least the carpet is soft and the floor is clean. I lie there for a few seconds, waiting for a piano or a safe to fall from the ceiling and land on top of me, because it's been that kind of a day.

When nothing else bad happens—for now—I pick myself up off the floor and decide the best way to deal with my suitcase is to slide it across the carpet to avoid making more of a racket than I have already. Unlike in a regular apartment building, there is no long hallway on the penthouse floor. Instead there are four doors in the open foyer—two on the left and two on the right—making it easy to locate apartment 4004. I guess that means it'll be quiet, if nothing else.

In the middle of the foyer is a glass-topped table with an enormous arrangement of flowers, which accounts for the heavy perfume smell. I skirt the table as I slide my bag across the carpet toward my temporary new home, then remember my purse is still sitting on the floor by the elevators.

The key card they issued at the front desk seems to have migrated to the bottom of my bag. I shift around the contents searching for it, but it's like it belongs to Mary Poppins with how much crap I have in there. I use my suitcase as a chair, the flimsy plastic exterior cracking loudly as my ass hits it. Oh well; it was destined for the garbage anyway with how mangled it is. A jagged piece pokes me in the butt, but I'm too tired to move.

The key card and my phone have both magically disappeared into a quarter-size hole in the lining of my purse. It takes me forever to fish them back out. I pull up the instructions on how to open the door, since apparently this building's key system requires a step-by-step explanation. After dragging myself to my feet, I key in the six-digit code, swipe the card, and turn the handle, but all it does is beep at me.

"I just want to lie down," I mutter to the door. I give the code a second shot, but I get another longer, louder beep. "What the hell? Why won't you open?" I whisper-yell. Each time I make an attempt to get in, the beep grows louder and longer while my patience wears thinner.

I yank on the handle, frustrated. I don't want to call RJ again because I should be able to open a damn door on my own. I'm probably missing something small. Also, it's late, and he has a toddler who doesn't always sleep through the night and loves to get up at ass o'clock in the morning. Kody is super adorable, though, so his rooster-level early rising is mostly tolerable.

The door directly across the hall swings open. Awesome. Now I've woken my temporary neighbor. Talk about bad first impressions. I turn with the intention of issuing an apology, but my mouth is suddenly desert dry.

A man stands in the open doorway. A very, *very* large man. My brother is a big guy; he towers over everyone with his six feet two inches. But this annoyed-looking man's head barely clears the door-frame. He's also broad. Excessively broad. He's an excessive amount of man in general.

Beyond being ridiculously tall and broad, and irritated based on his scowl, all he's wearing is a pair of boxer briefs. I might be able to get over his overwhelming size and his insanely gorgeous dark-brown, sleep-tousled hair complemented by fiery hazel eyes, a rugged square jaw, and full lips. I can also deal with all that toned muscle and his rippling abs and bulging biceps, finished off with a nice dusting of hair that leads my eye from his navel—it's an innie—down to his boxer briefs. But that's where I get stuck, because his crotch has the phrase **BEWARE OF FALLING ROCKS** with a rockslide right where his peen should be. So now it looks as if I'm checking out his package. I kind of am.

"What the hell is going on? It's almost fucking midnight, and you're out here making a goddamn racket. Some of us are trying to sleep." His voice is deep, gritty, and loud. He crosses his bulky arms over his cut chest, which should help cover up some of the nakedness but only seems to draw attention to how thick his arms are.

Also. Wow. Talk about hostile.

"Sorry. I'm having some problems with my key card and my suit-case." I flash the key card and motion to my destroyed bag. I'm suddenly super sweaty. Likely from embarrassment over getting chewed out by a hot guy in his underwear.

Hot-underwear man scoffs. He doesn't acknowledge my apology. Nor does he offer his assistance or tone down the dickbagness. "Where the fuck you get that key from?"

"How is that any of your business?" I scroll through my messages, trying to figure out what I'm doing wrong with the key card and the code so I can get into the apartment and away from this grade A asshole extraordinaire.

"It's *my* business because you're up here on *my* floor making an unnecessary amount of noise, and I'd put money on it that *you* paid someone off for that key card."

I pause my message scroll so I can glare at him more effectively. "Excuse me?" This guy takes the jerk cake with his asinine accusations. Such an epic waste of hotness.

He tips his chiseled chin up, glares down at me, and jabs a finger in my direction. He really is intimidating. "Which one of the security guys did you pay off? Or were there other favors involved?"

"Favors? What are you even talking about?" I'm super confused right now.

Underpants a-hole leans against the doorjamb, smirking as his eyes move over me. I'm wearing jeans and a T-shirt with a cartoon birthday cake on it. My hair is tucked into a beanie since I've been traveling all day and the humidity has not been kind to it. "You think I haven't seen this a million times? Chicks are always bribing security for keys to get up here."

"I did not—"

He cuts me off before I can put him in his place. "Look, sweet cheeks, I don't know what you've been snorting or mainlining or whatever, but there's no way you're getting in there without a code. And even if you do, I'm gonna go ahead and say that this whole shitshow"—he points to his face and motions toward me—"is one hell of a boner-killer, so stop embarrassing yourself and take your broke-down ass back the way you came."

Did he just say my face is a boner-killer? I have so had it with assholes tonight.

CHAPTER 2

WHAT'S YOUR DAMAGE?

Bishop

Okay, so the boner-killer comment may have been unnecessary, but it's midnight and I'm tired. I came out here thinking I would be confronting the dude who lives in 4001. Every time he's in town he throws a party that lasts for days. And then it's silence for at least a week, if not longer. Thankfully, he's gone more than he's here. Regardless, whenever he's around, there are also numerous scantily clad, potentially venereal disease–carrying women hanging out in the elevator.

Instead of the 4001 douchenozzle, I'm faced with this train wreck of a woman. Granted, as bad as she looks, she's still hot, but she's making all kinds of noise trying to get into my teammate's penthouse. The one he hasn't been staying in because he bought a house or something. With his wife and kid.

My conversations with Rook Bowman have been short and not entirely pleasant. I'm not his biggest fan. Almost every time we've played against each other in past seasons, one of us has ended up with some kind of penalty or other for being chippy. But my loathing for him hit an all-time high when he waived his no-trade clause and joined the Seattle expansion team at the last minute. It wouldn't have been so bad, but they also gave him the team-captain position that was supposed to be mine. His stupid fucking friendly "You can do it; we're a team!" attitude, and being in the coach's goddamn back pocket, only make me hate him more. I see through his do-gooder act. He also suggested that I be moved to defense, likely so I wouldn't be competition for his coveted first-line center position. Not that I'm bitter or anything.

And now it looks like he's got some sidepiece using the team-issued penthouse. What an asshole.

The woman sneers, her spine straightening. "I've had it up to here with dickbags." She motions to the top of her head. She's on the short side, so it's not very high. "Thanks for being so helpful and understanding with your insults and your assholery. That was exactly what I needed after this turdheap of a day, so really, much appreciation for your creative shit-slinging."

"I'm just telling it like it is. Not my fault if the truth hurts."

"Jesus, you really are an asshole, aren't you? Too bad your personality is in direct opposition to your exterior." She rakes her gaze over me on a huff. She almost seems irritated with herself for checking me out. As should I, if she's riding my married teammate in his spare time. "And why the hell are you out here in your goddamn underwear? Who even does that?"

Man, she's fired up, which would be semientertaining, except it's seriously late and I'm pissed off from having been woken up. I don't bother answering the underwear question, since it has no relevance to this conversation. "If anyone's being an asshole, it's you with all the noise."

She looks at her phone again while scrolling through messages. This time she scans the card and punches in a code. My annoyance spikes when she gets the green light. I guess Rook really does have a sidepiece, which proves he's not as perfect as he portrays himself to be.

The woman shoulders open the door and awkwardly drags her beat-up suitcase inside. "Thanks so much for your help. It's nice to be welcomed so warmly to the building." She shoots me the bird and disappears inside the penthouse.

For half a second I consider whether I should call someone, like our coach or maybe the GM, but I'm not sure there's a point. Rook is all buddy-buddy with our coach, Alex Waters, since they played together in Chicago for a number of years. And Waters is tight with the general manager. Besides, Rook's extracurriculars aren't my problem. If he's cheating on his wife, I sure as hell don't want to be in the middle of it.

I turn off the TV—which I'd fallen asleep in front of—and hit my bed. I expect to fall asleep right away, since I'm bagged, but I find myself wondering what the hell is going on across the hall for a lot longer than is reasonable.

The next morning I wake up late thanks to last night's hallway disturbance. I set a pot of coffee to brew before I grab the paper from the hallway. I don't read books, because they require a time commitment and I can't stay seated or focused long enough to finish one, but the newspaper is different. I can get all the basics from the sports section and scan the current events to keep up with what's going on in the world while I eat breakfast.

My semidecent mood sours as I open my door to retrieve my morning paper and glance across the hall. Now that I'm not being woken up from a dead sleep, I can admit that I was a jerk, although I believe I had a reason to be. Especially if Rook is keeping a pretty pet in his team-issued penthouse.

I'm about to go back inside when I notice my neighbor's door is ajar. My first inclination is to ignore it, since it really isn't my problem . . . but then I entertain several possible reasons as to why the door is open:

A. The hot train wreck from last night got lucky with the code and ransacked the place.

B. Rook stopped by to make use of his sidepiece.

C. Rook's wife somehow found out about his lover and decided to murder them both in the middle of the night.

If it's option A, then someone in security is about to be out of a job. But if it happens to be option B, and I catch Rook in the act, I could use it to my advantage. If it's option C and there are dead bodies in the penthouse, the hallway will eventually start to stink.

I slip the paper between the jamb and the door of my apartment to prevent it from closing all the way and pad across the hall. While I've seen a fair amount of blood thanks to on-ice accidents, dead bodies are a whole different story and something I'd rather not be subjected to. But in this case, a fresh body is better than one that's been hanging around for a few days, so really I'm doing my civic duty.

I knock on the door, and it creaks open several inches. I wait a full fifteen seconds before knocking a second time. When no one answers after another half minute, I peek inside and take a look around. No pool of congealed blood stains the floor. No obvious body lying anywhere. So I don't have to call 911 yet.

I listen for sounds of human occupancy, namely moans of pain or pleasure, but all I get is the whir of the air conditioner, so I call out, "Hello?" loudly. Still nothing. I really hope no one is dead. I enter the penthouse. It's exactly the same as mine layout-wise, but it's missing any personal touches, making it feel sterile, like a show home. Everything is pristine and untouched, so his guest hasn't ransacked the place, and there's no indication of foul play, although the latter might be more likely to be found in the bedroom, where the dirty deeds happen.

I shout, "Hello?" again but still don't get a response, so I continue toward the bedrooms. I'm halfway down the hall when a door swings open and the woman from last night appears. She's definitely in one piece. One freshly showered, towel-wrapped piece. A second towel is wrapped around her head. She looks a lot better this morning—less like last night's strung-out head case and more like . . . sex wrapped in black terry. She's athletic but curvy, the perfect balance of strength and femininity. Not waify and breakable. I'm annoyed by this observation.

"What the hell!" she shrieks when she sees me.

"The door was open." I raise my hands and also my gaze from where the short towel barely caresses the top of her very bare thighs. I bet if she lifts her arms I'll get a money shot.

She clutches the top of her towel, dragging it higher. Despite the internal battle to keep my eyes on her face, they dip down without my permission, checking for flash. I can't decide if I'm disappointed by the lack of it.

"So you thought you'd let yourself in and creep on me while I'm taking a shower? What in the actual fuck is wrong with you?" she yells while flailing her free hand.

I force my eyes back up to her face. "I'm not creeping on you. I knocked twice and said hello three times. Like I said, the door was open, so I was checking to make sure there weren't any bodies that needed removing."

"Bodies?" She makes a face. "Are you serious with this—" She shakes her head and waves a hand in the air, like she's erasing my words, or maybe trying to erase me. "You know what? It doesn't matter. There's obviously something wrong with you. You need to leave before I call the police."

Man, she gets worked up fast. Although I suppose I can see why she might not want a strange man in here while she's naked and wrapped in a towel.

I raise my hands in a show of surrender and take a few cautious steps backward down the hall toward the front door so she doesn't make good on that threat, but I can't resist needling her. "Maybe I should be the one calling the police. You show up here in the middle of the night and make yourself at home like you own the place, but I know the guy who's supposed to be living here, and he's not even in town." This is half bullshit. I have no idea if Rook's in town or not this weekend. For all I know, he's hiding out in one of the bedrooms.

"How do you—" She slashes a hand through the air while advancing on me as I retreat toward the front door. "You know what? I don't need to explain myself to you. You're the one breaking into *my* apartment."

"It's not *your* apartment." I nearly knock a lamp off a side table as I back my way through the living room.

"Oh my God! Get the hell out! I'm in a damn towel. I was in the shower. There are no bodies, as you can damn well see." She motions around the spotless, mostly empty room, still advancing as I get closer to the door.

"Maybe you were showering away the evidence." Now I'm messing with her. I don't know why. Possibly because she's so worked up. Maybe because I'm irritated that Rook seems like this golden boy, when he's just another asshole. "Who are you here with?"

"No one. I'm here alone, just like I was last—" She clamps a hand over her mouth but drops it just as quickly. "I have company on their way here right now. You need to get out."

I step back through the threshold so I'm in the foyer and not the apartment anymore. "I was checking to make sure you were alive and hadn't been turned into a knife block. I'm also not the least bit interested in taking advantage of the fact that you're alone."

"You made that quite clear with the boner-killer comment last night, but thanks for reiterating it." She pushes at my shoulder, aggressively this time, so I fake stumble back a couple of steps. "And why the hell would the door be open in the first place? I closed it last night, right after you were done insulting me."

"Did you see yourself last night? You were Queen of the Hot Mess Express."

"Do you ever shut up?" she shrieks as she shoves me with even more force. I have to admit, she's pretty strong for someone so small.

This time I stumble for real and bump the edge of the glass-top table. The giant vase of flowers threatens to tip over for a few seconds. Thankfully, it stays put. I don't feel like explaining a pile of broken glass to security. I straighten and run a hand down my chest, an action she follows raptly, like a hungry puck bunny. Maybe she's a legit stick chaser. "You're welcome for making sure you weren't murdered in the night."

"Buy a pair of pants!" She slams the door, but it doesn't close. Instead it bounces back open. "And a shirt!" She flips me the bird and slams the door a second time.

It bounces open. Again.

I smile and wave as she reappears. The towel has unraveled from her head and fallen to the floor, revealing a tangled mass of long . . . *powder-pink hair*? It had been tucked into a beanie last night, so it was hidden.

She grabs for the door, and the towel wrapped around her torso loosens, sliding down her body, which means I get a glimpse of a pair of nice perky tits before the door slams a third time.

"Nice boob job!" I yell at the closed door.

This time when it opens, a middle finger appears in the narrow gap. "They're real, asshole." The finger disappears, and the door slams again and remains closed.

She seems too feisty for Bowman. Too bad I have a moral compass. Otherwise she might be fun to play with.

CHAPTER 3

JERKS INC.

Stevie

"What a jerk!" I say to my boobs. I drop the arm barred across them, as it's no longer necessary to protect my nipples from being visually molested. Despite his size, and the fact that he's a virtual stranger, I didn't feel particularly threatened by his unexpected presence in the apartment. Maybe because of his ridiculous underwear?

Anyway, my boobs are very much mine and also very nice. Every single boyfriend I've ever had whom I've gone past second base with has pretty much fallen in love with my chest—which hasn't been a ton of guys because that's not how I roll. Apparently I have great boobs and nipples. Guys are oddly enthralled with them.

I press my face against the door so I can look through the peephole. The jerk is still standing in the foyer, wearing a stupid grin. He scratches the inside of his leg near his junk, mutters something I can't hear, and swaggers to his apartment door. I get to check out his fine, fine ass and incredibly defined back.

It's so unfair that someone with a personality so lacking is this ridiculously good looking. He bends to retrieve his newspaper before he disappears into his apartment.

After I get dressed, I check the cupboards for food. There is literally nothing, apart from a bag of noodles and four tea bags, which makes grocery shopping a top priority. I don't really want to leave the apartment, but I don't seem to have much of a choice.

I'm poised to open the door when my phone chimes in my purse. Joey has messaged relentlessly since I found him with his man unit lodged in someone else's vagina. It's the typical "Oh shit, I got caught" BS: *I'm so sorry, babe, it was an accident; it didn't mean anything; we can work this out.*

And maybe we could work it out, but if we did, then what? I'd spend the next however many months feeling insecure, wondering what he was doing when I wasn't home or if he was being faithful when I visited my family in LA. I can already see how that would play out, and it definitely wouldn't be good for me. I wouldn't feel good about myself if I got back together with Joey after walking in on him like that. I suppose now at least I know exactly where my line is.

I'm relieved, sort of, when my brother's name appears on the screen instead of Joey's.

"Hey." I put him on speakerphone and flop down on the couch.

"How are you this morning? Everything go okay last night?" RJ's parental-style concern is as endearing as it is annoying with zero caffeine in my system.

"I'm fine." That's a lie, but the truth is an entire therapy session, so we'll leave it at that. "You were right about the lock being tricky, but I figured it out. The guy across the hall thought I was trying to break in."

"Which guy?"

"Uh, the super-buff one?" I wasn't paying attention to the apartment number last night, and I'm too lazy to get off my ass and check.

"Most of the people up there keep to themselves, but if any of them give you problems, tell me, and I'll deal with it."

"It's fine. I was making a racket because I was entering the code wrong at first." I leave out the part where the guy insulted me and broke in this morning because I really don't need my brother knocking on his door, making a scene.

"What about the douche ex? Has he tried to contact you?"

Only about a million times. "He's messaged. I haven't responded." I change the subject because I can feel my eyes pricking with more stupid tears. "Where's the closest grocery store and coffee shop around here?" If I use Uber Eats, I could avoid leaving the apartment altogether until Monday morning, but that would be a waste of the limited funds I currently have available.

"There's a coffee shop on the first floor, and the grocery store is down the street. Sorry there's nothing in the penthouse, but you can use online delivery. The concierge will bring everything up for you."

"Isn't there some kind of fee for that? Besides, there's not much point in filling the fridge when I'll be moving out as soon as I find a new place."

"You don't need to find somewhere else, Stevie. I've already cleared it with management and explained the situation."

"Are you sure?" As much as I don't want to mooch off my brother, not having to search for another apartment or foot the rent bill on my own would alleviate one of my many stresses.

"Positive. I've got your back, Stevie. And don't worry about grocery-delivery fees. My card is already on file with them. I'll send you my log-in and password; then you can order what you need."

"You're doing more than enough by giving me a place to stay, and you already helped with furniture and stuff; you don't need to pay for my groceries too." I feel bad that I'm twenty-four years old and not self-sufficient, especially since RJ has been making millions of dollars since he turned twenty. Being fresh out of graduate school means my bank account is going to be light until I get a paycheck from my first-ever career-related job. On the upside, the salary and benefits are really great; on the downside, I'm working at the same clinic as my cheater ex.

"You don't need to worry about money when you haven't even started your job yet. Let me help. I can afford to take care of my family, so give me the chance to do that."

He has a point, since he makes eleven million a year. Racking up a credit card bill is another stress I don't need on top of everything else, so I concede. It's ironic how his fame and money are both a blessing and a curse in so many ways.

◆ ◆ ◆

The rest of the weekend passes in a blur of unanswered text messages and voice mails from Joey, many pints of Ben & Jerry's—courtesy of online grocery shopping—and several boxes of tissues. By Sunday night, my second suitcase still hasn't made it back from its trip to Alaska, but I ordered a bunch of clothes with express shipping—compliments of my brother's credit card—so at least I don't have to start my new job naked.

My stomach is in knots on Monday morning as I get ready for work. I pack snacks even though I'm too nervous to eat, pour a to-go cup of coffee, and make sure I have my key card before I slip on my shoes. A newspaper sits in front of my door when I open it, which seems odd, but I kick it into my apartment. Maybe it's complimentary or something.

As I pull the door shut behind me, the one across the hall opens, and out steps my jerkwad neighbor. Just like our first interaction, he's wearing only boxer briefs. This time they're a black-and-white checker print. A set of flags crosses over the peen pouch with the words **FINISH LINE** right over his junk. It's physically impossible not to look at his crotch. I force my eyes up, dragging slowly over his ridiculously cut abs on the way to his annoyingly attractive face.

He pauses when he notices me, eyes roving over my casual yoga-style pants and plain golf shirt in what feels a lot like silent judgment. It's probably the same way I assessed him but with less drooling and more disdain. When he reaches my backpack, his lip curls in a loathsome sneer. "Are you a *student*?" He says it like it's some kind of horrible disease.

I arch a brow and self-consciously adjust the strap. I could invest in a tote bag or something, but backpacks have better weight distribution and don't cause shoulder misalignment. "Good morning to you too." I head for the elevators without so much as a second glance in his direction. What a prick.

I'm grateful when the doors slide open almost immediately. I step inside, hit the lobby button, and fight with myself not to check to see if he's still standing there. I lose the battle half a second before the doors close fully. He's scratching the space between his navel and the waistband of his underwear. I roll my eyes and breathe a sigh of relief when the elevator begins its descent.

I wonder what the hell that guy's problem is. Sure, I made a lot of noise that first night, but I don't think it warrants his continued disdain. Whatever. It's not like I have to be friends with him. I don't even have to acknowledge him.

The bus ride to my new job is blissfully uneventful. The clinic is located at the edge of the university campus. They opened a brand-new center, which required a mass hiring in part because of the new expansion team in Seattle. Put a hockey team in a city, and all of a sudden hundreds of college kids want to go pro and are looking for every possible advantage to get them there.

I could've cashed in on my brother's connections and scored a position at one of the clinics that works directly with the professional teams, but I wanted to get the job on my own merit, not my brother's name.

I have a master's in physiotherapy with a specialization in sports rehab, and I graduated at the top of my class. That, along with the glowing recommendation from my professors and my clinic placement, as well as my interview skills, got me the job. And I didn't need my brother to do it.

So here I am, day one at my new job, praying I don't run into Joey and end up in tears. The good thing about starting two months after him is that he won't be part of my orientation. Also, the clinic is massive: there are more than a hundred people on staff, including physiotherapists, massage therapists, acupuncturists, chiropractors, and even a doctor, as well as a team of personal trainers—that's what Joey was hired for. I'm hopeful the size of the clinic means I won't run into him often—better yet, not at all—since I'm with the physiotherapy team.

I'm about twenty-five minutes early, so I sign in, pick up an orientation package of paperwork, and take a seat at one of the many empty desks in the seminar room. It's strange being in a university as something other than a student.

The seats around me fill with nervous bodies as I complete the forms. I'm not necessarily an introvert, but new situations where I don't know anyone apart from my cheater ex make me nervous.

Two women who look roughly my age take the empty seats next to me. One of the girls is tall and willowy with a pixie cut, and the other one is short with an athletic build, her long hair pulled back in a ponytail. We exchange hellos and names as they settle in. The willowy one is Jules, and the athletic one is Pattie. Apparently they're cousins.

My phone vibrates on my desk with new messages, but I ignore it. RJ sent me one this morning wishing me luck, as did my mom and my brother Kyle. I slide the device into my bag so it's not a distraction, but before I do, I catch the new name I've given to Joey's contact: Douche-Hole. His most recent message, sent seconds ago, reads look up.

The last thing I need or want this morning is to see his asshole face. I don't look up. Instead I flip distractedly through the orientation booklet.

"Hey! Stevie!" Joey whisper-shouts from the end of the row.

"For fuck's sake," I mutter.

"Do you know that guy?" Pattie asks on a whisper.

"Unfortunately, yes." I keep my head down, determined not to give him any kind of sign that will make him think he has half a chance of getting back on my good side. Ever.

"*Psst*, Stevie." His voice is closer now, like right beside my ear.

I glance at Pattie and mouth, *Is he behind me?*

She nods.

The tiny woman made of 100 percent muscle standing at the front of the room looks beyond me, her mouth twisting into a frown. "Mr. Smuck, did you need a refresher? Is that why you're gracing us with your presence?"

Yes, Joey's last name is Smuck. The irony is hard to ignore.

Every single person in the room is now looking at him, and I'm a sitting duck for whatever his response is going to be. I can feel the heat in my cheeks.

His hand, the one that was slapping the bare ass of someone other than me, lands on my shoulder. "Just saying hi to my—"

Embarrassment collides with incredulity and rage. I drop my arm, stabbing him in the shin with my pen. To his credit, he only half chokes on a groan, finishing with a cough and "Friend."

The room is pin-drop silent. I want to melt into the floor and disappear.

"Save your social calls for off-work hours, Mr. Smuck."

"Yes, ma'am. Sorry, ma'am." He lowers his voice and whispers, "You can't avoid me forever." Then he shuffles down the row and saunters out of the room with a slight limp.

Once he's gone, our orientation leader gets down to business as if the interruption never happened. And by business, I mean icebreakers. It's like being back in high school with the games she pulls out. I almost feel bad about everyone's complete lack of enthusiasm with how excited she is.

She has one of the new recruits in the first row pull a card from a top hat. We're supposed to shout out the first thing that comes to mind after it's been read aloud. Whoever gets similar responses will end up working in groups together for the rest of the day.

"What food is an absolute no-no on a first date?" the poor guy who pulled the question asks the room.

Several people shout out "Garlic!" or "Onions!"

I yell, much louder than necessary, "Bratwurst!"

At the same time, Pattie beside me shouts, "Hot dog!"

Jules follows it with, "Penis! I mean banana!"

Suddenly I'm not the most embarrassed person in the room anymore, and I think I've found my girl squad.

CHAPTER 4

UNDERWEAR CHALLENGE

Stevie

After orientation Pattie and Jules invite me out for dinner, but I'm supposed to go to my brother's for a combined post-birthday-new-job celebration, so I ask for a rain check. I join them for a quick drink, though, since we finished up with the orientation-day activities earlier than anticipated. It's nice to have friends already, especially with Joey working there and apparently wanting to be my shadow, based on the number of times I ran into him today.

My sister-in-law, Lainey, picks me up from the pub on her way home.

Kody, my nephew, is harnessed into his car seat, babbling away as he bangs two squishy hockey pucks together. "Evie!" he yells when I get into the SUV.

I twist in the passenger seat and tickle his foot, which is missing a shoe. "Hey, little man! I can't believe how big you've gotten!" I give Lainey a side hug. "Thanks for coming all the way out here to get me."

"It's no problem. We were already running errands, and this way you don't have to take the bus." Lainey's nose wrinkles. She's not a fan of public transit—not because she thinks she's above it but because she has an aversion to large crowds and confined spaces.

Lainey asks me how my first day at work was, and if I ran into the-jerk-who-shall-not-be-named. I skirt the uncomfortable parts of that conversation, mostly because the topic makes me want to cry.

Once we get to my brother's house, I play with Kody while Lainey prepares his dinner. When it's ready, I put him in his high chair and watch him shove food in his cute little face.

Lainey starts talking about preseason training, because it's safe conversation and that's where RJ is right now. She keeps trying to convince me to come to the arena with her, and while I love my brother and I'm actually a fan of hockey, I tend to shy away from attending his games.

I've had issues in the past with people using me to get to my brother. Being part of a brand-new expansion team in a city like Seattle is a big deal, so it's easier if I'm settled with friends of my own and the excitement of the start of the season has died down before I entertain the idea of going to games. I love my brother, and I don't begrudge him his success, but it can be hard to handle, and sometimes I succumb to inferior-little-sister syndrome.

Lainey gives me a sly look. "A lot of RJ's teammates are really nice. I know you're not ready to jump back into the dating pool yet, but there are a few cute ones who are probably close to your age, and single."

"Thanks, but I have zero interest in dating any of those guys."

"Dating what guys?" RJ appears in the kitchen, having just arrived home.

"The ones on your team," I reply.

RJ arches a brow. "No way in hell any of those guys would date you anyway."

"RJ!" Lainey smacks her spatula on the counter, an inch from his fingertips.

My brother raises both hands in the air. "Whoa, whoa, I don't mean because you're not datable, Stevie. If anything you're *too* datable."

"What the hell is that supposed to mean?" I'm not easy and I never have been. I get emotionally attached quickly, which isn't ideal, so I don't jump into bed with a guy right away, to avoid making it worse for myself if it doesn't work out.

RJ wraps his arms around me from behind in a big bear hug. "You've got the Bowman dimples, Stevie. They're lethal to the opposite sex. Isn't that right, Lainey?"

She nods somberly. "The dimples are hard to resist. I think what your brother is trying to say, however ineloquently, is that you're stunning and he would pull the big-brother card on any guy from his team who tries to date you."

Thankfully, no one mentions dating or RJ's teammates as viable options for the rest of the evening. RJ spoils me with unnecessary and extravagant birthday presents and my favorite cake, but the real highlight of my night is getting to put Kody to bed.

It's late by the time my brother drives me back to the penthouse. "You need me to help you get your rent money back from Assface?" he asks.

Every time he references Joey, it's with another creative insult.

"I can handle it." I smile, but it feels flat.

"I know you can, Stevie, but you shouldn't have to. I really hate that you're going through this. You can come stay at the house with us so you're not alone."

"Uh, that's sweet, but probably not something you should suggest without consulting Lainey first."

"We already talked about it. The pool house could easily be converted into a separate apartment, so you'd have your own space."

The idea of not being alone is alluring, but RJ's new house is a good forty-minute drive from the clinic, and I don't have a car; nor do I want my brother to buy me one.

"As nice as the offer is, RJ, you're newlyweds. I get that you have a baby and that you've been living together for a year already, but Lainey mentioned that you're looking to give Kody a brother or sister, and I would really rather not be in your living space while you're working on that."

"It's not like we're going to get it on at the dining room table."

"Not the point, and thanks for the totally unwanted visual. Besides, the penthouse is close to my work. Unless something has changed and I need to find somewhere else to stay?" The thought makes me suddenly panicky.

Despite my loathing of his neighbor and his ridiculous underwear, I'd rather deal with that than apartment hunting. And it would mean having to confront Joey about the rent I paid up front. I'll take care of that eventually, but I wouldn't mind a couple of weeks of mental preparation before I have to deal.

"Nothing has changed. The apartment is yours for the season."

"Okay, that's great. Can I pay you rent or something?"

"Absolutely not. It's part of my contract, and it would be sitting empty otherwise, so you can stay rent-free." He pulls up in front of my building, puts the car in park, and turns on the four-ways. "You want me to walk you up?"

"I'm good, but thanks." I give him a side hug. "Thanks for dinner, and for the upscale accommodations." I motion to the building as I get out.

"No problem, Stevie. And if you change your mind about needing my help with the asshole, let me know. I'd be happy to make him crap his pants for you."

"I know, and I appreciate it."

I use my card to enter the building and then again to get into the elevator, arms laden with bags of presents as I ascend to the penthouse floor. I love my brother, and I know he feels as though he has to step in and be like the dad we both lost a few years ago. Most of the time I need RJ my brother, not RJ the pseudodad, but I don't know how to tell him that without hurting his feelings.

The elevator dings when I reach the penthouse floor, and the doors slide open as a woman steps out of Jerkwad's apartment. Her black dress clings like a second skin and doesn't cover much. Her long dark hair is tousled, and her cheeks are flushed. She looks like she's been riding the orgasm train very recently. Of course my neighbor is *that guy*. I bet he's a walking, talking, womanizing cliché with a flavor of the week.

"Oh! Can you hold that for me?" she calls as she sashays across the foyer.

I don't know why I would need to hold the elevator for her, since there are so few people who use this one, but I smile, say "Sure," and keep a hand on the door to prevent it from closing.

"Thanks!" I exit the elevator as she brushes by me, her lipstickless smile firmly in place as she gives me a once-over. "I hope you had as good a night as I did!" She winks as the doors slide closed.

I throw a mental middle finger at my neighbor's door, irritated that despite his horrendous personality, he's getting action, and from someone who looks like a model. I assuage myself by imagining that he has a really small penis, even though she looked way too happy for that to be even remotely true.

Over the week that follows, several different women rotate through Jerkwad's penthouse. I also run into him twice more in the mornings. Well, *run into* probably isn't the right phrase. It just so happens that when I'm leaving for work, he conveniently appears in his weird underwear. It seems a lot like he's flaunting the fact that he has several different women who enjoy riding his joystick. At least that's what I assume he's doing. We don't exchange more than leering glares, so I'm going purely on speculation.

By the time I've been living in the penthouse for two weeks, I think I've gotten a handle on his schedule. The same blonde woman has been at his place on consecutive Wednesdays, so she must be his midweek screw. One afternoon I'm standing by the door, flipping through the mail, when I hear a woman's voice in the foyer. So I have a look through the peephole.

The jerk is nowhere in sight, but another woman, this one petite with a short brown bob, struts over to the elevator, phone in hand as she waits for the doors to open. It irks the shit out of me that this asshole screws whoever the hell he wants, whenever he wants, and none of these women seem to mind. Maybe he pays them. That would make sense. He seems like too much of a dickhead to have booty calls without compensating them somehow.

We fall into a routine of sorts over the week that follows. He collects his morning paper on Tuesday and Thursday at exactly the same time—as I'm leaving for work—always in his damn underwear. On Wednesday and Friday, it's already gone by the time I leave—those are my late-start days.

So the next Tuesday I wait with my eye pressed to the peephole for him to pick up the paper, to see if it's coincidental or not. The minutes tick by, and his door stays firmly shut, at least until I open mine. I don't step out, though. Instead I let it fall closed as his opens, revealing his ridiculously toned body wrapped in a pair of psychedelic boxer briefs.

What the hell is with this guy and his underwear?

He glances in the direction of my apartment, frowning as he picks up his paper. He's slow to disappear behind his door.

Today I decide to up my game, because it's obvious we're playing one. I'm not exactly sure what the point is, other than this guy seems to be an exhibitionist and a complete playboy. Normally I'm dressed for work by this time, but today I go as far as throwing on a pair of athletic running shorts—the kind that barely cover my butt cheeks—and my sports bra. Then I put a hold on completing my outfit.

As a physiotherapist I stay in good shape. I'm curvy but fit. Waif types look great in magazine spreads, but I'll own the hell out of every single one of my curves.

He opens the door at 7:03 on the nose as always—apart from the one time when he opened it at 7:05 because I'd held off until then—so I open mine. His underwear is Hawaiian print.

His gaze shifts my way, and his self-satisfied smirk slides off his face. It's ridiculously gratifying to watch his eyes nearly pop out of his head. I twist slightly so I'm giving him a rear view and bend at the waist to retrieve my paper. It's absolutely a blatant attempt to taunt him the way he's been taunting me, and based on the way he's gawking, it works well.

I toss a condescending grin his way. "Nice panties." And then I return to the safety of my apartment and press my eye to the peephole so I can see his reaction.

He's still standing there, mouth agape. He runs a hand down his chest and rearranges himself before he slowly bends to grab his own paper, eyes still on my closed door. He says something I can't hear as he looks over his shoulder once more before disappearing.

"So much for being a boner-killer." For the first time since I started my new job, I get ready for work with a smile.

CHAPTER 5

NEIGHBORLY

Bishop

Preseason training is something I usually look forward to, but right now it's the opposite. For the majority of my career I've played forward. I might be a big guy—bigger than most of the forwards on the team—but I'm fast and I can shoot the puck. Which is why I'm irritated over the way Bowman and our coach, Alex Waters, keep having these obvious side conversations where I end up being shifted around from forward to defense and back again.

I already had some less-than-warm feelings toward Bowman with his asshole moves on the ice and his fake I'm-so-nice bullshit, but now he's screwing with my game too. Plus, there's this woman living in what's supposed to be his penthouse, and I can't figure out what the hell is going on there. It's pissing me off. Although, to be honest, everything is pissing me off lately.

I'm in the lobby, on my way to my car, when I realize my favorite pair of preseason boxer briefs is still sitting on my kitchen counter where

I left them. I debate whether I can deal with wearing the ones I have on and decide I can't. My underwear is a thing.

Thankfully, the elevator is still at lobby level, so I hop right back on. Less than two minutes later I jam my favorite underwear into my duffel bag and leave my apartment once again. The elevator door is open, and there, in all her pink-cotton-candy-haired glory, is my team-mate's sidepiece.

Once again she's decked out in her "I like to pretend I work out" wear, probably on her way to her third-year psych class, oblivious to the fact that she's potentially ruining lives. Whatever. Not my monkey. Not my circus.

When she sees me, she starts jabbing the button, but I manage to slide a hand in to prevent the doors from closing. "Thanks for holding the elevator for me."

"You're so welcome." She shoots me a patronizing smile and moves into the corner as the doors slide closed again.

And then I'm trapped inside the small steel box with a thousand reflections of her. Now that I have a chance to actually look at her up close and she's not the train wreck she was the first time I saw her, I can admit that she's pretty. Fine, she's more than pretty, actually. I'd go as far as to say she's gorgeous, and she smells good, which is aggravating because of who she seems to be and where she's staying.

I've yet to see Captain Bowman here, but maybe he stops in at odd hours, or they meet up elsewhere. I have no idea why I care, other than I hate him and his lax morals. Also, she woke me up from a dead sleep the night she arrived. I take sleep very seriously.

"All dressed up for class?" If he's screwing a college chick on the side, I might feel a little bad for her, because it means she's probably getting played.

She sneers, and her eyes rake over me viciously, like knives slicing skin. "Look at you in *actual clothes*."

The way the tips of her ears turn pink along with her cheeks tells me that I'm making her uncomfortable.

I lean against the railing and stare at her profile. I'm being a dick. Obviously on purpose. She doesn't touch her hair or adjust her outfit, which is commendable considering how intently I'm looking at her. Her jaw clenches and her nostrils flare. I'm about to get a reaction in three, two, one . . .

Her head snaps in my direction, eyes vibrant with ire. "What in the actual fuck? How the hell do you manage to attract women with your horrible personality? I really don't get it. Unless they're all brain-dead idiots and they duct-tape your mouth shut while they're riding you." She tilts her head, as if considering that, and nods once. "That has to be it. I can see how that might be doable."

"What the hell are you talking about?" And did she just fantasize about riding me with my mouth duct-taped shut? Why is that hot?

"What am I talking about?" Her eyebrows shoot up. They're very light brown, almost blonde. She motions to me and then to the elevator. "The constant rotation of women in and out of your apartment. It's like a damn brothel."

I scoff. "That's rich, coming from you."

She makes a face that resembles confusion before she plasters on a fake, condescending smile. "I've seen the same woman go into your apartment two Wednesdays in a row, not to mention at least four other women. I hope you're smart enough to wrap it up."

It sounds like I need to have a chat with my brother about his ultraprolific love life. My brother's tactics for getting women into bed with him aren't exactly aboveboard, but he's also my best friend, so I let him get away with a lot of shit.

I don't particularly care if he sleeps with a different woman every day of the week; I just don't want to find them hanging out in my kitchen the morning after, wearing one of his T-shirts, bugging me for an autograph, and making other, less-than-appropriate requests. It's happened plenty of times.

Also, I run hot all the time, so my preference is to wear as little clothing as possible when I'm in the comfort of my own home. If he has some random over, I have to put things on, like shorts and T-shirts, which I don't love.

I suck in a deep breath, inhaling her sweet smell. It's making me hungry for cake, or a muffin. Or sex. Fuck. It's been a really long time since I've been inside a woman, and it irritates the shit out of me that I find her appealing. "Look at you, Little Miss Nosy. Why the hell are you so interested in the recreational activities that go on inside my apartment?"

The tips of her ears turn from pink to red, and this time she splutters her response. "I'm not interested in who or whatever you're doing. I happened to be coming home when your friend was doing the walk of shame on Wednesday. Two weeks in a row. Does she know you're a womanizing asshole?"

I mirror her condescending smile with one of my own. "Wednesday is the day my cleaning lady comes by, but it's nice to know you're keeping such a close eye on me." Before she can sputter out another response, the elevator dings and the doors slide open.

Little Miss Nosy bolts, speedwalking across the foyer and out the front door. I exhale a quick breath, make a surreptitious adjustment in my pants, and exit the elevator. I take a right toward the parking garage, unsure if I feel better or worse after that exchange, considering the way my body reacts to her proximity.

My already-questionable mood takes a fast dip south once I get to the arena. I'm almost suited up in my gear when my phone rings from somewhere under my discarded clothes. I intend to ignore it or send it to voice mail, but it's my brother.

When I left home, I assumed he was still asleep. He doesn't keep regular hours, even though out of the two of us, he's the one who should have a structured routine. He's in college part time and works part time. I don't often know when or if he's actually home.

"Hey, sup?"

"Shit. Hey, Ship. I thought it would go to voice mail."

"I'm about to hit the ice. Everything okay?" My brother doesn't call to chitchat, particularly since he lives with me.

"Oh, yeah, everything is fine." His tone tells me that's a lie.

"So you wanted to leave me a message to tell me everything was fine?"

"Uh, yeah, mostly. I wanted to let you know I took a trip to the doctor's this morning, and I might be here for a few more hours 'cause they're running some tests, so you shouldn't worry or anything."

"What? Why are you just calling me now? How long have you been there? Was it a scheduled appointment?" I always put those on the calendar. It's not like me to forget something like that.

"It wasn't scheduled. I haven't been here long."

I hate it when he gives me vague answers and forces me to drag information out of him. Nolan is five years younger than I am and acts like he's invincible, which he isn't. Not by a long shot. "So what's going on? Why didn't you wake me up?"

"Because it's not a big deal."

"How not big of a deal is it?"

"I woke up feeling off. I got a ride here from my friend Sasha . . . or Sandy? She was a lot of fun, regardless. Anyway, I probably worked it too hard last night. They're checking my levels and doing some tests. My insulin needs adjusting, or whatever. I figured I should call and let you know in case I'm here longer than I expected, so you don't get all worried."

"You're telling me you had one of your randoms, whose name you can't even remember, take you to urgent care instead of waking me up, and you think I'm not going to worry? What time did you even get in last night? And how many chicks have you brought home this month that you can't remember this one's damn name?"

"You need to dial back your dad, brother. Someone has to get some action, 'cause it sure ain't you. Look, I knew you had practice and I figured you needed the sleep. I promise it's not a big deal. They're making me better as we speak."

"I'll come get you after practice."

"Don't bother. I'll Uber."

"Message me the address. If you're still there when practice is over, I'll pick you up."

"You gonna read me the riot act?"

"Do I need to?"

"One of the pretty nurses is here to stab me with some needles. It's masochism at its finest. Have a good practice, Shippy." He ends the call before I can give him more shit. I hate it when he calls me that.

"Everything okay?" Ryan Kingston, better known as Kingston or just King, slips his folded khakis into his cubby.

We used to play together back in college and ended up on different teams once we hit the pros. This year we're back on the same team. It's nice to have an actual friend among this group of misfits.

"My brother's in urgent care."

"Is he going to be okay?"

I shrug, because that's always the question with Nolan. Is he going to be okay?

"He thinks his meds need to be adjusted."

Kingston pulls his helmet on. "And you think differently?"

The thing that really needs an adjustment is Nolan's lifestyle. "He says he's going to be fine, and if it was an emergency he wouldn't be able to tell me that." I push up off the bench and grab my stick, helmet, and gloves before following Kingston to the ice.

We start with warm-ups, and I try to stay focused, but now my head is all over the place.

If Nolan took better care of himself, I'd feel a whole lot better about this spontaneous trip to urgent care. Unfortunately, he treats his life like time is running out, so he's living it to the fullest, which would be fine if he wasn't a type 1 diabetic with compromised kidney function and vision problems.

There's a good chance, if he keeps living hard, he's going to need a transplant. Even if he doesn't live hard, there's still a good chance he'll need one anyway. Type 1 diabetes has a lot of potential for complications, especially when it's not taken seriously.

I'd like to keep my brother around as long as possible. He's already looking at a shorter life span, and that's if he manages his health carefully. But he doesn't.

I've done the research, read the articles, gone to countless doctor's appointments. My dad traveled for work, and even when he was around he wasn't present, so it was just me, Nolan, and our mom.

Her insurance plan only covered the bare minimum for Nolan's endless medical needs, so I solved that problem by having him live with me and listing him as a dependent. It's not a burden since we're tight, but I know that as he gets older, those needs are going to increase, so I need to save the money I'm making now so I can keep taking care of him.

It's why I wanted team captain. It would've helped when trade talks come around again. As it is, the shift back and forth from forward to defense is messing with my head and my game.

I'm way off during practice, screwing up over and over, since defense is not my preferred position. I let way too many pucks near the net, which pisses me off, and I can't seem to hide my animosity toward Bowman, who floats down the ice and scores goals like he's wielding a magic wand instead of a hockey stick.

I miss yet another easy pass and toss my stick across the ice. It's a stupid, hotheaded move, and it doesn't look good on me, especially when it's just us playing against each other as a team.

Bowman skates by and claps me on the shoulder, getting in close. It looks friendly, but it's not. "Don't take your frustration out on your own team, Winslow. Maybe you need a time-out so you can watch how the big boys do it before you pick up a stick again." Ah, here's the real version of Bowman, not that Captain America shit he tries to sell people on. This is how he and I are with one another.

"Is that your version of a pep talk, *Captain*? It'd be a hell of a lot easier if I was playing the position I trained for."

"And have your attitude messing up my line?" He cocks a brow. "You need to work out your issues somewhere other than the ice."

"This good-guy routine you've got going is bullshit." I shake him off.

Bowman frowns. "What the hell are you talking about?"

I shake my head and skate over to the bench before I do what I normally would when Bowman used to needle me on the ice—react with aggression. Instead, I grab a drink of water so I don't say or do something more regrettable than throwing a temper tantrum.

"Winslow, why don't you take two." Coach Waters pats the bench beside him.

Giving my team captain attitude is one thing, but giving it to the coach is another. I sigh and clomp over to where he's sitting, dropping onto the bench beside him.

"I'm not used to defense." I watch the guys on the ice, the puck sliding back and forth between Bowman and Bender, a forward who used to play for Colorado before the expansion draft.

"I can see that."

When he doesn't say anything else, I'm forced to look at him.

"Anything else going on that I need to know about?"

I figure I have to give him something. "Just some family stuff. Nothing I really want to get into."

He nods and flips a puck back and forth between his fingers. "I know it's tough getting used to a new team, especially when we're moving you around to see where you fit best. You got a lot of size and a versatile skill set, which I can see you want to use, but you can't be trying to score the goals and protect your goalie at the same time, eh?"

"Yeah, I know. It's just getting my head around the change, I guess."

"That's fair, but you gotta give it an honest shot here, Winslow. All these guys are in the same boat as you. I know it can be hard, morale-wise, especially when you're coming together with a bunch of guys you haven't played with before. Just remember we're all on the same side."

"Yeah, I get it. It all makes logical sense."

"If you need to talk it out, let me know. I'm here to problem-solve."

"Right, yeah. Thanks." I'm not interested in a therapy session with my new coach, particularly since Bowman is already tucked into his back pocket.

I hit the ice again, but I'm still distracted. Exhibition games start soon, and I need to get a handle on my position before that happens. The last thing I want is to end up being third or fourth line and getting less ice time, which would put me further from my goal instead of closer.

I have a two-year contract with Seattle, but they could trade me next year if I don't work out. Being moved again after one year on an expansion team won't look good for me. It could be the difference between not getting another contract or, worse, being dropped back to a farm team, especially if I can't manage the shift to defense, if that's where they plan to keep me. Which is something I can't afford when I have a brother who needs solid medical for as long as he's here. I need to give Nolan the best chance I can, and that means checking my attitude, as difficult as that might be for someone like me.

CHAPTER 6

EXHIBITIONIST GAMES

Stevie

Despite my asshole neighbor calling me out on my spyish behavior, and my accusing him of being a total man-whore, we continue the seminaked morning-paper-retrieval trend. In fact, it's escalated thanks to me. I can't even defend myself, because seeing him in his underwear every morning has become some kind of weird obsession. To the point where I get up early on Wednesdays so I can have my morning paper underwear competition.

He might be a jerk, but he's nice to look at. Also, since he's a huge dick, I don't feel even remotely bad for objectifying him.

Over the past several days I've started switching it up in the morning. I grab my paper five minutes earlier than usual on Tuesday, and half a second after I open my door, Jerkwad does too. The next day I'm seven minutes late, and still, there he is. Every single day I match his weird underwear with a different sports bra and running shorts. I even bought new ones so I could keep up with the ostentatious patterns he seems to favor. Like I said, it's borderline obsessive.

I'm pretty sure this is his way of trying to make me feel like an ass for keeping tabs on the women coming and going from his place. But come on—there were at least five women in the first two weeks, not counting the housekeeper, if that's even what she is.

I have a super-early morning on Friday. I'm helping out a client who desperately needs the PT but is going out of town for the weekend, so I schedule her in at five thirty. It means I'm out the door hours before the paper is even delivered.

Working at the clinic has been great. Pattie and Jules are becoming real friends I can rely on, and I'm generally able to avoid interacting with Joey because most of his clients are scheduled in the afternoons or evenings.

While I'm definitely getting over him, he seems to be having difficulty letting it go. Every time we're in a room alone, which isn't very often, thankfully, he makes nice with me. Once he tried to hug me, so I gave him a jab to the kidneys. That was the last time he attempted physical contact.

Today our appointments are opposite each other, so whenever he has a break, I'm with a client, and whenever I have a break, he's training someone. I may have orchestrated this on purpose.

At the end of the day I change into street clothes and grab my bag from my locker, wondering if Jerkwad missed our underwear fashion show today. Tomorrow I'll bring my A game to make up for it. I smile at the thought, but it quickly disappears when I turn to find Joey crowding me.

"Hey." He does that weird, awkward, pretend-shy thing where he jams his hands in his pockets and kicks the end of my shoe. It's very grade school. I used to think it was cute. Now all I want to do is kick him in the shin, hard, while wearing steel-toed boots. Unfortunately that's workplace harassment.

I shoulder my backpack and try to step around him, but he mirrors the movement. I sidestep the other way, and he does too. It's like a bad rendition of do-si-do. I fight the urge to maim him and sigh instead. "What do you want?"

He leans against the lockers, getting all up in my personal space, especially since mine is the last one in the row, which means I end up between him and the wall. "It feels like we haven't talked in forever."

I blink but don't respond, because really, what can I even say to that?

"Can we go for coffee or something?"

"No. We can't." I wish I had a cool superpower that would allow me to scale walls or jump really high so I could get away from him without having to make physical contact. It's been weeks, but I still don't have the desire or energy to deal with him, so generally I don't. I dislike confrontation, and I fear that I'll lose it on him when we finally do talk, and work would not be the ideal location for that to happen.

"Why not?"

"Because you were warming your dick in a vagina that wasn't mine."

He makes a face like he doesn't appreciate the image I've painted. I don't particularly like it either, but it is accurate. "Come on, Stevie. You can't be mad at me forever."

I put a hand in front of his face, and he takes a step back, possibly because he thinks I'm going to hit him. It's definitely something I'd consider if I wasn't so opposed to domestic violence. Self-defense is a whole different beast, though. "First of all, you don't get to tell me how to feel about any of this, particularly how long I'm allowed to be angry. As far as I'm concerned, I wasted a year of my life being your girlfriend, and I have zero plans to waste more time, emotion, or energy on anything related to you."

"I made a mistake." He's whiny rather than remorseful.

"How many times did you happen to make that mistake?"

"I was alone out here for two months."

Well, now I know it wasn't an isolated incident. "A mistake becomes a choice when you make it more than once. Looks like maybe you should've thought about the consequences before you made yours."

"Baby, I get that you're—"

"Hey! There you are!" Pattie and Jules, bless their hearts, manage to worm their way between us. They flank me like very pretty bodyguards and thread their arms through mine.

Jules flashes a smile I can only describe as extra syrupy with a side of fake at Joey. "So sorry to interrupt, but we need Stevie."

Joey's overly groomed eyebrows furrow. "We were talking."

"Really? Because it looked a lot like you were trying to corner her," Pattie says.

Jules shoulders him out of the way, and my feet barely touch the floor as they basically carry me through the staff lounge. We have to turn sideways to get through the door because they refuse to unlink their arms. I feel a bit like Dorothy with the Tin Man and the Cowardly Lion, minus the Yellow Brick Road, as we walk down the hall toward the front doors.

We burst out of the building, and still they keep their arms linked with mine as we bust it down the street, past university campus buildings. My bus stop is in the opposite direction, and I'd like to tell them this, but I don't want to appear ungrateful for the save.

Jules looks over her shoulder. "He's not following us; we're good."

They unhook their arms from mine, and we shuffle off to the side so students can pass us on their way to and from their afternoon and evening classes. Working at a university clinic is interesting. It straddles a line between nostalgic and wistful, especially since the three of us are fresh from graduate school and could still pass for students, even though we're not.

"Thanks for getting me out of there." I shake off the uneasiness I feel when thinking about confronting Joey.

"It looked tense." Pattie gives my arm a gentle squeeze.

"It's annoying more than anything." For the most part I can avoid him, but it seems like he's made it his mission to seek me out every time we're in the building together.

"He's more persistent than a case of crabs in a rent-by-the-hour motel," Jules gripes.

"And just as unpleasant, actually," I agree.

Jules and Pattie invite me to join them for dinner. If I go home now, I'll end up perseverating on my altercation with Joey. It'll be one of those downward spirals where I question all my past boyfriend choices while eating a pint or two of ice cream.

Then I'll start wondering if Jerkwad is getting his fuck on with his newest bedpost notch. Inevitably, I'll start fantasizing about duct-taping his pretty mouth shut and using him as my personal dildo, which will result in self-loathing. Nothing good can come from going home and being alone, so I agree to dinner.

We head down the street to one of the local restaurants. Everywhere seems to be buzzing tonight, and I suddenly realize why as my brother's form fills the multiscreen TV that takes up nearly an entire wall in the bar.

"Seattle's first exhibition game is tonight." Pattie motions to the screen. "I bet the guys are watching this at home."

"The guys?"

"You know, our brothers." Jules has three, and Pattie has two, I've learned. "They're all sports fanatics, and we are, too, so it can get out of hand sometimes," Jules explains.

"Especially when two different sports overlap at the end or the beginning of the season."

"I can imagine." All the tables near the TVs are taken, so we bypass them and head for the patio. We'll still sort of be able to watch the game. I can't believe I forgot that tonight is RJ's first game. I shoot him a quick message wishing him luck as we browse the menu.

I'm able to half pay attention to the game from our table, so I don't feel like a totally horrible sister. We order pints and a bunch of appetizers. I'm busy stuffing my face with nachos when a collective gasp from the entire bar has me looking at the TV screens. It's a flurry of action on the ice, players shoving each other as one from Seattle curls into a ball close to the net.

"Oh shit! That had to hurt!" some guy from two tables over says.

"That was a dodgy play. They better give LA a penalty for that shit," someone else says.

"Who got hit?" I ask Jules and Pattie, who both have a hand covering their mouths. "Was it number forty-four? Bowman?" I ask, my heart suddenly in my throat.

Jules gives her head a shake. "No, uh, number fifty-two. Winslow. Some trade from Nashville."

"Thank God." I breathe a sigh of relief and slump back in my chair, checking the score at the top of the screen before it goes to commercial break. At least Seattle is winning, so that's something.

"Wait a second. Isn't your last name Bowman?" Pattie's eyes dart around, possibly checking for eavesdroppers. She leans in closer and lowers her voice. "Are you related to *Rook* Bowman?"

I don't see the point in lying. We've been working together for close to a month, and they'll find out eventually. And it will also tell me what camp they fit into. "He's my brother."

Pattie blinks a couple of times; her lack of reaction is fairly impressive. "Wow, so Joey isn't always full of shit. Good to know."

"You already knew?"

"To be fair, Joey isn't the most reliable source of information. We take everything he says with a grain of salt, or more like a brick. Particularly the part where he keeps insisting you two are on a break while you adjust to living in Seattle," Jules replies.

"Of course he said that." I roll my eyes.

"It must be kind of annoying to have a brother who plays professional hockey, especially when it's suddenly so freaking big here." Jules shoves a loaded nacho chip in her mouth.

"It can be when people go all gaga over him." I love the hell out of my brother, but it sure can be frustrating to be his solidly average sister.

"I can sort of relate. My brothers play college football, and women are constantly throwing themselves at them," Pattie says.

"Sometimes they have stalkers." Jules nods somberly. "Girls get crazy over athletes."

"Right? It can be too much to handle." I roll my eyes on a laugh.

"Remember that time Mike forgot he invited like three girls to the homecoming game, and they got into a brawl over him?" Jules says to Pattie, then turns to me. "It was insane. They legit had a mud-wrestling match on the field because it had rained that day. The whole thing was videoed and ended up all over social media."

"Oh God. That would be horrible." I can feel my cheeks heat with shared embarrassment.

"I can't even imagine how it would be for you, though. The bunnies are the worst for posting stuff." The way Pattie says it doesn't sound like she's fishing; it's more like empathy.

I look around, checking to make sure no one is paying attention to us, and lower my voice. "I think the worst was the viral threesome video."

Pattie makes a face and Jules cringes. "I remember that. People wouldn't stop talking about it."

"I was in high school."

"Oh God."

"Yeah. It was . . . not the best." I remember that day so vividly. It set off a chain of events that made me avoid social media for the rest of the year. Even now, all my accounts are set to private, and I never use my last name. "I walked into class, and the teacher wasn't there yet. Everyone was huddled over their phones, and they all went silent the moment I stepped into the room. I knew it had to be something with RJ. I mean, all of a sudden all these girls in the popular cliques wanted to hang out with me when he made the NHL—girls who wouldn't have given me the time of day before that. But this was different . . . people started laughing and whispering. I ended up taking a week off school until the worst of it blew over. I really learned who my true friends were then." The whole thing soured me on my brother's fame. Any kinds of perks were suddenly eclipsed by the media backlash and the storm.

"I'm so sorry. I can't even imagine how hard that would've been. Having a brother who's a college football star is bad enough; I can't fathom what would happen if he made the pros."

It feels good to be able to share stories with new friends who actually understand. We spend the rest of the evening talking about what it's like to have brothers who play sports where women are constantly throwing themselves at them. Tonight I feel like I fit because I'm me and not because of my last name.

CHAPTER 7

OW

Bishop

I think I'm still in shock. I'm also in a lot of pain, and that's with all the drugs they've pumped into my system.

The white sheet barely covers my junk—not that I care about modesty, since I've been prodded and inspected by half a dozen people in the past hour. The verdict is unanimous and shitty: I have a groin injury. On a scale of not bad to really fucking awful, I'm sitting on the really fucking awful side.

I look down at the inside of my thigh. The bruising spreads from my groin all the way down to my knee, and it's already turned a horrible blackish-purple color.

"You're going to need at least six weeks to recover," the team doctor tells me.

"I can't be out that long."

"I'm sorry, Bishop, but this needs time to heal." He motions to my crotch.

"Six weeks, though?" I look to Waters, who wears a grim expression. "The season starts in three. I gotta be on the ice for that."

Waters runs a hand through his hair. "I understand that this is upsetting, Bishop, but if you push too fast, too soon, you're going to do more damage, and then you'll be on the bench for a hell of a lot longer than six weeks. We'll start rehab as soon as the swelling goes down and the pain levels are tolerable."

I know he's right, but the gnawing panic takes hold. I'm already having problems with this back-and-forth between defense and forward, struggling to manage the shifting roles. And now I'm benched for six weeks after the first exhibition game. This is the opposite of ideal.

I'm given a prescription for painkillers and anti-inflammatories. I assure the doctors I don't live alone and have someone to help me get to the bathroom and all the other bullshit. Thankfully, Kingston showed up at the clinic after the game, so I don't have to rely on Waters for a ride home.

The only silver lining among a sky of dark clouds is the fact that I saved the goal, and we won the game as a result.

I dress gingerly, and Kingston wheels me to the side entrance. Instead of letting him bring the car around, I insist on crutching across the lot, because I'm a stubborn idiot.

By the time I get my ass into the passenger seat, I'm nauseous with the pain and there are black spots in my vision.

"I'm sorry, Bishop. I know it's not a consolation, but Hessler got a five-minute penalty, and Bowman checked him pretty good in the third period." Kingston pulls out of the parking lot and heads toward my place.

The penalty and Hessler getting checked don't fix my problems, unfortunately. "How am I going to gel with the team if I can't be on the ice with everyone?"

"You'll still be at games and practice and training."

"But I won't be able to *do* anything." I bang my head against the back of the seat, which is a bad idea, since I already have a headache to go with the groin pain.

"Maybe it'll heal a lot faster than six weeks? It could look worse than it is."

"Maybe." Based on how it feels right now, I'm not sure that's the case.

I doze on the ride home, wiped out from the pain and the medication. When we get to my building, Kingston offers to come up with me and make sure I'm settled. I assure him I can deal with an elevator ride and that my brother will be home to manage the rest.

Mostly I just want to be alone with my shitty mood and my bad luck.

The pain is brain-meltingly awful as I crutch inside and across the foyer to the elevators. Kingston's car is still idling in front of the building, likely to make sure I don't do a face-plant. I swipe my card over the sensor, grateful when the doors slide open and I can hobble in before I pass out. Blinking through the spots in my vision, I swipe my key card again and give Kingston a thumbs-up before the doors slide closed.

I lean against the rail as I speed toward the penthouse floor, willing the meal I had several hours ago to stay where it is. I imagine there isn't much in my stomach, but vomiting would be more than I can handle. All I want is to lie down and not move for twenty-four hours, give or take a day.

I must nod off briefly, because between one long blink and the next I'm looking at the penthouse foyer. I'm woozy as I leave the elevator, and in my uncoordinated state I manage to lodge the end of my crutch in the stupid gap in the floor. I yank on it, which sends a violent shock of pain through my body, shorting out my brain and turning my vision into the Milky Way.

I groan a few expletives, and the crutch pulls free, causing me to stumble forward. I go down, because my brain and my body aren't able to handle the level of pain I'm still in, despite the excessive amount of medication they pumped into me before sending me home—which should definitely tell me something about the severity of my injury.

My entire body breaks out in a cold sweat, and my stomach roils. I heave a couple of times but manage not to throw up. I lie in a heap on the floor for a few long seconds. I know it's no longer than that because the elevator doors are still open.

My key card is lying on the ground, right over that stupid gap between the elevator doors. As they begin to slide closed, I roll over and try to grab the card. That movement causes another vicious spike of pain to shoot through my groin. I feel like my balls are going to rupture and explode. Through a haze of black and stars I can make out the edge of my key card. I catch it with the tips of my fingers and drag it toward me. The doors hit my hand, and I lose my grip. And my freaking key card drops down the narrow gap.

I don't have to look down the hole to know my card is gone. I roll onto my back and stare up at the ceiling, my body covered in sweat, and breathe through the nausea.

This really isn't my day. For a moment I think about my neighbor and the state she was in the first time I caught her out here in the hallway, with her broke-down suitcase and disheveled, slightly manic expression. I imagine I must look a lot like she did.

Eventually I drag myself into a sitting position. I arrange my crutches and slowly pull my body upright. Then I hobble pathetically over to my door. "Fuck," I say to the sock hanging from the knob.

My brother has company, and this is his very sophisticated Bat-Signal. I rest my head against the door and knock. I'm unsurprised when he doesn't answer. I also text but get no response. Usually on game nights I'm out pretty late, and I assume Nolan has decided to take advantage of that, despite my having talked to him about slowing down on the number of randoms he brings back here.

I need the key card to get in, and to obtain a new one I have to go back to the lobby. I don't think I'm capable of making the trip at the moment, so I decide to wait out my brother's company by taking a nap against the door.

CHAPTER 8

COUCH GUEST

Stevie

I don't get back to my apartment until almost midnight. The dessert place we went to after the pub was licensed, so we drank spiked coffee and ate cake on the outdoor patio. I don't have a client until ten tomorrow, so technically I can sleep in.

I'm greeted by an interesting sight when I reach the penthouse foyer. My jerkwad neighbor is propped against the door, a set of crutches lying next to him, head lolled awkwardly to the side. Maybe he lipped off to someone bigger than him and finally got the payback he deserves for being an ass. I smile at the thought.

The ding of the elevator doors doesn't rouse him, so he must be out cold. I note the white tube sock dangling from the doorknob as I pass. In college, it was the universal symbol for Do Not Disturb. I thought he lived alone. Other than the endless stream of women, he's the only person I've seen coming and going from his apartment.

I creep closer and grimace at the line of drool on his chin. I also notice what looks like a bruise on his left cheek. Maybe I'm right, and he did get into a fight. I consider leaving him out here, but if he has a concussion and dies as a result of a brain aneurysm, I'll feel guilty. Also, I've never seen a dead body, and I don't want to start now.

I knock on his door, hoping someone will hear me. No one answers after a full thirty seconds, so I try again, but still nothing. I kick Jerkwad's foot, which in hindsight probably isn't the best idea, considering the crutches.

He sucks in a gasping breath, and his lids flip open on a deep groan.

"Sorry about that," I say.

He blinks a bunch of times and looks around, apparently confused. He groans again and touches the side of his face where the bruise is.

"You okay?"

"Uh, yeah. Fine. Took a nap." He grabs the edge of the doorframe and tries to hoist himself up. Half a second later he's back on the floor, this time lying on his side, one leg completely straight and the other one pulled up closer to his chest as he groans.

"You don't seem fine." As far as observations go, it's a pretty obvious one.

It takes him a good minute of deep breathing, during which he breaks out in the sweats, before he can manage to right himself.

It's getting awkward with how long it takes him to recover, so I do what anyone else would do in such a situation, despite his having been a huge asshole to me. "Can I help you get into your apartment? It might be more comfortable than sleeping out here in the hall."

He clears his throat, but it doesn't do anything to help with the gravelly quality of his voice. "I'm waiting for my brother's company to leave." He motions to the sock on the door.

"Is your place the sex pad or something?"

"Only when Nolan's on a roll."

Nolan must be the brother. "So he uses your apartment for sex?" That seems . . . awkward. More awkward than our underwear battle.

"He lives with me."

"Oh." Huh. Maybe I'm wrong about him being a womanizing douche. Maybe he just has the douche part covered.

"I'll wait out here until his flavor of the night leaves, which will hopefully be soon." He leans his head against the door and closes his eyes. "What time is it, anyway?"

"Almost midnight."

He cracks a lid. "I've been out here for hours. I told him the sleepovers had to stop."

"It's nice that you're willing to give him privacy for his fuckfest or whatever, but I think it's safe to let yourself in at this point, don't you?"

He flings a hand out in the direction of the elevator and lets it flop to the floor. "I lost my card down the shaft; otherwise I would've let myself in a long-ass time ago."

Seeing him like this frames him in a different light. It doesn't make me dislike him less, but I feel kind of bad for him. He's obviously badly injured, and being stuck out here in the hall all night would suck a lot.

"Do you want to wait it out at my place until Screwpalooza is over? You're more than welcome to lie here all night, but I don't think it's going to be comfortable, and considering how late it is, you may be here until morning. Unless you'd rather me help you back down to the lobby so you can get a new card." He doesn't look like he's in any kind of shape to do more than lie there, but I figure I'll give him options.

He rolls his head toward the elevator and then in the direction of my door. "Your place is closer."

That one detail seems to be his tipping point. He tries to pull himself up. It's an arduous task, based on the amount of grunting and moaning he does. He stays upright with the help of his crutches and the wall while I unlock my door and let him in. He heads directly for the couch, spins around with an impressive amount of grace, and lowers himself gingerly.

He manages to get the upper half of his body supine and on the cushions, but he can't seem to do the same with his legs.

I'm still standing near the front door, unsure how bad an idea it is to have invited this guy into my space. I don't know anything about him, other than the fact that he has a brother who apparently holds the womanizing title and that he's been a jerk to me.

I watch him struggle for another minute before I finally offer him some assistance. He seems reluctant to take it but eventually acquiesces.

I start to lift one leg, but he shouts, "No!"

I drop it back to the floor, and his shoulders curl in on a groan. "Shit. Sorry."

He sucks in a bunch of deep breaths. I can't decide if he's being overdramatic or not. Or maybe he's on drugs. Who the hell knows? I'll be locking my bedroom door and sleeping with my phone under my pillow tonight, that's for sure.

"Both legs at the same time," he finally croaks.

"What's the magic word?"

He cracks a lid and glares at me from a single eyeball. "Please."

"Look at you, using manners and shit." I manage to get the lower half of his body on the couch. He barely fits. As it is, his feet hang over the armrest. "I'm going to get you a glass of water and a painkiller, okay?"

"Just the water is good. Thanks." His eyes fall closed, and he crosses his arms over his chest. Despite his red face and the fine sheen of sweat dotting his forehead, he's still a good-looking asshole.

I leave him there, somewhat assuaged by the amount of pain it causes him to move. I grab him a pillow and blanket, then stop in the kitchen to pour him a glass of water. I make it a plastic tumbler, since his coordination seems questionable.

By the time I get back to the living room, where he's sprawled across the couch, his breathing has evened out. I set the water on the coffee table and drape the blanket over his huge body. His feet still poke out, but at least he's mostly covered. I gently slip a hand behind his head and lift enough to slide the pillow under his neck so he doesn't wake up with a terrible crick. Well, no worse than the one he'll probably already have, considering how I found him in the hallway.

He hums in his sleep and frees one of his hands from the blanket. His fingers wrap around my wrist, lapping each other. I suck in a breath at the unexpected contact. A zap of electricity pings through my arm, like static.

His eyes flip open, locking on mine. They're hazy and glassy with pain and exhaustion. "Thank you."

"You're welcome." My voice is all breathy, like I've been running laps.

"I didn't want you to be this nice." He lets go of my wrist, and his eyes slide closed.

I don't know if I misheard that, or misunderstood it, or if it's supposed to make any kind of sense at all.

Regardless of how helpless he is, I lock my bedroom door before I go to sleep.

◆ ◆ ◆

I get up at eight the next morning, impressed with how well I slept for having had a virtual stranger in my living room all night. The fact that he's injured helps. I pad down the hall and peek into the living room.

There's no longer a giant of a man sprawled out on the couch. The blanket has been tossed on the floor. Awesome manners this guy has.

I shake my head, annoyed, and continue on to the kitchen. Once the coffee is percolating, the drip, drip, drip inspires the need to pee, and I rush down the hall to the spare bathroom, the urge sudden and strong.

I wrench open the door and come to an abrupt halt when I find my neighbor, one hand braced on the vanity as he relieves himself with a loud, low groan. It sounds like part relief and part agony.

I can only attribute my knee-jerk response to surprise. And my reaction is to scream. Because that's what a person does when they find a massive, very well built man unexpectedly relieving himself in their bathroom.

My piercing shriek startles him, and he twists in my direction.

I back out of the bathroom and slam the door shut, but it does not erase what I've seen. My jerkwad neighbor is well endowed. Not in a terrifying "Do you shoot porn?" kind of way but more of a "That would be a welcome stretch." It also appears that he was trying to manage relieving himself while dealing with morning wood. I didn't realize that was possible.

A bloodcurdling scream and a low thud follow as I slam the door. Since the noise didn't come from me, it means it came from him. Obviously I scared him as much as he scared me.

"Shit. What the hell do I do?" I ask the wall as I press my ear to the door. I can hear groans and whimpers from the other side. "Are you okay?"

"No." The single word is followed by more groaning.

"I'm coming back in," I warn. It's not like I can leave him in there anyway. I have to get ready for work.

I turn the knob and peek through the narrow gap. He's still on the floor. I push the door open farther and cringe. He's managed to pee all over the seat. And he may have sprayed the vanity. Gross. At least it doesn't seem to be all over the floor too.

I notice a few more details now that I'm back in "feeling bad" mode instead of "panic and shock" mode. Once again he's in only a pair of boxer briefs. These ones are bright yellow with **CAUTION** written all over them, like the tape they use at crime scenes. He was fully dressed when I left him on the couch last night.

From across the hall his body is a lot to handle visually, but this close, good God, this man is *stacked*. Muscles layer over muscles, everything tight and defined. He's just . . . a lot. And he takes up a considerable amount of space in this bathroom.

Based on the way he's breathing like an angry bull, he's also in pain. That still doesn't explain where the rest of his clothes went. I'll come back to that, though.

"What do you need?" Apart from a shower, most likely.

"I can't reach my crutches." He motions to where they lean against the wall on the opposite side of the vanity. It's not particularly far, but I'm assuming his level of pain makes him incapable of getting to them.

I reach over him and flip the toilet seat down first, then grab the crutches and position them on either side of him. It's awkward, since he's facing the toilet, and I'm forced to stand behind him. My feet are sort of touching his, which is weird, but there's not much I can do about that. He braces on the handgrips and swears a blue streak as he slowly hoists himself up.

As someone who is trained in injury rehab and physical therapy, I should know what to do, but usually the people I'm treating are wearing more clothes and haven't scared the shit out of me or insulted me on several occasions. Also, this guy probably weighs twice what I do. I slip my hands under his arms to . . . I don't know . . . provide support?

"What're you doing?"

"Helping you?" I'm fully pressed up against his back. His incredibly defined, very warm, very hard, muscly back.

"By humping me from behind?" he grunts.

I step away, because screw him. He stumbles and loses his hold on one of his crutches, forcing him to use the counter to brace his weight again. I hope his hand is in his own pee.

"Will you sit down before you break something?" I snap.

"I'm trying. You're all up in my personal freaking space."

"I'm not even touching you anymore! And I was helping. God, why are you such an asshole?"

"Because I'm in pain! Why are *you* such a morally defunct home-wrecker?"

"What?"

He spins around, and again it's more graceful than I'd expect for someone his size, in his condition. I temporarily forget the home-wrecker comment when he bashes me in the shin with the end of his crutch. It might be covered in rubber, but it hurts like hell.

I drop to the floor and clutch my shin as he sits on the closed toilet seat. "Ow! Seriously?" This is what I get for being nice to someone with a pretty face and the personality of a praying mantis.

My current position puts me right between Jerkwad's spread thighs. I'm also almost at eye level with his **CAUTION** crotch. As distracting as his underwear is, I finally understand why this guy is in so much pain. "Holy shit! What the hell happened to you?"

The inside of his left thigh is a mottled mass of mostly black, purple, and a lot of blue spanning all the way down to his knee.

"I hurt myself."

"How the hell do you get a groin injury like that? What were you *doing*?" I've never seen one this bad—not even in my textbooks from college, or the videos I've watched online.

"Fucking around, obviously."

"Sex caused this?" Jesus. What kind of shape was the woman in if he's this messed up?

He rolls his eyes. "Not sex. I was playing hockey."

"You play hockey?"

"Yeah." He looks at me like I'm an idiot.

"What kind of hockey?"

His lip twitches. "The professional kind."

I can feel my eyebrows pop. "Like NHL? For Seattle?"

"Yeah." He seems as though he's waiting for some kind of reaction.

It would've been nice if my brother had told me my neighbor was also his teammate. Although maybe I should've put two and two together. Then I remember the hit we saw yesterday. "Are you Winslow? Number fifty-two?"

"Uh-huh."

"Well, by the look of things you're going to be watching the action from the bench for a while. You need to ice this."

I move in closer, the physiotherapist in me taking over as I brace my hands on his knees and inspect the bruising. I smooth my hand up his hard thigh. The muscles tense under his warm skin as I palpate around the edge of the discoloration with my thumb. This is a really bad injury. The kind I'd love to have a hand in rehabilitating.

"Ow! What the hell are you doing?" Jerkwad growls.

"Don't worry. I'm a professional."

CHAPTER 9
MAYBE I WAS A LITTLE WRONG

Bishop

I'm in a lot of pain, the kind that makes bile rise in your throat, gives you the sweats, and puts black-and-white dots in your vision. Partly because I haven't taken any pain meds since last night, and also because Rook's sidepiece is on her knees between my legs.

She's dressed in one of those tanks with straps I can shred with my fingertips and a pair of sleep shorts that rival those running ones she parades around in when she's getting her paper in the morning. Her nipples are peaked against the thin fabric. And there's cleavage. So much cleavage.

My body is trying to react to her state of semiundress and how close her face is to my dick. It's fucking agony. And also a serious moral dilemma. I'm pissed that my body is responding when clearly it should not.

"Puck bunny isn't a profession, sweetheart," I grind out.

Her head snaps up, eyes meeting mine. They're clear and blue like the ocean. I can see the allure. My dick agrees that she's hot, since I'm still halfway hard even though it's viciously painful.

"Excuse me?" Her grip on my thighs tightens, which means she's digging her fingers into my bruises.

It makes me woozy. I grab her wrist, because I need her to stop touching me for a number of reasons, ethical issues and pain being at the forefront.

"You think you can jump from one player to the next, and no one is going to give a fuck? Christ. You might as well be sucking on my balls with how up in my space you are. Where the hell is your moral compass?" Okay, that was extra graphic, but seriously, her nose is almost pressed up against my junk, she's so close.

She uses my thighs to push to a stand, which feels pretty damn awful. She's not particularly tall, so her nipples are pointing right at my face. "What the hell are you talking about? Who are you to call me a puck bunny?"

"You're banging the team captain, who has a fucking *wife and kid*, and now you're all over my jock." I motion to my crotch.

"Banging the . . ." Her brows furrow and her nose scrunches up. She makes a gagging sound and then throws her head back and laughs. It's a nice laugh, even if it's full of sarcasm. "Oh my God. Rook is my *brother*, you asshole!"

"Yeah, right."

She rolls her eyes and grins widely, pointing to the dimple high on her cheek. "See the resemblance?"

"Not really. No," I say truthfully, because I haven't paid enough attention to Rook's face in the time I've been on the team, which hasn't been long. Also, on the infrequent occasions I do make eye contact with Rook, both of us are usually scowling.

Her hair smacks me in the face as she spins on her heel and stalks out of the bathroom. I loathe admitting I stare at her ass. She returns less than a minute later with a framed photo and a few pieces of paper. She tosses the papers at me—they turn out to be envelopes that read **STEVIE BOWMAN.**

"Is this supposed to mean something to me?"

"Stevie is my name." She points at her chest, which draws attention to her cleavage and her pert nipples. Her tank is white, and even though it has one of those built-in bra things so there's an extra layer of fabric between her nipples and my eyeballs, I can still see the outline of her areolae. They're small and delicate, and the whole thing would easily fit in my mouth. *Why the hell can't I stop thinking about sex?*

I roll my eyes. "Nice try. Stevie is a guy's name."

"I'm named after my dad." She holds the framed picture an inch from my nose.

It's too close for me to make out the actual faces, so I take it from her, somewhat forcefully. It's an older photo, based on how young Rook is, but beside him is the woman standing in front of me, hair light blonde instead of pale pink. They're both smiling, and I see now the resemblance she was talking about.

I look up at her and then back down at the picture. "Shit. You're Bowman's baby sister?"

"I'm hardly a baby." She crosses her arms, pushing her tits up and highlighting her cleavage.

"Yeah, I can see that." I force my eyes back up to her face. At least I feel slightly less bad about noticing how hot she is.

"I can't believe you thought I was his, what . . . mistress?" She flips her hair over her shoulder and sneers.

I throw my hands up in the air. "Well, what the hell was I supposed to think when you show up in the middle of the night looking like something the cat dragged in, being all evasive and noisy and shit?"

"I wasn't being evasive."

"You could've said you were Bowman's sister from the start, though. It would've cleared up a lot of shit."

"Would it have changed how much of an asshole you've been?"

"Well, yeah, of course." If I'd known who she was, I wouldn't have been such a giant dick.

She props her fist on her curvy hip. "I shouldn't have to announce that I'm related to my famous fucking brother for people to be nice to me."

I drag a palm down my face. She's missing the damn point. "That's not—"

Her hand shoots out in front of my face, startling me. I almost fall off the slippery toilet seat. "As fun as this conversation has been, I have to get ready for work, so now is probably a good time for you to get your shit and head back to your asshole headquarters. You're super welcome for taking care of your rude ass last night." She spins around and stalks out of the bathroom.

"I thought you were a morally deficient stick chaser! And I'm always an asshole," I yell after her.

A door slams from down the hall.

"Dammit." I drop my head in my hands and mutter a string of curses. This is not awesome. I've been a total dick to Bowman's sister. I mean, I'm a dick most of the time, but I was extra dicky with her. And I pissed all over her bathroom. Plus I've insulted her a bunch of times. If she tells him, it's going to make my life even more miserable. Maybe she already has.

I use my crutches to pull myself up. I do a half-assed job of cleaning up the mess I made all over her toilet seat, and the side of the vanity, and the floor. I even managed to get the damn mirror. I might have to send my cleaner over to deal with this.

I debate whether I should leave but decide it would be better to try to smooth things over and lessen the chance of her ratting me out to her brother. I crutch down the hall, slowly. I need to take some painkillers and lie down again.

I reach what I'm assuming is her bedroom and knock on the door. "Hey, uh, Stevie?" It's a weird name, but it seems to fit her.

"Are you *still* here?" The door swings open. "And still in your damn underwear. Where the hell are your pants?"

I follow the movement as she pulls a shirt over her head, covering her sports bra and her smooth, toned stomach. She has an incredible athletic body, one I no longer feel guilty about ogling now that I know she's not screwing my married team captain.

"I think we got off on the wrong foot. If I'd known you were Rook's sister—"

"You would've toned your asshole down." She brushes by me and heads toward the living room.

I can't keep up because moving too fast makes me feel like I'm going to vomit. "Look, I'm sorry," I call after her.

"You're only sorry because my brother is a big deal."

I crutch after her, grunting through the pain. "That has nothing to do with it. I just don't want to make waves with my team."

She spins around angrily. "Oh, now I get it. You want to make sure I won't tell my brother about this. Well, don't worry. I'm not really dying to share the whole boner-killer comment with anyone, let alone RJ."

Shit. I forgot about that less-than-flattering insult. "You were a hot mess."

She glares at me, then forcefully gathers my clothes and shoes from the floor and stalks to the door. I must have gotten hot in the middle of the night and taken everything off, although I don't remember that. She unlocks it with a jerky movement and tosses them into the hallway. "Leave. Now."

I blow out a breath; clearly I'm not making things better with my apology. I hobble past her and turn with the intention of telling her I don't think she's a boner-killer at all, but she slams the door in my face.

"That went well." I bend and snag my jogging pants. As I drape them around my neck, I feel around for my phone and slip it out of my pocket so I can check my messages. My brother has finally gotten back to me. Apparently the door is unlocked now, so I can let myself in. I pick up my discarded shirt and fumble with my shoes but manage to keep ahold of everything until I reach my door.

I'm a whole lot stunned as I shoulder my way inside. My broth-er's most recent lady friend comes sauntering through my living room wearing last night's dress, a pair of heels that are way too high for this early in the morning, and what's left of yesterday's makeup.

She gives me a slow once-over, her smile widening. "Oh! Hi!"

I point in the direction I just came from. "The door's that way."

My brother appears at the end of the hall, wearing blue pants and a white golf shirt and staring at his phone, possibly setting up tonight's date. It wouldn't be the first time. "Shippy isn't a morning person. Just ignore him."

"We talked about this," I gripe as I crutch past him.

He finally drags his eyes away from the screen, and they widen when they land on me. "What the hell happened to you?"

"Hockey." I continue down the hall, leaving him to deal with his date.

Once I'm in my room, I toss yesterday's clothes on the end of the bed and root around in the pocket again until I find the painkillers. All I want is to lie down and sleep until my body doesn't hurt anymore.

There's a glass of water on my nightstand. It's two days old, but I'm too lazy to get fresh water, so I use it to swallow the pills. Stevie's right: I should ice my leg . . . but I don't feel like going back to the kitchen, so instead I stretch out on top of my comforter and wait for the painkiller to kick in, along with the drowsiness.

My bedroom door swings open a few seconds later. My brother points at my crotch and cups his own with his free hand. "Dude, that looks bad."

I drag my gaze away from the ceiling. "It feels worse than bad. Can you grab me an ice pack from the freezer?"

"Sure." Nolan disappears down the hall and returns with one of my gel ice packs and a hand towel.

I drape the towel over my leg and set the pack on top, cringing as the cold skims my balls. They immediately attempt a hasty retreat, causing a shock of pain. I groan and tense, making it worse for a few terrible, mind-bending seconds.

"So what happened exactly?" Nolan jumps onto the bed with his lunch box of medical supplies. Thankfully, it's a shock-free mattress, so I don't feel the movement at all.

Dicken, his black-and-white cat, follows suit. He rubs himself on Nolan's leg, then plunks himself down beside me and rests his paw on my arm. He starts kneading at me, claws digging in, his way of telling me he wants pets.

I rub Dicken's head while I fill my brother in on the hit I took last night and the splits I shouldn't have done, which was followed by the trip to the clinic and the six-week hiatus from the ice. I finish up with how I lost my key card down the elevator shaft and ended up on the couch at our neighbor's across the hall.

"You should've messaged when you were at the clinic, and I would've gotten rid of my date."

"I was a little preoccupied." I drag a hand down my face and cringe. My cheek hit the goalpost when I went down, but the groin injury is far worse, so I didn't notice the other pain until this morning. "So you know how I thought she was Bowman's sidepiece or whatever?"

"You've been bitching about it since she moved in weeks ago, so yeah."

"Turns out she's Bowman's little sister." Which actually makes a hell of a lot more sense.

"No shit? Is she single?"

I turn my head only enough so that I can glare at him. "Don't even think about it."

He stares right back, one brow arched. "Oh man, now this all makes sense. You have the hots for her, don't you?"

"No. I don't." I return my gaze to the ceiling. She's got great nipples, though, and a seriously sweet rack.

"I don't believe you." He pricks himself with his blood sugar–tester device so he can check his levels before giving himself his shot. It's the first of five he'll administer today.

"And that should matter why?"

"You've been bitching about this woman incessantly since she moved in. First it was because she was so damn loud and because you didn't approve of her moral standings or whatever. Then you bitched about her being a student and wearing too much perfume. After that you started moaning about how she's always in workout gear and doesn't she have real clothes, blah blah. I'd also like to point out that unless you have to leave this apartment, you're always in boxers. I'm so familiar with the outline of your junk I could identify it in a lineup before I could my own."

"I don't see how my observations can be construed as having the hots for her." I ignore the part about my junk because it's my place and I can wear whatever I want. If Nolan wants to wander around in his boxers, he's free to, although he gets cold because his circulation isn't the best.

"You haven't talked this much about a woman since Penny."

"That name is banned; don't bring her up again." Penny was my last semiserious girlfriend. That ended because Penny was more concerned with how many likes her posed photos with me had on her social media profiles than she was with me as an actual person.

"Just sayin'. It's been a long time since anything but hockey has lit a fire under your ass."

"An annoyance is not the same thing."

"You keep living in denial, Shippy." He lifts his shirt and catches the hem with his chin. He pinches a roll of skin between two fingers—he has to hunch forward because he's lean—and stabs himself, depressing the needle.

"It's not denial."

He drops his shirt and rubs the injection site. "I've seen you with your face pressed against the door in the morning, waiting for her."

"That's not because I have the hots for her."

"Uh-huh. You know, if you need dating tips, I'm here for you, bro."

"I don't need dating tips. I can pick up women fine. If I feel like putting in the effort." Which I often don't.

"I'm just saying, your pretty face isn't going to last forever, and eventually your hairline is going to start receding." He ruffles my hair, and I bat his hand away. "One day you'll have to work on your interpersonal skills and learn how to flirt, unless you're content with self-love for the rest of your life."

"Based on this"—I point to my groin—"I don't think I'm going to get any kind of lovin', self-imposed or otherwise, for a good while."

"Yeah. That's gonna suck." He packs up his insulin kit and slides off the bed. "You need anything before I head out? My shift is only four hours, and I don't have class, so I'll be back early this afternoon."

"Nah, I'm good. Thanks for asking, though."

I stare at the ceiling and think about my neighbor. Rook Bowman's baby sister.

For the past several weeks I've been taunting her. At first it was mostly curiosity and the perverse enjoyment of making her uncomfortable. Because I thought she was someone she's not. Because who I thought she was offended me on a moral level.

Nolan is right about me waiting around in the morning with my face pressed against the door. I didn't realize he'd seen me doing that. I've felt half-guilty, half-vengeful over the fact that I'm enjoying the strange underwear competition we have going on. Like we're both trying to get a reaction out of each other.

This frames everything in a whole new light. And I'm not sure what to do about that. Or the fact that I've been getting hard over her in that freaking workout gear.

Maybe Nolan is right. Maybe I do have the hots for her. I mean, physically she's nice to look at. She's got a great body and a sharp tongue. She smells good. All things I can appreciate in a woman.

Except she's the baby sister of my team captain. Who I loathe.

If I was a vindictive person, I might use that to my advantage.

CHAPTER 10

APOLOGIES AND FAVORS

Stevie

I arrive at work with only minutes to spare before my first client arrives, which is not how I like to start my day. I'm always at the clinic a good half hour early so I can review my schedule and pull treatment plans before my clients arrive. I also like to chat with Pattie and Jules and my other colleagues—aside from Joey, whom I staunchly try to avoid.

And who also happens to be the first person I run into as I jam my stuff in my locker.

"Hey." He props his forearm on the locker beside mine.

"What do you want?" I don't bother to look at him, because then I'll have to see his smarmy expression, and his armpit hair will be right in my face. He always wears muscle shirts between clients. I used to think it was endearing, but it's gross.

"I signed us up to work on the fundraiser gala together. I said we could handle the decorations part, 'cause you're all crafty and stuff. I thought it would be a good idea, since you're new and it'll make us look good. Plus it'll give us a chance to hang out."

All I want to do is punch him in the nuts and make him cry, but instead I grit out, "Awesome. Thanks." Clearly it's full of sarcasm and disdain, which he either doesn't pick up on or decides to ignore.

"I know you're still angry with me, Stevie, but I really think this will be good for us."

I slam my locker shut and stare at the gray paint for a few seconds while I take some calming breaths. What I should do is tell him to fuck off and find someone else to work with. As much as I'd rather have my fingernails ripped off one by one in lieu of working with Joey on anything, I recognize putting up a fight will create complications.

I slowly turn to face him, forgetting that his arm is positioned above his head. It looks like one of those troll heads is sprouting from his armpit. There's also a small clump of deodorant tucked in among the hairs, like his troll has dandruff. "For you, you mean; it'll be good for *you*," I say to his armpit troll. Joey is the opposite of crafty, so I'm assuming the workload is going to fall solely on me.

"Stevie." He drops his arm.

"I have a client." I sidestep around him and head for the door so I'm not tempted to do something that will get me written up for workplace harassment.

Pattie and Jules grab me before lunch and steer me away from the staff room. "We need to talk to you," Jules says as we step out into the warm September afternoon and drop our stuff on the closest picnic table.

"Joey already cornered me this morning."

"We're so sorry. He's never here early, but today he was, and he signed you up right in front of Loretta, so we couldn't do anything about it." Pattie looks as distressed as I felt when he corralled me by my locker earlier.

I pat her hand reassuringly before I continue to unpack my lunch. "It's okay. I appreciate the attempted save."

"Maybe we could talk to Loretta and explain the situation so you can get out of it."

I shrug off the idea. Complaining to my boss about working with my ex-boyfriend won't look great on me, and I'm not particularly keen on explaining my personal life to the people who issue my paychecks. "Honestly, it's probably best if I deal with Joey. If nothing else I can make his life miserable while he's forcing us to spend time together. Plus he owes me money, and it'll be easier to get it out of him this way." I hope I'm right about that. Joey isn't known for his great money-management skills, hence the reason I had to front all the first month's rent in advance. The more time I have to think about it, the more I realize how poor a boyfriend choice he really was.

Pattie makes a face. "What if we sign up too? So you could come over to our place to work on it. Can you imagine how uncomfortable Joey would be, surrounded by our brothers?"

As alluring as the idea is, I'm not sure it's a good one in the long run. "I appreciate the offer, and if I need backup, I'll let you know. Anyway, change of topic from one douche to another. You know that guy I told you about who lives across the hall?"

"You mean Billboard Balls?" Jules asks.

"That's the one." I nod.

Pattie props her chin on her fist. "That is literally my favorite nickname ever. What kind of panties was he sporting this morning?"

"Caution tape, but there's more." I fill them in on what happened last night: how I was nice enough to let him sleep on my couch despite his being a giant a-hole and that I found out this morning that he's my brother's teammate, Bishop Winslow, the guy who was injured in last night's exhibition game.

"Whoa, wait, you're telling me you have a professional hockey player living across the hall from you with a groin injury?" Pattie's eyes light up like a disco ball.

"Who is on my brother's team and who thought I was my brother's mistress until this morning, yes."

Jules makes a face. "That's just . . . ew."

"Very ew," Pattie agrees, "but I guess I can kind of see where he might have gotten the idea."

"That I was a puck bunny?"

"Yes. No. I mean, why else would a hot woman suddenly move into an empty penthouse in the middle of the night that is supposed to be for your brother, right? It's not like you broadcast that you're related to Rook. You don't have any pictures of him on your social media, and all of these guys are new to each other. I'm just saying I can kind of see how he might make that mistake, and if you think about it, maybe it's a good thing he was an asshole to you."

"How is him being an asshole a good thing?" I pop a grape into my mouth.

"He thought you were screwing a married guy with a family. At least you know he has a moral compass."

"Ooh, good point." Jules nods her agreement.

I hadn't thought of it that way, but I guess it sort of makes sense, especially with his "morally defunct" and "home-wrecker" comments. "He called me a boner-killer."

Pattie makes a face. "You are definitely not a boner-killer. My guess is he said that because he thought you were a bunny. Anyway, I have a spectacular idea." She pauses, maybe for effect.

"Which is what?" Jules quirks a brow.

"You should offer to help him with PT." Pattie smiles widely, as if she's handed me the Holy Grail.

"Why would I do that when he's been nothing but a huge jerk?"

Pattie grins. "If for no other reason than his being a jerk is the top of the list."

"That makes no sense." I pluck another grape from my container. "Besides, the team will already have a physiotherapist working with him."

"Yes, but groin injuries are hell, and they take weeks to heal. It's Seattle's first season. Every single player on that team—apart from your brother, who waived his no-trade clause—has something huge to prove. They're all seconds. They weren't good enough to save, but they're good enough to start a new team. That has to mess with a player's head."

"Especially when he gets injured in the first exhibition game of the season," Jules adds.

"Exactly." Pattie points her carrot stick at me. "He's going to want to be on the ice sooner rather than later."

"Okay, I can see what you're saying." I imagine if RJ were the one with the injury, he'd do everything he could to get back in the game.

"I bet all it would take is the suggestion that more PT is better than less to get him to agree. And if he does, you'll have experience working with an NHL professional, which is more than anyone else on our staff can say. Also, you said he's hot, and you'll get to help him stretch out his groin, which will be hella uncomfortable for him and payback for you. It's all win."

"There's no guarantee he'll agree to let me help him."

Jules snorts. "Do you want to know why seventy-five percent of your current clients are either women over fifty or girls with injuries?"

"Because I'm new?"

"Because the managers don't trust the jocks not to hit on you." Pattie takes a long sip of her iced tea.

"Or fake groin injuries so you'll rub down the inside of their thighs." Jules waggles her brows.

I roll my eyes. "Oh, come on."

"Seriously, we overheard two of the managers talking about it yesterday because you had like five thousand requests, and every single one is a dude."

"I'm sure you're exaggerating."

"You're hot, Stevie. It's a blessing and a curse."

Jules clinks her iced tea against Pattie's. "Might as well use it to your advantage."

◆ ◆ ◆

I don't get home until after seven. Thankfully, I don't run into Joey again, although he does text me, asking when we can get together to start planning for the gala. I ignore the message rather than respond with something along the lines of *When the eleventh circle of hell opens and clowns are running the show.*

I'm barely in my door when there's a knock. I press my eye to the peephole and find my neighbor's chiseled jaw taking up the window of space. I can't imagine what he could possibly want, unless he's left something in my apartment.

I unhook the chain latch, turn the lock, and school my expression into something that I hope looks unimpressed before I throw open the door. He's wearing a worn gray T-shirt with some vaguely familiar logo on it and equally worn navy sweatpants. I'd like to say he looks a lot better in his underwear than he does clothed, but that might be a lie.

The T-shirt stretches across his broad chest, contouring to the muscles. His pants, which might be baggy on a different body type, hug his muscular thighs.

"Oh look, you do actually own clothes." I'm going for bitchy-slash-sarcastic to offset the fact that I have openly ogled him.

"Uh, yeah. I just don't like wearing them unless I have to leave my apartment." He thumbs over his shoulder.

That's an interesting thing to admit to someone he hardly knows. "So you're what? A home nudist?"

The image of him this morning, holding his trouser snake—and subsequently peeing all over my toilet seat—pops into my head. I have enough of a visual, minus what his ass looks like *not* covered in fabric, to almost perfectly imagine him swinging free.

"If my brother didn't live with me, I might be." He slips his crutches out from under his arms and leans them against the wall. "Anyway, I wanted to bring you a peace offering." He braces a hand on the doorframe and grimaces as he bends forward.

That's when I notice the pizza box from Sammy's Pizzeria and the potted plant on the floor by his feet. I've ordered from there a couple of times in the past week because there was a brochure stuck to the fridge with a magnet that boasted a free pizza. "Why don't you let me get that?"

"I can do it," he grunts. He's folded over, trying to bend at the knees and lower himself enough to pick the stuff up.

"Even if you can, I'm going to go ahead and say you probably *shouldn't.*"

He ignores me and manages to catch the edge of the potted plant. He rights himself and thrusts it at me with a groan. "This is for you."

"You're giving me an aloe plant?"

"I noticed you didn't have any plants in your apartment. My brother has a green thumb, and we have like fifteen aloe plants. They're hardy and useful." His eyes dart around, and the tips of his ears go red.

"Okay. Well, thanks?" I can't decide whether it's a thoughtful gift or just convenient. Either way, it's unconventional. And possibly a little odd that he noticed my lack of plants.

"You're welcome." He starts to bend again.

I crouch and pick up the pizza box before he gets too far and ends up face planting into my feet. "Do you need help getting into your apartment with this?"

"It's for you." His cheeks have turned the same color as his ears.

"You brought me an aloe plant and a pizza?" I set the plant on the side table by the door so I can take a peek inside the box. It's the exact same kind I've ordered both times since I moved in: pepperoni, bacon, ham, pineapple, green olives, and hot peppers. It's an odd combination, but the sweet of the pineapple with the salty of the olives and the heat of the peppers is delicious. At least I think so. The question is, How the hell does my neighbor know *exactly* what I like on my pizza?

He must read the question on my face, because his goes even redder, if that's even possible. "I saw a couple of boxes from Sammy's in your recycling, so I called and ordered whatever had been delivered last."

That's a lot less creepy and a lot more resourceful than any of the other scenarios I entertained, like him going through my garbage and performing a sniff test. "Thanks for bringing me dinner and a plant?" I don't know what else to say to him. It's a nice gesture, even if it's a strange one.

"I ordered the pizza like an hour ago, thinking you'd be home earlier, so you might need to reheat it."

"Okay." I don't make a move to close the door, and he doesn't make a move to leave.

He chews on the inside of his lip like he's waiting for something. Maybe he expects me to invite him to share the pizza with me. Or this is supposed to be his way of wiping the slate clean.

"Is there something else?"

He blows out a breath. "I, uh . . . I could kind of use a favor."

Well, that explains the plant and the pizza. "A favor?"

"Yeah. Uh, my car is still at the arena, and I left a bunch of stuff in it that I need, but I can't drive." He rubs the back of his neck. "If you're not busy, maybe I can ask you to come with me to drive it home?"

I stare at him for a few seconds, trying to figure out if he's serious. This actually works perfectly with the whole idea Pattie proposed, but

I'm still reasonably wary. "Why wouldn't you ask your brother? Unless he doesn't actually exist."

"He exists; he can't drive me, though." He fidgets, adjusting his stance again. Perspiration breaks across his forehead. I wonder if it's pain induced or caused by embarrassment, or something else.

"Can't you wait until he gets home?" It would be far less awkward than being stuck in a car with me.

"He's home. He doesn't have a license."

"Oh." He doesn't offer more information, and I don't press for it. "Yeah, I guess I can help you pick up your car. You wanna go now?"

"You can eat your pizza first." He motions to the box, which I'm still holding.

"That's okay. I went out with friends after work and we ordered appetizers, so I'm not super hungry right now. Let me put this in the fridge and grab my purse. Unless you want a slice or something?"

"Uh, no, thanks. That combination of toppings is pretty gag worthy."

"Don't knock it until you try it." I leave him standing in the hall, put the pizza in the fridge, and consider stopping in the bathroom to make sure I look okay but decide against putting in the effort, since he's not asking for help for any reason other than I'm convenient.

He's leaning against the wall, head bowed with his phone in his hand, when I come back out. "The Uber will be here in a couple of minutes."

"Great."

The ride down to the lobby is awkward. He leans against the mirrored glass with his eyes closed and breathes heavily through his nose.

"Are you okay?"

He cracks one lid. "Yeah. I'll be better when I'm sitting down again."

I don't bother with more chitchat on the short trip to the lobby. The Uber is already waiting. Bishop opens the door and motions for me to get in. I guess he does have some manners.

"Why don't you go first?" I suggest.

He looks like he wants to argue but decides against it. He lowers himself slowly into the back seat and grunts as he lifts each leg in, folding himself into the sedan. He's huge and it's a Civic, so there isn't a ton of room for his long legs or the rest of his body.

I lay the crutches over his lap and get in on the other side, putting me behind the driver. The arena isn't terribly far from the apartment, and rush-hour traffic is long over. During the short trip our Uber driver tells us all about his plan to become a famous musician. He even hands me a postcard when we're stopped at a light and proceeds to tell us he's the lead singer of his band, and he plays the guitar. "You should totally come see the band this weekend." His gaze shifts to Bishop in the rearview mirror, but Bishop's eyes are closed. "You can bring your boyfriend too."

I snort. "He's not my boyfriend."

Bishop cracks a lid and eyes me from the side but doesn't comment.

"Oh?" Uber Driver, whose name is Jett, according to the tag hanging from the rearview mirror, perks up. "Well, in that case maybe you wanna come see me play, and we can get a drink afterward?"

Bishop scoffs. "Are you seriously trying to pick her up?"

"Are you guys, like, a thing?" Uber Jett's eyes dart from me to Bishop.

"No, but it's pretty tacky, don't you think? First of all, you have no idea what's going on between us. Just because she told you I'm not her boyfriend doesn't mean I'm not *something*. I'm not, but that's beside the point." Bishop's annoyed gaze locks on the side of my face. "Also, what's she gonna say when she's trapped in this car with you until we get where we're going? You're almost forcing her to say yes, even if she doesn't want to."

"It's really okay." I pin Bishop with a "What the fuck?" look and slip the postcard in my purse.

"It's really not," Bishop says.

Thankfully, we pull into the arena parking lot, and Bishop gives him clipped, irritated directions to his car, ending whatever that was.

CHAPTER 11

SMALL SPACES

Bishop

I don't know why I'm being such an asshole to the Uber kid, other than he's being ballsy with the way he asked out Rook's baby sister. I'm tempted to one star him, but then he might one star me back.

He might one star me anyway. Not that I honestly give a shit.

Stevie doesn't offer to help me get out of the car, which is a lot harder than getting in. Uber Kid takes off as soon as I close the door.

"Well, that was fun." Stevie's arms are crossed, and it draws attention to her perky tits, the nipples of which are burned into my memory for all eternity.

"You're out of his league, and he's not even remotely your type."

"You have no idea what my type is," she snaps.

"I know it's not a chain-smoking Uber driver who probably snorts blow." I dig around in my sweats pocket until I find the keys to my SUV. The lights flash as I unlock the doors and hand the keys to her.

She looks my car over. It's not flashy or overly expensive. It's practical, decent on gas, and fits all my hockey gear. I like my money in my bank account more than I like fast cars. Would I enjoy driving around in a sweet sports car? Maybe, but dropping a quarter of a million dollars on a vehicle is a stupid way to burn through money when I have no idea how long my career is going to last. I'm pragmatic and I don't have a five-year contract with an $11-million-a-year salary like her brother does. All I have is two seasons at five mil a year, and I'd like that to last the rest of my life and Nolan's if it needs to.

I toss my crutches in the back while she adjusts the driver's seat so she can reach the gas and brake.

I'm about to get in when Kingston comes jogging across the lot. His hair is wet and parted on the side. He looks a lot like Captain America and dresses like a golf pro. It fits his personality. "Hey! I'm surprised to see you. I figured you wouldn't be moving around for at least a couple more days."

I lean against the side of my SUV. "Just coming to pick up my car."

"I would've brought it back for you." His Volvo SUV beeps from the next spot over, and he tosses his hockey bag in the back seat. He peeks over my shoulder and tips his chin up. "Who's driving?"

"Just a friend." I shift so I'm blocking the passenger-side window. "What're you doing here so late?"

"Running ice drills with a few of the guys—you know, keeping sharp for tomorrow night's game." He's still trying to see around me. "Is that a *girl*?"

"Uh, yeah." King and I might be friends, but there's no way I'm going to tell him it's the team captain's little sister driving my car.

"Since when do you have a girlfriend?"

"I don't. She's a friend who also happens to be a girl." She's not even really that.

"You're being awfully cagey about her if she's just a friend. Don't think I can't tell you're trying to hide her." He opens his driver's-side door and climbs in. "Miss you on the ice, buddy. Give me a call if you need anything; otherwise I'll stop by later in the week, 'kay?"

"I'll make sure I'm stocked up on two percent milk."

"Does a body good." He actually means it like the commercial, not like he's full of himself. I wait until he closes his door before I turn back to my SUV. I have to open mine all the way so I can get in, but my body blocks most of King's view.

"Does that guy play for Seattle too?" Stevie leans forward, like she's trying to see around me.

"Yeah. That's Ryan Kingston; he's a goalie. Why?"

Stevie shrugs. "No reason." She watches him pull out of the spot. He waves as he passes us, so she waves in return.

"He's a super-straight arrow, and there's no way in hell he'd be interested in you."

She glares at me, full top lip pulled up in disgusted sneer. "Could you be any more offensive?"

I hold up a hand. "That came out wrong. You're the team captain's little sister. He's a rule follower, so even if he was interested, he would never make a move, because it would go against his moral code. Also, he has a girlfriend, and they've been together for years."

"Right. Okay. Let's also not forget that I'm a boner-killer."

I sigh. I should probably learn how and when not to be an asshole. "I only said that because I thought you were screwing your brother." I cringe. "I mean I thought you were his other woman, not his sister."

"Uh-huh."

She has to know she's hot. I don't see how she couldn't. She sees her own face in the mirror every day. It's not hard to look at, and neither is the rest of her. "You're not a boner-killer. You got hit on by the damn Uber driver with me sitting right next to you. That has to tell you something about your appeal to the opposite sex."

"That guy looked like Justin Bieber's emo brother." She types the address to our building into the GPS while I shift around, trying to get comfortable—which isn't easy, considering my pain level.

It's been six hours since I took anything for the discomfort and swelling, partly because I want to see how bad the pain gets. The medication the doctor prescribed is good for taking the edge off, but it also keeps me from knowing exactly how severe the injury is. Based on the black spots in my vision every time I make a sudden move, I'm thinking it's pretty damn bad. I groan as I stretch my leg out.

"Did you ice your injury today?" Stevie flips through my music presets until she finds something she presumably likes.

"Yeah."

"What about heat and stretching?" She shifts the SUV into gear.

"Nope."

"When do you start rehab?"

"Probably in a couple of days."

"You should stretch and massage the areas around the injury site that aren't too tender to keep the muscles from seizing."

"I'll take that under advisement." I don't get why she's suddenly on a worried-mom-style inquisition. It's frustrating that I can't escape the questions, because I'm trapped in this vehicle with her.

"You'll be back on the ice sooner if you start taking care of it right away."

She said she was a professional, but I never asked what kind. "What is it you do?"

"I'm a physiotherapist. I work in sports rehab."

"Guess that makes sense, with Bowman being your brother and all."

"My brother has nothing to do with the reason I'm a physiotherapist. I like sports, both playing and watching, and I like the challenge of helping athletes who need rehabilitation."

I should not find that trait appealing at all. Nor should I be scanning her body or noting how toned and defined her shoulders and arms are. She also smells good. Like cake and berries or something. I crack a window so I don't start huffing her. "What kind of sports do you play?"

"All kinds. I played hockey when I was a kid. In high school if there was a team, I was on it, and in college I played soccer. I was on scholarship, but I pulled my groin in third year. I ended up with a tear and a hernia and had to have surgery. I probably could've kept playing, but that was sort of the deciding factor for me. Rehab was hard, but I had a great physiotherapist, and it made me want to help athletes recover from injuries."

"That's what you do now, then? Rehab athletes?"

"Sort of. Yeah. I finished grad school in the spring. I'm working at a clinic affiliated with the university campus, so our client base is primarily the athletes on school teams and the professors and their families. Sometimes they come in for conditioning and strengthening, sometimes for rehab. Being new means I don't get to work with the kind of cases I really want to, but hopefully with time that will change."

"Cases like what?"

"Like yours." We're stopped at a red light. She squeezes the steering wheel and looks at me. Her tongue darts out, sweeping across her bottom lip. She's not wearing any makeup. Her lips are full and pink, and they look soft. "I could help you," she says.

I drag my eyes away from her mouth. "Help me?"

A horn blares behind us, and we both startle. The light has turned green, so Stevie focuses on the road again, but apparently she's not moving fast enough because the car behind us honks a second time. I roll my window down and flip them the bird at the same time she does.

"With rehab for your injury. I know exactly what it's like to recover from a bad groin injury and how much work it takes." She signals right and pulls into the underground parking lot.

"Why would you want to help me?" I've been nothing but a dick to her, apart from my lame attempt at an apology tonight. And it's not like it wasn't steeped in ulterior motives, since it came with my asking a favor.

"Because it's the only way I'll get to work with an actual professional athlete. All I'm getting right now are freaking cheerleaders and older women with neck and shoulder strains from typing too much."

"I'm sure your brother can pull some strings and get you into a clinic with professional athletes."

"He's already offered to do that, but I'd like to get the experience without using his fame—you know, doing it on my own merit, the way most people have to." She backs my SUV into the designated spot, which is impressive, and shifts into park. "So, is it a deal? You let me help you with rehab, you get back on the ice sooner, and I get experience with a professional athlete without nepotism?"

Is it a good idea to have my team captain's hot younger sister help me with rehab? The answer to that is probably no. But she makes a good point, for both of us. The sooner I'm back on the ice, the better it will be for me and the easier it'll be to gel with my teammates. My social skills aren't the best, so I have to rely on my ability to pull my weight on the ice to show my worth. "And we keep it between us?"

"Yup. But if I actually help your progress, I want a letter of reference. Do we have a deal?"

This has the potential to backfire, but it also has the potential to get me back where I need to be. Will Coach like that I'm doubling up on rehab? Probably not. But what are my alternatives? Is it ideal that it's Rook's little sister doing the rehab? Not really, but she's offering, and it's convenient since she's my neighbor. In the end, the longer I'm off the ice, the less opportunity I have to show the team my value as a player, which ultimately tips the balance in Stevie's favor.

She holds out her hand, and I take it in mine, noting how soft and warm her skin is. "Yeah, we have a deal."

CHAPTER 12

PUT YOUR HANDS ON ME

Bishop

Apparently Stevie is super serious about starting PT right away. As soon as we get in the elevator, she's on me. "The first thing we'll do when we get upstairs is go through some range-of-motion tests. Then you'll soak in a hot bath, and depending on how you're feeling after that, we'll follow it up with a few more range-of-motion tests and a cold compress. Sound good?"

"Uh, sure?"

"Great." She taps her bottom lip. "What did they give you to manage the pain and swelling?"

"An anti-inflammatory-based painkiller."

"Okay, that's what I figured. Obviously it's nonsteroidal. When was the last time you took it?"

"Around lunch."

She frowns. "That was seven hours ago. How's your pain right now?"

"High."

"On a scale of one to ten, what would you rate it?"

"Like, an eleven."

She makes a disapproving face. "You have to take the medication."

"I don't know how bad the injury is if I can't feel it."

"You also can't control the swelling, or heal or function, if you're not taking the medication. New plan. Gentle heat therapy before anything else." The elevator doors slide open, and she motions for me to go ahead of her. "Your place or mine?"

My doorknob isn't decorated with a sock tonight. "Mine, I guess?"

"Lead the way."

She's oddly all business, like some professional switch has been flipped. She holds the door open, allowing me to go first. Design- and layout-wise, my place is the same as hers—the kitchen is modern, with dark wood cabinets and black granite countertops—but that's where the similarities end. My place looks like two guys live in it. A black leather couch, dual leather recliners, and a seventy-inch flat-screen TV take up the majority of the living room. A large table that never actually gets used is set up close to the kitchen in what's supposed to be the formal dining space.

I haven't bothered with art yet, aware that I'll only be here for a year, and then my brother and I will likely need to find a new place, unless we decide to take over the lease or buy the place outright, which is an option.

A low thud comes from the cat tree across the room, and Dicken waddles over to rub himself on my leg, meowing loudly.

"Look at you . . . what a sweet chonky kitty!" Stevie drops into a crouch. "Is he friendly?"

"Exceedingly."

He abandons me and rubs himself across Stevie's legs. He circles her and purrs when she scratches under his chin. "We used to have barn cats when I was growing up. What's his name?"

"Dicken."

"Like the author?"

"That's one interpretation." That's not at all why we named him that. "But his middle name is Balls."

Her nose scrunches up. "That's not a very nice name for your cat." She takes a closer look at him, and then her eyes go wide. She gestures to his face, which is decorated in a white pattern. "Oh my God. He has—"

"A dick and balls on his face. Hence the name Dicken Balls."

She bites her lip as if she's trying to decide whether she wants to laugh. She rubs between his eyes, where the figurative shaft is. "That's a horribly awful and perfect name for you, little Dicken." She gives him one more affectionate scratch under the chin and rises. "Let's get some medication into you and get you in the tub."

She follows me down the hall to my bedroom. So does Dicken, meowing loudly behind us. I didn't bother making my bed, since I spent the majority of the day lying in it. Three ice packs are scattered over the comforter, and my clothes from yesterday are lying in a heap in the middle of the floor, but it's not too much of a shit sty otherwise.

It's odd to have a woman in my bedroom for nonrecreational purposes. And it's been a damn long time since that's happened. Based on the state of my groin, my unapproachableness, and my lack of finesse with women in general, it's probably going to be a damn long time before it happens again. I'm lucky I'm decent looking or I'd be totally fucked. Or not fucked. Ever.

"The layout is exactly the same as my bedroom. Is the bathroom through there?" Stevie points to the mostly closed door.

"Yeah. Just let me check and make sure it's safe." I hobble past her and stick my head in. The towels on the rack are askew, and a couple litter the floor, but like my bedroom, it's not bad. "Okay, good to go."

"Great." She claps her hands and rubs them together. "Bath time! In you go!"

She prods me forward and slips around me. It's a fairly spacious bathroom—a lot bigger than the one she found me in this morning. I flip the lid down on the toilet and take a seat. My prescription is sitting on the counter, so I fill the glass sitting on the vanity and pop the cap. I'm supposed to take two every four hours, so I shake out three pills and down them with some water to partially make up for the missed dose.

"Do you have epsom salts?" Stevie asks as she opens cupboards and peeks around.

I point to the linen closet. "Should be some in there."

She runs the water and puts the stopper in the drain, then opens the linen closet. The epsom salts are on the top shelf. Stevie isn't particularly tall, maybe five four at best, so she has to stand on her tiptoes to reach it.

She manages to get the epsom salts down and dumps a healthy amount into the water, swirling it around to help it dissolve.

"All right, time to strip down," she says when the bath is half-full.

I wait for her to give me some privacy, but she just stands there, one eyebrow arched, hands on her hips.

"You want me to get naked in front of you?"

"You've been flashing me your panties for weeks."

She has a point. I pull my shirt over my head and drop it on the floor. I have to brace my weight on the counter so I can rise up enough to pull my sweats over my hips, which really hurts. I sit back down with a groan and slide them past my knees. Bending over causes more pain, so Stevie steps up and helps take them off the rest of the way.

I can't even make it from the toilet to the tub without crutches. I sit on the edge and take a few deep breaths, waiting until the worst of the vicious stabbing pains ease.

Stevie settles her palms on my shoulders. "You okay?"

I lift my head, which isn't the best idea, since her tits are right in my face. They're covered by a T-shirt and a bra, but still. They look like they'd be a comfortable place to rest my head. I look down instead of doing that, except now I'm staring at her crotch. Again, covered in black yoga pants, but she's female and gorgeous, and I'm full of testosterone. Pent-up testosterone, some latent rage, and a high level of frustration over being benched for six weeks. And for the first time in what feels like four million eons, I think I might actually like this woman beyond the surface. I wonder if she's wearing a pair of those shorts she favors under the yoga pants. I wonder if she'll wear them for our physio sessions.

"Bishop, you in there?" She snaps her fingers.

"Huh?" I look up, all the way to her face.

Her brow is arched. "You were off in la-la land."

"Sorry." The la-la land of her yoga-pants-covered pussy. "Are you gonna leave me alone to soak?"

"I'm going to help you into the tub first."

"I can get in without help."

She props a fist on her hip. "You couldn't get your feet up on the couch last night without help."

"I'll be fine."

"Okay. Well, go ahead and get in, then." She takes a step back and motions for me to have at it.

"With my boxers on?"

"Yes, Bishop. With your boxers on. You're not going to burn candles and sip wine while reading your favorite trashy book. You're going to sit in a warm bath for fifteen minutes, and then we're going to assess the damage and see how stiff you are."

"Fuck. Fine." I brace my hands on the edge of the tub and turn my body, thinking it'll be easier to get my good leg over first, and then I can lift the injured one in.

In theory it's a fantastic idea. In practice it's a terrible idea. I manage to get my good leg up and over, but the pain is excruciating. I scream and grab Stevie because she's the closest, most stable thing I can hold on to. The water in the tub is warm, but it's got nothing on the fire in my goddamn groin.

"Fucking Christ, it feels like my balls are trying to detach from my body," I groan.

"Would you like some help getting into the tub now?" The "I told you so" is clear in her tone.

"I need a minute." I take several semishallow breaths, waiting for the sick feeling and ball burning to cease.

It isn't until I'm no longer blinded by pain that I realize I'm full-on hugging Stevie and that her arms are trapped at her sides. My cheek is also pressed against her boob. I was right about it being a soft place to rest my head.

"Sorry." I release her.

"Maybe next time you'll stow the alpha 'I can do it on my own' bullshit and save yourself some unnecessary pain."

She makes me lift my arm and drapes it over her shoulder. She's incredibly small compared to me. She tucks one arm under my knee and gently grips the back of my calf with the other. "On the count of three," she orders. I tense up when she hits three. She gets my leg about six inches off the floor, which is when I scream bloody murder again and grab on to her with both hands.

"Okay. That's not going to work. The angle is too awkward." She taps her lip and holds her finger up. "I have an idea."

She ducks out from under my arm and hooks her fingers in the waistband of her yoga pants.

"What the hell are you doing?"

"Calm down. Some bathing suits have less coverage than my underwear. Besides, it's nothing you haven't seen before."

She kicks off her yoga pants, leaving her in a T-shirt and panties. They're plain cotton boy shorts, which should be a good thing, but apparently my body doesn't care that it's not a satin or lace thong. All it cares about is the proximity of almost-naked pussy.

Rook's sister is standing in my bathroom in her underwear. If I had a sister who looked like Stevie and I knew that she was standing in one of my teammate's bathrooms half-naked, I would probably kick the shit out of the guy. Thankfully, I have a brother.

I try to keep my eyes averted, sort of, but I catch her reflection in the vanity mirror.

She has fantastic legs. Athletic. Strong. And her ass. Goddamn. She definitely does a lot of squats, based on how round and firm it looks. The ache in my groin turns into that stabbing pain again because I'm getting hard. I think about my grandmother in a bathing suit to counteract the effect of Stevie being partly undressed.

She steps into the tub, and I force myself to keep my eyes down, bringing up the image of that hot chick in the tub who turns into a rotting old lady in *The Shining*. That helps a bit. At least until Stevie moves into my personal space and starts touching me again. I mutter a string of profanity, especially when I feel her boob pressed against my arm for a few seconds. I have no choice but to latch on to her shoulder as we lift my leg over the edge of the tub. I'm sweating, I'm angry, and I hate my dick.

"I need you to stop touching me!" It's stupid because I'm still holding on to her, not the other way around.

"Why are you yelling at me?" she shouts back.

"Because you're half-undressed in my tub, and I'm a guy, and apparently my dick is a fucking sadist. It honestly feels like my balls are on fire right now. A semi has never been this painful."

"Well, close your damn eyes and think about dead things."

"It doesn't matter if I close them. The image of you in panties is burned into the back of my lids, probably for the rest of my fucking life. It's all I can see."

"You'd think you'd never seen a set of bare legs before." She helps me lower myself into the tub and steps out.

"It's been a long time since I've seen a pair up close," I grumble.

"Such a surprise, with your warm, fuzzy personality."

I try not to look as she aggressively yanks a towel free from the bar and swipes it down her toned, wet legs. They look smooth and soft. Also, I used that towel yesterday. So she's sort of wiping my junk on her legs. It quite literally feels like my balls are filled with acid instead of semen, which I'd like to now unload all over her bare thighs.

She nabs her yoga pants from the floor and heads for the door.

"Hey! Where are you going?"

"To get a cold compress ready and give you some time to calm the hell down."

She's gone for a while. Long enough that I start to wonder if she's left me here for the night. I can probably get out of the tub on my own, but it won't be easy, and it'll hurt like a bitch.

I must doze off, because when she comes back, Nolan is with her, and I'm too out of it to string a sentence together that makes sense. It's another reason I don't like the meds. Together the two of them manage to get my groggy ass out of the tub. I shuck off my wet boxers and leave them on the bathroom floor, not caring what Stevie sees anymore.

"Christ, you're heavy, Shippy," Nolan gripes.

"Shippy?"

"It's his favorite nickname," Nolan snickers.

"I hate that nickname." I sound drunk.

"How much medication did you take, Bishop?" Stevie asks as they turn me around and tell me to sit.

"Three pills. I half made up for the missed dose." All the *s*'s blend into the other words.

"Well, that explains a lot. Let's get him on his back." I think Stevie is talking to my brother. My eyelids are hella heavy, too heavy to open more than a slit.

"My balls don't feel like they're on fire anymore," I tell her.

"That's great, Bishop."

A shock of cold against the inside of my thigh makes me temporarily alert, and I ask about the exercises I'm supposed to do.

"What the hell is remotion sex?" Nolan asks.

Stevie laughs. "I think he's trying to say 'range-of-motion exercises.' We'll get to those tomorrow."

"Oh. That makes a lot more sense, 'cause I don't think he's gonna be in any kind of shape to have sex in the foreseeable future."

"Probably not, if getting excited makes him cry." She pats my shoulder. I know it's her hand, because it's soft and warm and it seems to have a direct, semipsychic connection to my dick, making it stir. "See you tomorrow, Shippy."

"I hate that fuckin' nickname," I grumble. And then it's lights out.

CHAPTER 13

PRETTY PAINFUL

Bishop

"Hey, Shippy, rise and shine." Those words are followed by a repetitive poke at my shoulder.

"Would you fuck off?" I slap my brother's hand away. "And stop calling me Shippy." I pry one lid open, slowly. It's a challenge. My brain and body are not interested in doing things like moving or being alert.

"You have company."

"Huh?" I glance at the clock on the nightstand. It's nine in the morning. I've been out for a lot of hours.

"Company. You have a visitor." Nolan is grinning, like an asshole.

"Stevie?" I attempt to sit up in a rush, forgetting that I'm not really in any kind of shape to be doing anything quickly. I bite out several curses and flop back down on the mattress.

"Look at how excited you got there for a few seconds. I mean, I get it. That chick is hot."

"That chick is off limits, brother, so keep your hands to yourself. And don't flirt with her," I snap.

"I can't *not* flirt. That's like me telling you not to be an asshole."

He has a point. "Just stay away from her. If she's not here, who is?"

"Ryan."

"Who?"

"King."

"Oh." No one ever addresses Kingston by his given name, apart from his parents. Not even his siblings. He's always been King or Kingston for as long as I can remember. "What's he doing here?"

"Picking you up for a team meeting or something. Or maybe going door to door trying to recruit people into his Polo Army."

I ignore the dig at Kingston. He's a good guy. Super straightlaced. Like, the straightest arrow I've met. Guy still drinks milk with dinner, and often at the bar, or whenever he can, really. He rarely has more than one beer, and he doesn't drink at all if he's driving. He honestly looks like he should head up the chess club, with his uniform of polos, khaki pants, and polished dress shoes.

"Can you tell him I'll be out in a minute?"

"Sure thing. You need help?"

"I'm good."

Nolan leaves me to manage getting my ass out of bed. I notice that my bathroom looks a lot cleaner than it did last night. It takes me a full ten minutes to get ready. Kingston is sitting at my kitchen island, drinking a glass of milk.

"Sorry to keep you waiting."

"It's no problem. I came early since I know you're not moving fast these days." He finishes his milk, rinses out the glass, and puts it in the dishwasher. "You ready to go?"

"Yup." I pocket my wallet and phone. Since I'm on crutches, King takes my to-go coffee, and we head for the elevators. I glance at Stevie's door; the paper is gone, which means she's already left for work. I wonder if we'll still have our morning underwear competition now that she's helping me with PT. Guess I'm not going to find out today.

"How was practice yesterday?" I ask once we're in Kingston's SUV. He drives the speed limit dead on and keeps his hands at ten and two, like he was taught in driving school. While he may be a rule follower, he doesn't expect that of anyone else. He accepts people for who they are—rule breakers and all.

"Okay. You getting injured shook the team up, though. You know how it is: some of the guys are superstitious. How you handling things?"

I wish I wasn't one of the superstitious ones, but losing team captain and being out with an injury after the first exhibition game is shit luck. "I'm not happy, obviously. I don't want to miss the beginning of the season."

"I get it, but that's a bad pull. You don't want to rush it and reinjure, either." King flicks his blinker on a full block from where he has to turn.

"I know. It hurts like hell. I've never done this kind of damage before. I wish they hadn't put me on defense. It wouldn't have happened if I'd been playing forward." I lift my hat and run a hand through my hair. "I can't afford to have a bad season, you know? I only have a two-year contract, and if I screw this season, I could be sent somewhere else—or worse, the farm team."

"You're too good of a player to get sent back to the farm team," Kingston says.

"I'm only good to the team if I'm on the ice. Warming the bench for five mil a year isn't going to get a contract renewal. I need a few more years at least to make bank, especially if Nolan keeps living his life like it's going to end tomorrow."

Kingston knows about my brother's health issues. "He's not taking care of himself?"

"Not the way he should." I blow out a breath. "I'm worried about the long game, you know?"

"I get it, but you'll only be out for the first few weeks of the season, so you'll have lots of time to prove your worth to the team."

"I really hope so."

We pull into the parking lot, ending the personal conversation. The team meeting is a whole lot of morale-building bullshit. The GM, Jake Masterson, is well respected despite being young for his role. He and Waters will be pumping up the team, so it'll be a lot of rah-rah crap today, which I'm not in the mood for, considering I get to watch all the action from the bench.

Apparently Waters is going to be hosting a party for the team prior to the official start of the season. I'm not big on parties, or lots of people and socializing outside of the rink, but I can't exactly avoid these kinds of things when it's pretty much the only way I can mesh with my team.

After the meeting there's a training session I can't take part in, so I'm sent to work with one of the team physiotherapists instead. I will say that Stevie is much nicer looking and smelling than the guy I'm dealing with. He's professional and efficient, and those are the only good things I can say about him.

We go through range-of-motion exercises, and he pokes and prods me for a good forty-five minutes. By the time he finishes his initial assessment, the verdict is that I'm going to need intensive sessions, starting tomorrow.

I head to the locker room, where the rest of the team is suiting up for ice time. I'd like to call an Uber and take my ass home, since my groin feels like it's on fire again from all the unpleasant attention, but I realize I need to stick around. If I can't play, I should be watching my teammates, getting a sense of how they work together.

I take a seat on the bench while the guys do warm-up drills. This is fucking depressing.

Waters drops down beside me. He's dressed in a suit, which is pretty much what he wears all the time unless he's in the gym training with us. He's a hands-on coach, in the middle of everything. Super friendly and just . . . nice. It's irritating since I'm in such a shit mood. "How you holding up?"

"I'm all right. Not happy about the situation, but we're starting rehab tomorrow, so hopefully we'll beat the six-week healing time."

Alex claps me on the shoulder. "Just don't push yourself too hard, too fast. I know when I screwed up my shoulder, I wanted to be back on the ice for playoffs. Injuries like this can mess with your head and your morale."

"I remember when you took that hit. It was bad." I'd been playing in the minors, waiting to be drafted, and it was all the hockey world could talk about. The top player in the league being out for the end of the season because a rival player had had a beef with him and took him out of the game. Cockburn has since retired from the league, although maybe *retired* isn't the right word. At the end of the season that followed, his contract expired, and no one would renew.

Waters nods his agreement. "If I'd pushed rehab the way I wanted to, I wouldn't have had the last few years of my career, and the only reason I didn't was because my best friend was there to keep me from being an idiot. So listen to your body and make sure you don't do more damage than good when you're pushing the recovery angle."

I don't want to hear all the ways I can ruin my career, even though I get what he's saying. "I'll take that under advisement."

He cocks a brow. "I know it's been a rough start, but one injury doesn't have to dictate the rest of the season for you."

I track Rook on the ice, watching him move seamlessly between players as he heads for the net with the puck. He's flawless out there, quick and fluid. He manages to slide it past Kingston. He skates around behind the net, coming to a stop in front of him. King gets along with everyone, and nothing really ever seems to rile him up. We're pretty much opposites, apart from both liking routines. Rook puts a hand on Kingston's shoulder, and they talk for a few seconds. King nods, probably eating up whatever advice he's being given.

I should hate Rook less, knowing that he doesn't have a sidepiece living across the hall from me, but I find I loathe him more. He acts like a golden boy, when really he was the furthest thing from it at the beginning of his career.

He skates over to the bench and grabs his water bottle. "How you doin', Winslow?"

"All right."

"It was a good save the other night." He tips his head back and squirts water into his mouth, eyeing me from the side.

"Thanks," I grind out. I can't tell if he's being sarcastic or being seminice because Waters is here and listening.

"When you're ready to get back on the ice, you should spend some time working with the other guys on defense."

I bite back an asshole reply and force out, "I'm sure that'll be part of the training plan."

"Actually, I'm not convinced defense is necessarily the best place for Winslow."

Rook and I break our stare down and give Alex our full attention.

"What? But I thought you agreed that Winslow would be better guarding the net than trying to score on it," Rook spits out.

Alex pins him with a look that seems a lot like a warning. "Don't put words in my mouth, Bowman." He turns to me.

"You have a lot of size, Winslow, and I felt like defense could be a good fit, especially with how tight you and Kingston are. With time and practice, you'd make a great defensive player, and maybe that's something you'll want to focus on later in your career, but I think it may have been a mistake on my part to move you there now. I've been studying your performance on the ice with Nashville, and you have a lot of speed for your size, so for now we'll shift you back to forward, where you're more comfortable."

I nod and fight a smile, because I can practically feel Rook seething. "Who's going to take his place on defense?"

"You can let me worry about that, Rook, since that's my job." Alex smiles tightly.

"Right, yeah. You know what's best for the team," Rook replies.

"Actually, I have an idea." Alex steeples his fingers and looks between us.

"What's that?" Rook leans on the boards, trying to appear casual, but his tension is obvious.

"Once Bishop is back on the ice, I think it would be good for the two of you to work together."

"Are you serious?" And Rook is back to looking like he wants to punch me. Or Alex. I'm not sure which.

"Very." He turns to me. "With more speed training you'll be second line, and since Rook is the best forward we have, it makes the most sense for you to work together when you're ice ready."

Rook smirks and cocks a brow. "I'm not the best; you are. Maybe you should lace up your skates and get back on the ice, Coach."

"I lost that title last year when you blew my scoring record out of the water."

And now it's turning into a fucking lovefest. Rook is such a brown-noser. "Do you two want a minute alone?"

Both of their grins drop, and they pin me with the same unimpressed look.

"Kidding. It was a joke." I'm not kidding at all, but I don't need to piss off my coach and my team captain with more of my asshole remarks.

"You're being given a golden opportunity here, Winslow. I get that you're unhappy about the situation, but don't screw yourself over because of pride." Waters pushes to a stand, and Rook gives me an arched brow before he skates away, as if to say he won that round.

I wish I could stop digging holes for myself.

I consider how pissed off Rook would be if he knew his sister had offered to help me with physiotherapy. Not that I care. I want back on the ice more than I want him to like me.

"Everything okay?" Kingston asks on the way home.

"Waters wants me to work with Bowman when I'm ready to get back on the ice."

"That's not a bad thing, is it? He's got the best scoring record in the league."

"Not you too." I roll my eyes. "Why is everyone so up this guy's ass?"

Kingston shrugs. "He's a great player. Plus he waived his no-trade clause so he could be part of a new team and so his wife could be closer to his family. He's a good guy."

I chose to come to this team, too, but that doesn't seem to matter to anyone but me anymore.

"You should've heard him and Waters. They're so far up each other's asses it's ridiculous. 'You're the best.' 'No, you're the best.'" I mock their voices. "I'm surprised they didn't offer each other goddamn blow jobs to go with the lovefest."

"They both have wives. And kids."

Sometimes Kingston can be super literal about things. "I know that. I don't honestly mean I think they'd blow each other. I just mean it was a mutual and annoying lovefest. I should probably shut up. I'm in a bad mood."

"Do you want to grab lunch?" Food is Kingston's way of changing this subject.

"Nah. I'm tired. I need a nap."

I take the meds like I'm supposed to when I get home and fall asleep on the couch with a cold compress on my thigh.

My brother is home this afternoon, so I do myself a favor and run a bath so I can manage the heat-therapy shit. Stevie left me a short list of things to do today, among which are to take another epsom salts bath, alternate with cold compresses, and keep a detailed record of the exercises I do with my team physiotherapist.

I try to get into the tub on my own, but I can't do it without causing myself more pain, so I get Nolan to help me. He won't shut up about how crappy it must be to have a hot chick all over my jock when getting hard feels like someone is stabbing me in the balls with a fiery poker.

The highlight of my shit day occurs when Stevie shows up at my door at seven. She's holding a piece of the pizza I brought her yesterday in one hand and a rolled-up yoga mat in the other hand. Today she's wearing a pair of athletic shorts and a tank top. It's a lot of skin on display. Tanned skin wrapped around toned muscles. She clearly works hard to stay in shape, which I can appreciate, because I have to do the same thing.

She looks me over with pursed lips. "I see we're out of clothes again."

"I get hot."

"I'm sure you do, Billboard Balls." She flips her hair over her shoulder—it's now pale blue—as she slips by me.

"What did you call me?"

"It's what me and the girls call you at work."

"You talk about me at work?"

"I talk about what an asshole you are, so don't let that inflate your ego." She shoots me a look. "Did you take an epsom salts bath and use ice therapy this afternoon like I told you to?"

"Yeah."

"Great. Now give me a rundown of what you did with your team therapist today. I'm assuming you saw him? Her?" She drops down on my couch and stretches her legs out. Her feet are bare, toenails painted the same shade as her hair.

"Him, and go right ahead and make yourself at home," I grumble.

She gives me a syrupy smile. "Watch the 'tude, dude, unless you want today's session to suck more than a sex worker on Saturday night."

I lower myself into one of the recliners. "Mostly he poked at my legs and did range-of-motion exercises until I was at risk of vomiting."

She makes a face. "Can you not talk about throwing up while I'm eating?"

"You asked."

"Not for references to regurgitated food."

Dicken jumps up on the edge of the couch and headbutts her. Then he jumps onto the cushion beside her, making his broken-squeaky-toy sounds and getting all up in her face, sniffing her pizza. She gives him a scratch under the chin, but he doesn't stick around. Instead, he jumps off the couch and trots over to his dish to check out the contents.

She pokes at my brother's insulin kit sitting on the coffee table, her expression shifting to concern. "Are you a diabetic?"

"No, my brother is." I wish he'd put that stuff away, but it's always lying somewhere: coffee table, kitchen counter, bathroom. I ended up getting him a spare, which I keep in my medicine cabinet on the not-so-off chance that he can't find his.

"Type one or two?"

"One." I don't love talking about my brother's health issues, mostly because they seem to stress me out more than they do him.

"Is that why he doesn't have a license?" Stevie picks an olive off her pizza and pops it in her mouth.

"Pretty much, yeah." He had a license, but he's had too many visits to the hospital in the past year for unregulated insulin issues, and they took it away. He has to be clear for a year before he gets it back. His vision isn't great, either, which is another strike against him.

"That happened to my dad too."

"Your dad's a diabetic?"

"Was. He passed away from complications a while back."

"Shit. I'm sorry."

"Thanks. Me too." She stuffs the last of her pizza slice into her mouth.

I want to ask her more questions, like what kind of complications and what happened for him to lose his license, but she bounces up off the couch like she has springs in her ass and plasters on a huge, very fake smile. "Enough about that. Let's get this party started." She gives me her back as she rolls out the yoga mat.

I stare at her ass and ponder the layers of her personality. She's sarcastic and bitchy, she's sweet and helpful, but I think she's also got some broken pieces she tries to hide behind all the other parts. She's the younger sister of an NHL player, her dad passed away, and she's living in her brother's unused penthouse for reasons I'm unsure of, other than it's rent-free.

"All right, grumpy pants, let's see how stiff you are today."

Lying down on the floor isn't easy, and Stevie promises to bring her portable massage table tomorrow. She starts off the same way the team physiotherapist did this morning, checking to see how far I can raise and bend my legs and at what point the pain goes from a dull ache to a vicious throb.

It's pretty miserable, but even though she's causing me pain, I don't absolutely hate having her hands on me.

The range-of-motion shit feels horrible, as do the stretches, but it's nothing compared to when she starts palpating the muscles around the injury site, checking for tightness. She's good at finding the worst spots and working on them until they loosen up, but I'm tense, and every touch sends violent pain shooting through my groin.

Stevie sits on the floor beside me and shifts, positioning one of her legs under my injured one. It's meant to take the pressure off so none of my muscles will be doing the work. She presses her fingertips gently along the edges of the bruising, starting at the inside of my knee.

It doesn't feel good, but my body seems to be reacting to the physical contact in a way that's going to become a different kind of painful if I can't get a handle on it. I pull up the same images from *The Shining* again and then Charlize Theron when she was a murderer in *Monster*, because rotting corpses and female serial killers should help prevent my dick from reacting in ways I would prefer it wouldn't.

But Stevie's boob is pressed against the outside of my thigh, and her long, pale-blue ponytail tickles my skin, and her fingers keep moving higher, so my control starts to slip.

"You need to stop."

"Am I causing you a lot of pain?" Stevie flattens her palm against my inner thigh, which doesn't help at all.

"There's too much contact. Too much of your skin on my skin. It's distracting. Can't you cover up?" And I'm back to being the asshole again. Not that I ever really stopped.

"What?"

I motion to her outfit. "Are you trying to taunt me? Is that what this is about?"

She frowns, and her nose wrinkles. It's almost cute, which is not good. I can't be thinking about her in terms like *cute*.

"What the hell are you talking about?"

I flail a hand toward her. "You. This. The half nakedness."

"You're in a pair of underwear."

Okay, she has a valid point. "You showed up unannounced."

"Well, I don't have your phone number, so how else would you propose I contact you? And it wasn't like you didn't have plenty of opportunity to cover yourself up. And why is this even an issue? What does it have to do with your level of pain?"

"You're making me hard!" I snap.

She blinks a few times, and her eyes dart down to my crotch. It's pretty damn obvious I'm sporting a semi. "How is that my fault?"

"I can feel your boobs on my legs, and your hands are near my dick. It's not like I have control over it."

"Well, maybe next time you should rub one out before we do this so you don't embarrass yourself."

"You think I haven't tried? It feels like someone is stabbing me in the balls with a rusty steak knife."

Stevie huffs and throws her hands in the air. "What do you want me to do? Stop? It's not like it's any skin off my back if I don't help you."

She starts to move away, but I grab her wrist. "Wait. Just . . . maybe you could put on a sweatshirt or something? There are bound to be a couple clean ones in the laundry room. Please?"

She rolls her eyes. "Fine. But don't get pissy with me because you can't control your body parts."

She comes back a minute later wearing one of my hoodies from college. It really doesn't help. It's still a lot of physical contact, and now the sweet smell of her lotion mixes with my laundry, so it's like she's wrapped in me. "Can you talk, please?"

"About what?"

"Anything. Why'd you move to Seattle?"

"My ex-boyfriend got a job here, and so did I."

That doesn't make a lot of sense. "Why would you want to move where your ex lives?"

"Because he wasn't my ex until I moved here." Her voice is somehow softer and harder at the same time.

I'm trying to piece this all together with half my brain functioning thanks to the pain in my groin and my inability to stop focusing on how nice it is to have an attractive woman touching me, even if it's supposed to be in a professional capacity. "But you've only been here for what, a handful of weeks?"

"Yup." Her expression remains purposefully neutral.

"I don't get it."

"We were supposed to move in together. He came out a couple of months early to get settled into the apartment and start his job. I flew in a couple of days earlier than I planned to so we could be together for my birthday, and he was already celebrating."

I feel like I'm missing some important detail here. "What does that mean, that he was 'already celebrating'?"

"It means I walked in on him screwing someone who wasn't me, on my birthday."

This guy is clearly a brain-dead idiot. "What a dickhead. This guy must be a special kind of stupid to pull something like that."

"And now I have the pleasure of working with him every day."

A heavy feeling settles in my gut as I watch her face. Her lips are pressed in a thin line, her jaw tense, but her cheeks are flushed, and there's a slight tremble in her chin. "Why don't you quit? Get a job somewhere else?"

"Because then he wins, and there's no way I'm going to let that happen. Besides, I was the one they hired first. I got him the stupid interview, so if anyone should find another job, it's him. I have friends there now, and it's a great clinic, apart from him." She slides her thumb along my IT band, which hurts like hell. "Anyway, I called my brother, and he said I could stay here, so here I am."

"Hold on. All of that happened the night you first showed up here?" She was riding the Hot Mess Express: blotchy face, red eyes, uncoordinated, loud.

"Yup."

"On your birthday?"

"Correct."

I push up on my elbows. It's not easy, and it makes a lot of body parts ache. "I'm sorry I was such an asshole to you."

"I was making a lot of noise; you thought I was my brother's mistress. You had no idea."

"But if I had—" If I hadn't already strongly disliked Rook, I might not have jumped to conclusions about her. She still woke me up in the middle of the night, but I might have been less of a jerk.

She pushes to a stand. "I think we're done for tonight. You should ice it again so it doesn't get too aggravated from all my prodding."

I grab her wrist. "Hey." I try to get my ass off the floor, but I don't have my crutches and it's awkward as hell.

"Sorry. I wasn't thinking. Hold on a sec." Stevie gets them for me and helps me up. She quickly rolls up her yoga mat and heads for the door like her ass is on fire.

"Stevie." I feel like I should say something helpful. Like her ex is an idiot, because clearly he is. Stevie is gorgeous and feisty and probably way too nice for his cheating ass. She's way too nice to be helping me.

She spins around, flustered and looking a lot like she's hovering on the edge of tears. Shit. I better not make her cry. I don't know how to handle tears.

"Don't be nice to me right now, Bishop."

Obviously she's psychic, or I'm wearing my panic on my face. "But—" I try to think of something to say that isn't nice but isn't dick-ish, either, as she puts her hand on the doorknob. "I still don't have your number."

Her head falls forward, and she glances over her shoulder, a rueful grin making a brief appearance. "Same time tomorrow night. I'll wear a muumuu, and you wear some actual clothes so you can keep yourself in check."

I stand in the middle of the living room for a long time after she's gone, trying to figure out what I could've said to keep her from leaving upset.

Half an hour later I slip a piece of paper under her door with my number on it. It sounds like it's not a big deal, but it hurt like a bitch to bend over, even if it was only for a few seconds.

An hour later I get a message from an unfamiliar number.

Did you ice your leg?

I fire one back:

Stevie?

It doesn't take long for a response to appear:

No. It's a random person asking about your leg.

Yes. It's Stevie.

Bishop: Are you okay?
Stevie: Fine.
Bishop: Your ex is a fucking idiot.
The dots appear and disappear a bunch of times before she finally responds.
Stevie: Ice your leg, Shippy.
Bishop: Don't call me that. Lying in bed with ice on my leg right now.
Stevie: So you can follow orders. Good to know.
Bishop: Just depends on who's doing the ordering.
Stevie: See you tomorrow.
Bishop: Okay.
I stare at the series of short messages for a long while, wondering what the hell is wrong with her ex and how someone as strong and feisty as Stevie could have ended up with someone like that in the first place.

The next night Stevie shows up at seven and acts like she didn't tell me someone screwed her over recently. She also wears a huge hoodie and oversize jogging pants. She looks ridiculous. It should help, but it doesn't.

I want to ask personal questions about her ex and her dad, but there's no way for me to bring it up without it being awkward, so I leave it alone.

The week that follows is a weird form of torture. The daily double PT sessions are definitely helping the healing process. The bruising begins to fade from the horrible black to more of a purple green with some nice yellowing patches at the edges. It's ugly, but it's improving, and my team physiotherapist keeps praising me for all the hard work I'm obviously doing outside our sessions to help with recovery.

It's all Stevie. If I'm in a mood—and let's face it, I'm perpetually in a mood—she keeps pushing, dishing out the attitude the same way I give it to her.

For the first few days she wore baggy sweats, but it didn't seem to have an impact on my physical reaction. So she stopped with the oversize clothes and went back to those athletic running shorts and tanks layered over sports bras.

And unless we're in the private gym specifically for the people who live on the penthouse floor—which means it's rarely ever used—I stick to my uniform of boxer briefs and sometimes basketball shorts.

Tonight I'm thinking maybe once Stevie gets home, we should order in dinner and get down to the PT. I'm feeling good, and tomorrow I have a checkup with my doctor, so I want to go in all loose and limber. We can work on some stretches, and Stevie can massage my leg, and I'll finish with heat and ice.

Tomorrow night is the get-together at Alex's place. I don't really want to go because

A. I don't love all the social shit;

B. it means I won't get in a PT session with Stevie.

The season starts in a week, so I need to put some effort in with my teammates, since I won't be on the ice for at least the first few games, and that's me being optimistic. I'm hoping that with the extra PT, I won't miss much more than that.

I'm in my living room, waiting for Stevie and flipping TV channels with the sound off so I can listen for the elevator. Yes, I'm aware it's borderline creepy. I messaged her more than half an hour ago, but I still haven't heard back yet.

The sound of the elevator dinging puts me on alert. I grab my crutches and pull myself up, pleased with how much less it's hurt over the past few days. I hear a knock in the hallway, but it's not my door. I make it to the peephole in time to see a guy disappear into her apartment.

A fucking *guy*. Who isn't me.

I wait with my eye pressed against the peephole for the guy to come back out.

"Have you moved in the past half hour?" Nolan startles me.

"What?"

"I've walked through here three times, and you haven't moved. What the hell are you doing?"

"A guy went into Stevie's apartment, and he hasn't come back out."

Nolan's eyebrows rise, and he smirks before he schools his expression. "And that's a problem because . . . ?"

"Because we're supposed to have a session tonight, that's why. And she hasn't answered my texts. I have to see the team doctor tomorrow. I need to go having made progress so I can get back on the ice, and now she's leaving me hanging!"

"So you're pissed that she has a life outside of sessions with you, which she doesn't get paid for, unless you parading around in your underwear has somehow become a form of reimbursement?"

"I'm comfortable like this, and she doesn't care. Besides, she offered to help me. It benefits her too."

Nolan leans against the couch, and Dicken jumps up, sauntering along the edge until he can rub himself on Nolan. "Does it, now? And how might this little arrangement you set up benefit her?"

"She gets experience working with me."

"So she learns how to best deal with assholes?"

Dicken meows, like he's in agreement. He's only loyal to the person most willing to feed him.

"Screw you. I'm not always an asshole. She gets to rehab an NHL player. She learns what works and doesn't, what helps me make progress, how hard to push. It's good for her, career-wise."

"Why doesn't she use the fact that she has an NHL-playing brother to get her into a clinic that works with professionals in the first place?"

"Because she doesn't like using her brother's connections to get things."

"Well, she's living in that apartment, isn't she?"

"Only because her dickhead ex-boyfriend cheated on her and she didn't have anywhere else to stay. It better not be him in her apartment. I will beat his ass." I don't care if I have to break his nose with my crutches; I will take that motherfucker down. I pull out my phone and compose a message to Stevie, but I'm agitated, so I have to delete it a bunch of times and start over again.

I finally go with:

You ready for me? Should I come to you?

It's not confrontational, and there are no death threats, so I think it's good. Nice and neutral.

"You sound a little territorial for someone who swears he doesn't have the hots for our neighbor."

"I'm not being territorial. I need her for my rehab."

Nolan snorts. "You keep telling yourself that, Shippy."

I don't bother responding to Nolan, because he's baiting me, and inchworm dots appear on my screen. I frown when I read her message:

Not a good time. Msg l8r.

"Not a good time? Message later? What does that mean?"

"It means she's busy and she'll get back to you when she isn't. I told you to stop being a pussy and just claim the pussy."

I motion to my crotch. Today I'm wearing boxers that say **DANGER: CONTENTS UNDER PRESSURE** on them. I figured Stevie would find them funny, because it's true. At least it doesn't feel like I've dipped my balls in acid every time I get hard anymore. "I can't claim the pussy."

"Your tongue and fingers aren't damaged, though." Nolan shakes his head. "You're an idiot. If she has a date, you have no one to blame but yourself."

He wanders down the hall, complaining about how I'm wasting my good years being celibate.

I stand with my eye at the peephole and wait. And wait some more. It's almost eight by the time the door finally opens. So I step out into the hall, ready to do exactly what my brother said I should before someone else does: claim the pussy.

CHAPTER 14

SERIOUSLY?

Stevie

The second I step out into the hall, Bishop's door flies open. He leans on one crutch, eyes narrowed and homed in on me. "We still on for tonight, or you busy with something else?"

I can feel RJ behind me. "Winslow, this isn't the damn locker room. What the hell are you doing in your goddamn underwear?"

My brother's giant hand clamps over my eyes, and his pinkie nearly goes up my nose.

I bat his hand away and spin out of his reach. "Like I've never seen a guy in his underwear before."

"Rook?" Bishop's somewhat angry expression softens when his gaze shifts to me. "Why didn't you say your brother was over? I've been waiting for like two hours."

"I didn't realize I needed to give you a play-by-play of my evening plans."

"What the hell is going on here?" RJ's blazing eyes are fixed on Bishop.

Based on the way these two are glaring at each other, I have a feeling they don't like each other very much. It may explain why my conversations with Bishop that revolve around hockey are only ever related to his PT and his friend Kingston. Bishop actually seems like he might be a bit of a loner. Or a homebody. Or both.

RJ's lip twitches. "Are you *hanging out* with this guy?"

"I'm helping Shippy with PT." I use the nickname on purpose, to let Bishop know I don't appreciate whatever the hell drama he's about to cause me.

"Shippy?" RJ looks like his eyes are about to bug out of his head and roll across the floor.

"Kody needs to go to bed, and Lainey's waiting on you." I grab my brother by the elbow and lead him to the elevator, jabbing the button four hundred thousand times in less than three seconds. Thankfully, it opens right away. I use my brother's shock, or whatever it is, to push him into the elevator. He drags me in with him, though.

I jam my thumb on the button for the parking garage, repeatedly, and fire a glare at Bishop, who's still standing in the hallway in a pair of red underwear, looking super pissed off. As if he has a right. Christ.

My brother points a finger in Bishop's direction as the doors slide closed. "What the hell is going on? You better not be dating him."

"Excuse me?"

RJ crosses his arms. "You can't date a hockey player."

"Are you kidding me?"

"You just had your heart stomped all over, Stevie. Do you really think you need to be getting involved with someone right now? Especially someone who travels for more than half the year? Not to mention that guy is an ass clown."

I rub my temples, trying to keep a lid on my anger, but I don't think it's a battle I'm going to win. "Okay, first of all, Rook, you don't get to dictate what I do or who I do it with. I'm not a kid. I'm an adult, and I can make adult decisions without consulting you or anyone else. Secondly, I'm not dating Bishop."

RJ scoffs. "Come on, Stevie. Do you think I'm an idiot? He was in his underwear in the hall saying he's been waiting on you for two hours." He runs a hand through his hair and tries to pace in the very confined space. It's not effective because he's at one end and then the other in two strides. "Are you hooking up with him?"

"He has a groin injury, RJ. He can't have sex."

"Thank fuck for that," he snaps.

The elevator doors slide open, and I push him out into the parking garage. "I'm helping him with PT, not trying to ride his broken dick. Not that it's any of your damn business." I've thought about it, though. During our sessions I've gotten to know Bishop, and under that surly exterior and his poorly thought-out comments that often come across as seriously rude insults is what I'm beginning to think is a genuinely nice guy.

Plus he's insanely hot, so I would have to be asexual not to have dirty thoughts about him. The kind I use as fodder for my private one-hand clapping parties after our nightly PT sessions. My vibrator has been getting one hell of a workout lately. Not that I'm going to share that with my unreasonably angry brother.

"He already has a team therapist working with him. He actually has a full staff helping him rehab, so why would he need you?" RJ's eyes narrow with suspicion.

I'm pretty sure he doesn't mean for it to sound as dismissive as it does, but it still gets my back up. This is the exact reason growing up as Rook Bowman's baby sister is a curse. Like what I do is so paltry and unimportant I couldn't possibly be helpful in any real capacity. "I'm helping because he wants to heal faster, and it's a good opportunity for me, career-wise. I get to work one-on-one with an injured NHL player."

"I've already offered to get you a job working with NHL players, if that's what you want. All I have to do is talk to our GM, and you're in, Stevie. I have connections that could get you in to work with the women's team. Then you can rehab and condition hockey players in a professional setting that isn't Winslow's apartment." RJ keeps running his hands through his hair, gripping it at the crown.

"I already told you, I don't want you to get me a job. I want to do it on my own merit, not because I have some high-profile brother who can pull all these strings for me. I'm damn good at my job, and I don't need my brother swooping in to do everything for me. I'm better than that." I try not to raise my voice, but I'm pretty annoyed by this whole thing.

"Why do you think Winslow is letting you rehab him?"

"Because I offered, and he wants to get back on the ice."

RJ sighs and rubs the spot between his eyes. "Come on, Stevie, you can't be that naive."

"What are you talking about? Naive about what?"

"He's *using* you, Stevie."

"I'm the one who suggested it. Besides, it's a mutually beneficial arrangement, so I don't see how that constitutes me being used," I snap.

"He's doing this to get back at me."

"That doesn't even make sense. To get back at you for what? Not being injured?"

"Because he's had a beef with me for years and because I became team captain when I chose to come to Seattle. It was supposed to be him."

I throw my hand in the air. "Of course it has to be about you."

"He's been an antagonistic ass since preseason training has started. He's jealous and he doesn't like that I'm tight with management and our coach. Fuck!" He paces around like he's a caged MMA fighter waiting for the bell to ring. "I bet he did this on purpose. I bet he knew this would piss me off when I found out. That's why he's letting you rehab him. I doubt him coming out into the hall, dressed the way he was, asking if you two were still on for tonight, was an accident."

"Are you serious with this?" I can't believe what I'm hearing; more than that, I don't want to believe it, because I honestly feel like, shitty attitude aside, Bishop may actually be benefiting from my help.

"I'll get the pool house set up for you, and you can move in there. There's no way I'm letting you live across the hall from Winslow if he's going to pull this kind of shit."

The anger I try to keep a lid on most of the time pops off. "Do you even hear yourself? Not everything is about you, RJ! For the first few weeks, Bishop thought I was your *mistress*. He had no idea I was your sister. So whatever plot you think he's hatching against you is in your head."

"You don't understand, Stevie—"

I slash a hand through the air. "No. *You* don't understand. You have no idea what it's like to be your little sister. It's always been about you. How much better you are at everything, how much attention you always got. Is it so hard to believe Bishop is letting me help him because I'm actually capable?"

"It's not that I don't think you're capable, Stevie. I know you are, and I don't want you to feel like I'm trying to make this about me—"

"Then stop, because it has nothing to do with you."

He blinks a bunch of times, probably shocked by my outburst, and his expression softens. "I don't want you to get hurt." His phone goes off. Judging by the ringtone, which is the refrain from a sappy song, it's Lainey.

I'm on the verge of really losing it on him, so this interruption is perfectly timed. "You have to get home."

"Stevie."

I step out of his reach. "I love you, RJ, I really do, but this is my life, not yours. No one stopped you from making your own choices, bad or good, so you need to let me do the same."

This time he doesn't try to stop me from getting back on the elevator. Once the door is closed, I drag my palms down my face and exhale my frustration. I don't want to second-guess Bishop's motives for letting me help him, and now that's exactly what I'm doing.

What if he is using me? I let my head drop back against the glass and stare up at my reflection in the mirrored ceiling, annoyed that one conversation with my brother would make me reevaluate everything.

When the elevator doors slide open, Bishop is there, in all his ridiculous underpants glory, waiting for me.

I don't have the mental or emotional energy left to deal with him right now. "Session canceled." I brush past him.

"What? You can't do that. I have an appointment with the team doctor tomorrow."

"Have a bath, do some stretches, and follow it up with an ice compress, and you'll be fine. You don't need me for that."

He's right on my heels, literally. His crutch nearly lands on my foot. "What the hell is going on? What did Rook say to you about me?"

"Nothing. He said nothing." I unlock my door, and of course, because Bishop is a giant of a man, he bulldozes his way in before I can shut him out.

"Bullshit. If he didn't say anything, why are you flaking out on me?"

"Because I'm not in the mood to deal with your level of asshole."

"He said something. Why won't you tell me?"

He grabs for my wrist, but I smack his hand away. "Because my conversations with my brother are none of your goddamn business."

He stabs at the floor with the end of his crutch, like he's stomping without using his feet. "If the conversations are about me, then it is my goddamn business."

I throw my hands in the air. "What is it with you hockey players and your fragile, overinflated egos?" I don't wait for a response, because it doesn't warrant one. "You know what? I'm done with this bullshit. Go home." I skirt around him and yank the door open, motioning for him to leave.

"So you're bailing on me when I need you?"

"Like I said, you don't need me. Take a bath, stretch if you want to, or don't. Just give me some space, please and thank you." I'm looking at the floor because I'm on the verge of tears, and I do not need Bishop here when that happens.

His crutch appears in my vision and then his bare feet and his junk. His underwear is ridiculous tonight, with the whole **CONTENTS UNDER PRESSURE** warning. His abs are also ridiculously amazing, and they're right in my face. I want to run my hands over the smooth planes and trace all the dips and ridges.

I'm realizing now, after that blowout with my brother and Bishop's current line of questioning, that I might actually be starting to like this guy. Which isn't great for a lot of reasons, not the least of which is that my brother seems to hate him, and he's also a high-profile NHL player: something I generally try to avoid.

"Stevie?" Bishop's voice is low.

I watch his hand lift in my peripheral vision, and for a moment I think he's going to tip my chin up and force me to look at him. In which case I'll most definitely lose it in front of him.

Shit. I really do like him.

His rough fingertips barely graze my cheek before his hand falls back to his side. "I'm going to leave, not because I want to, but because I don't know what to do or say to make this better, and I don't want to make it worse."

He crosses the threshold, and I let the door fall closed behind him; then I turn the lock and secure the chain latch. I listen for the sound of his door, but after a few seconds of silence I give in to the urge to check the peephole. He's still standing in front of my door, frown fixed in place, looking a whole lot confused.

It makes me want to invite him back in, and not for a therapy session.

CHAPTER 15

PARTY TIME

Bishop

I haven't seen or heard from Stevie since last night. I'm pretty sure she was on the verge of tears when I left her apartment. I wanted to do something to make it better, but I had no idea what that something would be, so I did nothing.

Maybe I should've hugged her. That would've been something. But I didn't want to screw this up, and she seemed really pissed off. And now I'm waiting for her to message me, because she asked for space. I don't know what that means. So my brother's claiming the pussy idea is on hold until I can figure it out. Also, Rook's reaction to the whole thing hasn't been great. I really hope he's not going to mess this up by making her not want to work with me anymore.

Tonight I have to go to Waters's house for his morale-building team party. I'm not in the mood for it, since it means being social and friendly for a lot of hours. But I can't build rapport on the ice right now, so I need to show my face. At least for a couple of hours.

Kingston picks me up at seven thirty. Waters lives on the outskirts of the city in a huge house that verges on being a mansion. A lot of the top earners on the team live out here. I think Rook might be one of them, which would make sense, since he's pretty much up Waters's ass all the time.

Kingston pulls into a driveway lined with our teammates' cars and parks behind an SUV. The inside of Waters's house boasts top-of-the-line finishes and appliances and modern furniture.

Waters's wife, Violet, greets us in the kitchen. She's a tiny woman with brownish hair and a really big rack. She's dressed in a pair of black leggings and a Seattle T-shirt with the logo stretched across her chest. She also looks like she's pregnant. Either that or she's smuggling a basketball under her shirt.

"You must be Winslow." She motions to my crutches. "I saw that happen, and my beave cried in sympathy." She points to her crotch, as if that needs more of an explanation. "I can't imagine how much that hurt. You know, Alex has had his share of on-ice injuries over the years, but never a groin pull, thank the Lord for that. I can't imagine what I'd do if he was out of commission for six weeks. He took a bad hit back when he was playing for Chicago and messed up his shoulder, but all the important parts were still in working condition, you know?" She pats her rounded belly. "And obviously those parts work incredibly well."

I've been warned about Waters's wife. We all have. By Waters. He explained that Violet has zero filter and pretty much says whatever is in her head. I thought he might be exaggerating, but obviously not.

"I guess that's a good thing?" It comes out more like a question than anything.

"Alex seems to think so, and usually so do I, but he keeps knocking me up, so right now I'm on the fence, since it means I can't have a glass of wine for another year, again. Speaking of booze, can I offer you boys something to drink?"

I'm no longer on pain meds, so I accept a beer, but Kingston declines.

"Wine? Cocktail?" She motions to the endless supply of alcohol. "Oh! I have Jell-O shooters! You boys should do one!"

Rook appears beside her, out of nowhere, holding a beer. "Kingston, Winslow, glad you could make it." He gives us both a nod, but his gaze lingers on me for a couple of extra seconds. "You sure you wanna start passing out the Jell-O shooters already, Vi? If I remember correctly, the last time you had Jell-O shooters at a party, there was an impromptu karaoke session. I have a video of your rendition of 'I Like Big Butts' saved somewhere on my phone."

Violet points a manicured nail with little sparkly jewels on it at him. "I'd just finished breastfeeding and hadn't had anything to drink in almost two years. Also, you were supposed to delete that. And one Jell-O shooter for these boys won't lead to karaoke." She passes one to Kingston.

"What's in it?" He sniffs it.

"Mostly Jell-O," Vi replies.

"And vodka," Rook explains.

"Oh, thank you, but I'm driving, ma'am." Kingston offers it to me. I don't want to be rude, so I take it, toast the beginning of the season, and suck back the lemon Jell-O shot, coughing as it burns its way down my throat.

"Is it really strong?" she asks.

I have to clear my throat before I answer. "A little."

"Maybe I didn't get the ratio right this time." She pats her belly. "I can't try them, so it's possible I overdid it on the vodka." She turns her attention back to Kingston. "Kudos for being super responsible. Can I get you water, sparkling water, soda, orange juice? Pretty much if you want it, we have it."

Kingston surveys the bar. "I'd love a glass of milk, if it wouldn't be too much trouble, please, ma'am."

"Oh my God, that's awesome." She throws back her head and laughs, but when none of us join in, she stops. "Wait. Are you serious?"

Kingston's ears go red, and he slips his hands into the pockets of his khakis. "Yes, ma'am, but I can have water if that's not possible."

"We have milk, but you have to stop calling me ma'am. You're making me feel old."

"Sorry, ma'am. I mean Mrs. Waters. It's a habit and not meant as an insult."

Violet turns to Rook. "Is this guy for real?"

"Kingston is from Tennessee. They're bred with manners down there," Rook explains. His gaze slides to me. "Most of the time, anyway."

"Maybe you should introduce him to your sister. It's Evie, right?"

"Stevie," Rook and I say at the same time.

Violet gives me a questioning look, and Rook pins me with a glare.

"She doesn't date hockey players." Rook directs the comment at me.

So of course I respond. "Does Stevie know you dictate who she can and can't date?"

Rook sneers. "I don't dictate anything for Stevie. That's her choice. She doesn't like the attention that comes with someone in the media spotlight, which includes my teammates."

"Not all of us live in the spotlight, though," I argue, which is an admittedly stupid thing to do.

Rook shrugs. "She just got out of a long-term relationship. It wasn't an easy breakup, and she's not ready to get into another one."

"Okay, well, I guess no introductions for you, then." Violet points at Kingston. "Which is too bad, because she's stunning and good with kids, from what Lainey tells me. And you look like the kind of guy who probably wants to have at least a dozen children."

"I have a girlfriend, and she's not ready for kids yet." Kingston runs a hand over his chest and looks down at his outfit. "But twelve would be a lot."

"Sure would, but making them is fun." Violet grabs the milk from the fridge. "Is two percent okay?"

"Yes, ma'am . . . I mean Mrs. Waters."

"Please, call me Violet." She pours him a pint glass of milk and slides it across the counter.

Alex comes up behind his wife and kisses her on the cheek. "Kingston, Winslow, glad you could make it. It's good to see you on your feet! Injury's healing great, I hear."

That must mean he's spoken to my therapist after today's session.

"That's 'cause he's pulling double PT." Rook takes a hefty sip of his beer.

"Double PT? With the team therapist?" Alex's brows pull down. "He didn't mention that."

Shit. Well, now I know exactly what Stevie told him last night.

"With my sister," Rook says flatly.

"I thought she was working at the college clinic. Did she change her mind and decide she wanted you to put in the recommendation? I would've put in a word if I'd known."

"She's still working with the college clinic." He tips his chin in my direction. "Bishop here thought he would take it upon himself to coerce her into helping him out so he could get back on the ice sooner."

"She offered. There wasn't any coercion, 'cause you know she thinks for herself."

Alex looks between us and claps Rook on the shoulder. "Why don't the three of us take this conversation to my office?"

Rook rounds the counter without another word, and I follow him and Alex out of the kitchen and down the hall. The high pitch of children's voices comes from somewhere close by. We pass an actual movie-theater-style room, complete with rows of seats that look way more comfortable than any theater I've ever been to. A Disney movie is playing, and kids are jumping from seat to seat, not paying attention to what's on the screen.

Alex's office is actually more like a library with a desk. There's a couch and club chairs. Pillows, blankets, a table lamp, and a stack of books take up one end of the couch. Based on the covers, I'm assuming they're Violet's books.

Alex motions for us to take a seat. "Scotch?"

"Please." Rook downs the rest of his beer in one gulp.

I hold up my mostly full bottle. "I'm good with this, thanks."

He turns his back and pours expensive scotch into lowball glasses. He passes one to Rook and one to me, even though I declined. I'm not going to say no twice, so I take it.

Alex settles into the chair across from us and sips his scotch pensively. Then he stares at us for what seems like forever until he finally speaks. "Violet's brother was on my team when she and I started dating."

"I'm not dating Stevie. She's helping me with PT." I keep saying this, and no one is listening. Would I like her to help me with other things? Like some relief for the perpetual hard-on I'm always fighting off when I'm with her? Of course. She's hot and I'm full of testosterone. But at this point what I'm saying is true.

"How often is she helping you?"

"Every day. Except yesterday and tonight." I shoot a look at Rook, because it's his fault last night didn't happen.

Alex taps the arm of his chair while staring at me. He's usually a friendly guy, so it's kind of unnerving. "As I was saying, when Violet and I started dating, her brother, Miller, was on my team. We didn't exactly get along. And then when he started dating my sister . . . well, that didn't help things."

"Is this supposed to be a pep talk?" I sip the scotch. I don't like the way it tastes, but if I'm going to get a full story about my coach's dating history with his now wife, I might need to up my alcohol consumption.

Rook crosses his arms over his chest. "No, he's making a point. He ended up marrying Butterson's sister, and Butterson married his sister.

What Alex doesn't understand is that this isn't the same, since you're using Stevie to get back at me."

"Using her to get back at you for what?"

"Because I'm team captain and you're not."

"Oh, for fuck's sake. I'm not using Stevie!" I snap. "This isn't about you getting team captain. Am I pissed about that? Sure, but you would be, too, if I was the one who got captain and you didn't. She offered to help me. I didn't ask. She wanted an opportunity to rehab an NHL player without having to go through you. And honestly? I get why, and so should you. But that's all she's doing. Besides, it's not like I can make a move on her." I motion to my junk. "I can't fuck my own hand let alone another person right now."

Alex coughs and sips his drink. "He has a point, Rookie."

"Why keep it a damn secret if there's nothing else going on?"

I cock a brow. "I can't speak for Stevie, but it's not like you and I have heart-to-hearts on the regular."

Alex interrupts. "Here's what I think. The team physician had a look at your scans, and he and the team physiotherapist have cleared you for light workouts."

"Seriously?"

Alex nods, smiling slightly. "He says you're a good week ahead of what they expected. Looks like the double PT is working, even though you should've run it by me and the team therapists first."

"So I might be back on the ice in the next few weeks?" This is really good news. The kind I want to share with Stevie. Except I'm not sure she's talking to me.

"It's a possibility." He spins his scotch glass on the arm of his chair. "Since you've been cleared for light workouts, Rook is going to handle those with you."

And there goes my awesome mood.

"Whoa, what? I thought I was training with Bishop when he's back on the ice." Rook sounds about as happy as I feel over this new development.

Alex motions between the two of us. "Obviously there's some hostility between you, and the only way to resolve that is for you two to work together."

"But—"

He cuts Rook off. "There are no buts. Bishop is working with Stevie, and that's not going to change because I'm authorizing it to continue."

"What the hell, Alex?"

Alex arches a brow. "Obviously whatever she's doing is working. And correct me if I'm wrong, but if Stevie wants to work with him, that's her call, not yours." He shifts his attention back to me. "And apparently you'll listen to Stevie, so from here on out I want to see written treatment plans. You can email them to me and cc the team therapist so he can give feedback and adjust accordingly."

"I'll run that by Stevie when I talk to her later."

"I think we need to have a chat, Alex, privately," Rook says through gritted teeth.

"I'm sure you do." Alex's attention stays fixed on me. "I know you've said it's only PT, but I have to wonder if it's going to stay that way."

"The fuck?" Rook sounds appalled.

I open my mouth to defend myself, even though yesterday I was ready to make it known that I'd like her to massage more than the inside of my thigh.

Alex holds up his hand. "These two are spending a lot of hours together, and Stevie's volunteered to do it in her free time. What does that tell you?"

"It's a smart move for her, career-wise," I say, because it is.

"You keep working that angle, Bishop, but we both know you're not big on following orders you don't like, and yet you're following my sister's," Rook snaps.

"Because it's helping. Did you both miss the part where I said I can't physically make a damn move on her, even if I wanted to?" I motion to my crotch.

"But it doesn't mean you don't want to." Rook cocks a brow.

"I want to earn my salary by doing more than warming the bench."

Alex holds up a hand. "Settle down, both of you. All I'm saying is that Rook might not be so opposed to the PT or whatever is going on if he doesn't think you're trying to pull one over on him."

"There's nothing going on. And even if there was, it'd be none of his business. I don't owe him anything. This isn't high school." I try not to sound like my usual dick self, but this whole conversation is frustrating as hell. "Stevie and I have an agreement, and it's mutually beneficial. End of story. My goal is to get back on the ice, and hers is to help me get there."

Rook flails a hand in my direction. "How do you know he's not telling you what you *want* to hear?"

"Because Bishop is making progress that proves he's working his ass off and because Stevie graduated at the top of her class," Alex says pointedly before turning back to me. "I'm holding you to it that while Stevie is working with you on rehab, that's all that's happening. This would apply to any member of our staff. Keep this professional. Your next session with the team physiotherapist is Monday, before the team workout, eh?"

"Yup."

"He'll have a workout assignment for you. Rook, your job will be to make sure he doesn't push it too hard, too fast, and undo the progress he's made. The faster he heals, the sooner he's back on the ice and the PT ends. And Rook, be the team captain I know you can be. Don't bring the personal shit into the session. If he has a setback, I'm holding you personally responsible." He tips back his glass and drains the rest of his scotch. "All right, there's a party going on, and I need to make sure my wife hasn't given out all the Jell-O shooters in the first hour, or your teammates are going to be a mess. Good talk. Enjoy the party."

And that is apparently the end of that.

Alex leaves us sitting in his office. I'm still on crutches, although I don't have to use them all the time anymore. If I was faster getting off my ass, I could escape before Rook has a chance to corner me, but I'm not that lucky.

"You better not mess with my sister," Rook snaps.

"Stevie's a big girl. She can make her own choices." It's a noncommittal response—one I know is going to piss him off, even if it's true.

"This has been a rough transition for her, so don't take advantage of her niceness by screwing her over, or you'll be answering to me."

"Got it. Don't screw with your sister. Anything else?" I adjust my crutches, aware my attitude isn't winning me any prizes.

"I mean it, Winslow. She's lost a lot in the past few years, and the last thing she needs is someone else dicking her around."

"I heard you loud and clear, Bowman. I'm not planning on dicking her around, so find some chill."

After that impromptu meeting, I'm not feeling the whole "being social" bullshit, so I don't head back to the party right away. Instead I make a pit stop in the bathroom, mostly to escape Rook and avoid people for a while longer.

Kingston doesn't do late nights, so I'm banking on him being ready to head out fairly soon. I decide I should try to make nice with my teammates, especially since I'm on the captain's shit list. On my way back to the living room I run into Stevie, whom I definitely didn't expect to be here tonight.

She comes to an abrupt halt when she sees me, although to be fair, I take up most of the hallway, so there really isn't a way for her to get around me.

"Hey."

She does a head-to-toe scan. I'm wearing black dress pants and a polo. "I didn't realize you owned anything apart from jogging pants and T-shirts."

Her sarcasm isn't unexpected. In fact, I think it might be her go-to response when she's uncomfortable, like mine is to be a dick.

"I even own a couple of suits, surprisingly enough."

"Huh."

We stare at each other for a few seconds before I finally say, "I didn't realize you were coming tonight."

"I'm here to pick up Kody."

"Who?" I mentally flip through all my teammates' names. There isn't a guy named Kody. Karl, yes, but no Kody. Besides, Rook just finished telling me that Stevie wasn't interested in dating hockey players.

"My nephew. My brother's kid."

"Oh." Well, that's a relief. "So you're not staying?"

"No. These parties aren't really my thing."

"They're not mine either."

"Is that why you're hiding out in the hallway?"

"I'm not hiding. I had a meeting with Rook and our coach."

Her eyes flare. "What kind of meeting?"

"Just to talk about my progress."

"Bullshit. I don't buy that for a second. Did my brother get you in trouble because you're working with me? I'm going to kill him." She spins around as if she's planning to hunt him down and confront him.

I grab her by the wrist to prevent her from running off half-cocked. "He didn't get me in trouble." Although he tried. No sense in sending Stevie on the warpath, though. "I'm a week ahead of what they predicted for healing, so I'll be starting workouts next week."

"Seriously?" Her anger melts into excitement. "That's so great, Bishop!" She throws her arms around me in what seems to be an impulsive hug.

The feel of her entire body flush with mine is unexpected, and it seems to short out the connection between my brain and body for a few seconds. I wrap an arm around her waist as she starts to loosen her grip around my neck. Every muscle in her body tenses briefly before she softens against me. I drop my head, inhaling the fruity scent of her shampoo.

Stevie's fingertips drag down the back of my neck, making goose bumps rise along my skin and the hairs on my arms stand on end. She steps back, palms smoothing over my shoulders and down my biceps until they fall to her sides.

"Does this mean you won't need my help anymore?" Her expression doesn't tell me if that makes her happy or not.

"Actually, my coach wants me to keep working with you."

"Oh." She seems surprised. "You told him you're working with me outside of team PT?"

"Rook did." I squeeze the back of my neck. "My coach also wants Rook to help me with workouts."

"But you two hate each other."

I shrug. I don't know that I hate him, but I definitely don't like him. "He thinks it'll help smooth things over."

"Has he met you?" She half smiles.

"Maybe he's setting me up for failure." I blow out a breath, gearing up for an apology. "I'm sorry about last night. I didn't mean to piss you off more than you already were. I shouldn't have been such a dick."

"I'm used to it by now."

"Does that mean you'll still help me with rehab?" I need her to say yes to this; then I can work on the rest, like not being a jerk all the time.

She sighs and rubs her forehead. "RJ thinks you're only letting me rehab you because you're trying to get back at him or whatever."

He's certainly made it clear he believes I have ulterior motives. "And what do you think?"

"I think I'm not always the best judge of character, my ex-boyfriend being prime example number one."

"My goal has always been to get back on the ice as quickly as I can. I have my brother to take care of, and I can't afford a lot of fuckups. This injury is one of those fuckups I can't afford. And using you to get back at Rook seems a lot like something that could screw things up for me even more."

She tips her head to the side. "He said you were supposed to be captain, except he got it when he came to Seattle."

"This is true." No point in lying.

"This would be a lot easier if you two didn't hate each other so much."

"It would also be a lot easier if your brother didn't think I'm just in this so I can get into your pants."

Stevie purses her lips and looks away. I thought I was being kind of funny, but apparently not. She's about to reply when a woman who looks vaguely familiar appears in the hallway with a toddler perched on her hip.

"There you are! Kody's all ready to go, aren't you, little man?" She kisses the kid on the cheek, and he giggles and drops his head against her boob, nuzzling in.

"Sorry, Lainey. I was just talking to . . . a friend." She thumbs over her shoulder at me. Her face lights up as the woman—Lainey—approaches, and Stevie holds out her arms.

"How's my favorite nephew? Are you ready to hang out with Aunt Stevie? I am so ready to hang out with you! We'll drink milk and eat arrowroot cookies until we pass out. Sound good?"

The little guy squeals shrilly when she takes him from Lainey and gives him a raspberry on the cheek.

I've never been comfortable with kids. It's not that I don't like them; it's that I don't have any experience and I don't know what to do with them.

Lainey gives me a slow once-over, her gaze shifting between me and Stevie, before a wry grin pulls up the corner of her mouth. "You must be Bishop."

"Uh, yeah, and you're Rook's wife, right?" I hold out a hand, aiming for polite.

"I am. That was a rough hit you took. I hear you're on the mend, though, thanks to Stevie."

"She's been a big help."

"Okay, well, I should really take Kody home, since it's past his bedtime." Stevie's voice is high pitched and annoyed.

"Thanks again for watching him for us." Lainey gives her a side hug. "I know it's important for RJ to be at these kinds of things. I honestly don't know how you do it."

"Alcohol and Alex's wife, Violet, are my saving graces so far, and not necessarily in that order." Kody yawns loudly, and Lainey leans in to kiss him on the cheek. "You be a good boy for your auntie. I'll see you back at the house, Stevie. I'm not sure how late we'll be, but you know how RJ is when he gets into the scotch with Alex. There's a very good chance I'll be home before him."

Stevie adjusts Kody on her hip and turns to me. "Have fun tonight."

"Will I see you tomorrow?" I need some kind of confirmation that she's not going to keep ditching me like she did last night.

"Uh . . ."

"For rehab?"

"Oh, right. Um, tomorrow's a bit of a clusterf—" She grimaces. "I have a thing in the afternoon I don't think I can get out of. I'll text you, okay?"

"Sure. Okay." It's the least-committal response she can give, and I don't like it.

They walk down the hall together, whispering to each other, with Lainey looking over her shoulder, before they disappear around the corner.

I head back to the party, pausing as I pass the room that was full of kids a while ago. Now it's full of wives and girlfriends. Violet is at the front of the room, clicking on a PowerPoint presentation—of what looks like shirtless male celebrities.

She points across the room. "No peens allowed. Not even hot, young, broody ones."

The entire room turns to look at me.

"Move along, Winslow. Your girlfriend isn't in here, and if she was, I'd still send you packing."

"I don't have a girlfriend."

Violet smirks. "You keep telling yourself that." Then she addresses the women sitting in the front row. "I present you with exhibit A. The broody, antisocial, injured hockey player with lots to prove. I give him a month—two, tops—before he has a girlfriend in our ranks."

A murmur of agreement comes from the women in the room.

She makes a shooing motion. "Off you go so we can start placing bets."

I'm not sure if she's serious about placing bets or not, but I do as she asks and then run into Lainey on the way back to the party.

"Did Stevie leave?"

She tips her head to the side. Her long dark hair hangs in a braid over her left shoulder. She regards me with deep chocolate eyes. She's exactly the opposite of Stevie, dark to her light. Lean and willowy to her athletic build. "She did."

"She'll be okay getting there on her own?" Honestly, I'm looking for a reason to bail on this party, and Stevie is a good reason to get out of here.

"We live three houses down. She'll be fine."

"Oh. Okay." Of course Rook does. Always up Waters's ass.

"RJ worries about her. She has a tough exterior, but her heart is soft, and she's been through a lot in the last few years. It's not easy living in the shadow of someone you love, especially when it's not by choice. Just something to keep in mind." She pats me on the shoulder and heads down the hall, toward the roomful of women.

CHAPTER 16

EVERYONE HAS AN OPINION

Stevie

Lainey intentionally orchestrated pickup so I would have to go to Alex's house. I tried to sneak in and out as quickly as possible, mostly to avoid my brother, which I've been doing all freaking day because I'm still pissed off at him—hence Lainey being the one to organize Kody's pickup.

Of course, RJ was on me the second I walked through the door. And he only added to my irritation and my embarrassment by introducing me to his teammates as his *baby* sister, with his arm around my shoulder, while he glare-smiled at most of them. It was ridiculously uncomfortable. Also, babies don't have boobs or master's degrees, thank you very much.

Thankfully, I had a valid reason to bail. And then I ran into Bishop. Who was wearing dress pants and a polo. I didn't realize that clothing combination could make my lady parts so excited. He also smelled really, really good. It only reinforced my irritation with my brother over the fact that he'd planted those stupid seeds of doubt in my head.

Which don't seem to apply to Bishop. He doesn't strike me as the kind of guy who would go to that much trouble to piss someone off.

"Why are boys so complicated?" I ask Kody as I change him into his sleeper back at RJ's house.

He babbles at me, random words sprinkled in with nonsense, his expression serious as if he's truly giving me advice. Once he's changed, I give him his nighttime snack and read him a story before I put him to bed. It's past his bedtime, so he goes down without a fight.

I turn on his monitor and head back downstairs to chill out. The fridge is full of my favorite foods accompanied by a note in RJ's rushed scrawl to help myself to whatever I want. I pour myself a glass of his expensive, organic, freshly squeezed grapefruit juice, grab a snack, and flop down in front of the TV. I spend a good twenty minutes flipping mindlessly through channels, but my mind keeps wandering to Bishop and the fact that he's only a few houses away from me right now, hanging out with his teammates and their wives and girlfriends. I wonder if he's miserable there. He's not big on crowds or small talk, and he has no tact. I smile, thinking about how he might accidentally stick his foot in his mouth with one of his excessively honest comments.

Joey was never good in those situations. The few times he met my brother's teammates, he fanboyed so hard it was mortifying.

As if Joey can sense me thinking about him from across the city, his name flashes on my phone. Tomorrow I have to deal with him, and I'm not excited about that at all. Before I can check the message, the alarm system gives off a warning beep, and the front door opens and closes.

"It's just me!" Lainey calls out softly from down the hall. She appears a moment later in the kitchen. "Is Kody down?"

"Sure is."

"Did he give you any trouble?" Lainey shrugs out of her jacket and drapes it over one of the chairs lining the kitchen island.

"Tons. Drank his bottle, let me read him a story, then told me he was tired and forced me to cuddle with him until he passed out."

136

She smiles, opens the fridge, and pulls out a few things. "I wonder if the next one will be half as easy as he is."

"I'll cross my fingers for you."

"I appreciate that." Lainey opens a tallboy and splits it between two glasses, then tops them off with grapefruit juice. She passes me a glass and drops down onto the other end of the couch. "RJ thinks you're still angry with him."

I shrug. "He thinks it's always about him."

Lainey nods and smiles behind the rim of her glass. "Often it is."

I roll my eyes. "Not you too. Bishop isn't using me to get back at RJ. It's a mutually beneficial arrangement, and we both get something out of it."

"Mmm." Lainey's eyebrows rise.

"His man stick is pretty much broken. I'm not getting a ride out of this, if that's what you're thinking."

Lainey's smile widens. "Well, that's what your brother is worried will happen."

"It's none of his damn business who I ride."

"I agree. However, he and Bishop have a bit of a standing rivalry, and you did just get out of a bad relationship, so his worry isn't completely unfounded."

I sigh and tip my head back, staring at the whirring ceiling fan. "I hate it when you do this."

"Be reasonable?"

I roll my head in her direction so I can glare effectively. "Make me feel guilty for being mad at RJ. You weren't there last night. He basically ordered me not to date Bishop, which is ridiculous, and that's not even what's happening, so his dramatics were totally unnecessary."

She arches a perfect eyebrow, her chocolate eyes lighting up with mirth. "Oh, Stevie, who do you think you're fooling here? Because it certainly isn't me."

"What are you talking about?" My voice is all pitchy.

"Bishop is a good-looking guy, and you two have been spending a lot of time together. Besides, I saw the way he looked at you."

"And how does Bishop look at me?" I try to sound flippant, but really I'm curious as to what she sees, because at this point I've convinced myself that any flirting is all in my head and a result of Bishop's raging testosterone and his inability to manage his situation.

"Like he wants to hold your hand." She pauses, her smile widening at my eye roll. "And shove it down the front of his pants."

I bark out a laugh. "Lainey!"

She shrugs. "It's true. I'm sure he wants to do both things."

"Well, he's broken right now." I motion to my crotch area.

"He won't be forever."

"There's still nothing going on."

"Yet."

My phone buzzes on the table, and we watch the screen light up. I half expect it to be Bishop, messaging to ask again if I'll still work with him, since I never really gave him a straight answer. It's not Bishop, though; it's Joey. Again.

Lainey motions to my buzzing device. "What's going on there?"

"Nothing."

"Based on the way it looks like you want to blow that phone up with your eyeballs, I'm going to go ahead and say I don't believe you."

"He still thinks we're going to get back together."

"Is that something you're considering?"

"Absolutely not. I will never get back together with him."

"Does he know that?"

I pause at that. I mean, it should be obvious, but I haven't had this conversation with him yet. Up until now I've been avoiding it.

As if seeing my discomfort, she continues. "It can't be easy to work with him."

"I'm managing fine. I don't see him that often." I can avoid him for the most part.

"It's okay if you're not managing fine. You gave up a lot to come here, and things didn't exactly go as planned."

I sip my drink, trying not to let the visual of what I walked in on form in my head. "At least I didn't move in with him and find out after the fact that he was screwing around on me."

She gives me a soft smile. "That doesn't necessarily make what happened between you any easier to get over, though, does it?"

My phone lights up with another message from him. I flip it over so I don't have to see them. "No. Not really."

"Well, for what it's worth, I think it's good that you're spending time with Bishop, even if it's for rehab."

"Can you convince RJ to look at it that way for me?"

Lainey laughs. "I can try, but I doubt I'll be successful." She stares into her glass for a few long moments before she looks up at me, her expression soft and knowing. "Your brother carries a lot of guilt around with him. He has a hard time letting go of his past mistakes, and it manifests as concern and overprotectiveness. I know he needs to learn how to let things go, but I think you might need to do that too. He continues to punish himself for his past sins, even though who he was when he was first drafted to the NHL isn't who he is now."

What she says makes sense. He never pushes me to come to games; he always makes sure I'm protected from the media stuff because it was so hard on me as a teenager. And I see it in the way he is with Lainey, so doting and head over heels in love with her. Always trying to make up for the time he missed when they lost touch after their summer in Alaska together.

I also see how that extends to me.

The sound of Kody rustling around in his bed draws our attention to the monitor. We're both quiet for a few moments, waiting to see if he'll settle. "Da-eee!" he calls out groggily.

Lainey gives me a wry smile. "It's as if he knows his dad is out. I'm going to check on my little man."

"Okay. I'm going to go to sleep."

She gives my shoulder a squeeze as she passes. "I'm always here, Stevie, in whatever way you need me. A sister, a confidant, a mediator for you and RJ. We both love you so much."

"Thanks." A lump in my throat makes the rest come out in a whisper. "I love you too."

I'm up early the next morning with Kody. RJ doesn't come down until after eleven, and he and Lainey make a greasy breakfast of bacon, eggs, and hash browns. I stay out of the kitchen while they cook because they're super touchy, and I don't need to see that.

Once we've eaten, RJ and I take Kody outside. We set up the hockey net, and RJ tends goal while me and Kody take shots at him. It's fun and honestly cathartic. Lainey eventually comes out to get Kody and put him down for his afternoon nap, and RJ and I keep passing the puck. It's been a long time since he and I have played sports together.

He stays in net while I keep firing shots at him, enjoying the way he has to keep dodging them when they almost connect with his groin. A charley horse in the thigh takes him down.

He curls into the fetal position on the ground and grumbles a litany of juicy curses.

"Sorry. You all right?"

"It's like you're purposely aiming for my balls." He groans and sits up.

He grabs my outstretched hand, and I help pull him up. "That's because I am."

"I'm sorry."

"For what?"

"For making the thing with Winslow about me, for trying to tell you what to do, for making you feel like I don't think your career has value, or that you're anything but amazing. It's just . . . me and Winslow haven't seen eye to eye, like ever, and I worry about you."

"I know you do, and I get it, but he's been really focused on rehab and getting back on the ice, not on trying to get into my pants."

"I just don't want you to get hurt, that's all."

"I can appreciate that. But I need to make my own decisions."

"I know. So am I forgiven?" He gives me the famous Bowman half smile that pops his dimple.

I roll my eyes. "Yeah, you're forgiven."

He pulls me into a big bear hug that makes it feel like my ribs are bending.

"But if he does end up hurting you, I'm probably going to beat his ass."

I try to jab him in the ribs, but he hugs me tighter.

"I love you, kiddo."

"I love you, too, even if you're a pain in my ass."

RJ drops me off at home late in the afternoon. I'm 100 percent not looking forward to dealing with Joey, which is why I stayed at my brother's so long. I'd hoped Joey might be inclined to give up, but apparently not. He said he'd be over by four thirty. The only reason I agreed at all is because my suitcase was forwarded to his place, and he promised to bring it with him. He's already had it for more than two weeks now.

I'm gritty with sweat from playing hockey, and I haven't washed my hair recently, so it's nice and greasy. I add an oversize sweatshirt to my dirty-sweats-and-tank ensemble and pull my hair up in an extra-messy bun, highlighting the stringy greasiness. I wash any residual makeup off my face—there wasn't much to begin with—and do an armpit-sniff test. I'm definitely ripe. I want to be as disgusting as possible for Joey.

At a quarter after four there's a knock on my door. He's early. I take a few centering breaths, school my expression so it looks annoyed more than nervous, and open the door. Except it's not Joey. It's Bishop.

He, too, is wearing sweats and a T-shirt. The sweats hug his thighs, and the shirt, which has holes in it—not the strategic kind either—pulls tight across his chest. Is there anything this man wears that doesn't look good on him?

I glance over his shoulder at the elevator, almost expecting Joey to show up at this exact moment.

His gaze sweeps over me, pausing at the text across my chest that reads **F THIS S** and then lifting to my hair. "Are you feeling okay?"

"Huh?" I did not expect him to say that or for him to look so concerned.

"Are you sick?" He motions to my outfit. "You usually dress differently."

I look down at my outfit. "Oh. Uh . . . this is on purpose."

"Oh. Okay." He shifts from foot to foot like he's nervous about something. "I, uh . . . I have pizza for you. I thought maybe it would make you less mad at me."

"I'm not mad at you. I'm annoyed with the circumstances and the way everyone keeps overreacting."

"I'm sorry." He bites his lip. "If you're not mad anymore, does that mean we can still work on rehab?"

"We can still work on rehab." I wasn't clear about that with him last night, mostly because I was fixated on how good he looked in dress pants and also because I needed to get the Joey crap out of the way.

"Great." He takes a step forward, as if he wants to come in, but I stay where I am, firmly rooted in the center of the doorway.

"Now isn't the best time, though."

"Oh. You're busy?" His gaze moves over me again, his confusion apparent.

It's understandable: I'm dressed like I'm homeless, not like I have something important to do. "I have this thing, and I can't get out of it."

"What kind of thing?"

"I got suckered into volunteering for something for my work."

"Maybe I could help?" He looks somewhere between hopeful and unsure. It's almost cute.

"I wish you could, but my stupid-ass ex-boyfriend signed us up for it, and then he invited himself over here to work on it. I've been putting him off, but it needs to get done."

That hopeful expression turns dark. "Wait a second. The asshole who cheated on you is coming here?"

"Yeah. One of my suitcases got misdirected to Alaska when I flew in, and it's now at his place because that was the forwarding address, so as much as I would rather he not set foot in my personal space, I could really use the rest of my wardrobe." I rub the space between my eyes where a headache threatens to make my afternoon that much worse. "I need to get this over with. Once he leaves, we can do rehab."

"How long will he be here?" Now he sounds frustrated, which would make two of us.

I lift a shoulder and let it fall. "Hopefully not long, but I'm sure he'll find a reason to drag it out." Unless I can find a way to get rid of him. I take in Bishop's somewhat angry expression. I'm not sure if it's because it's the douche ex who's coming over or because it interferes with his rehab, but I plan to capitalize on it either way. "I have an idea . . . if you want to help shorten his visit."

"Sure. Yeah. What do you need?" He gives me a quick, somewhat jerky nod.

"He's supposed to be here any minute. Maybe in, like, half an hour you can come back with the pizza, and I can pretend like I forgot we have a session? That way I won't have to be alone with him for long, because I know he's going to try to plead his case for us to get back together."

"I'm sorry, what?" Now he looks seriously pissed. And I'm anxious, because Joey will be here any minute and I don't have an exit strategy for him yet.

"Never mind. I'll figure out an excuse. I'll get Pattie to call and pretend there's an emergency or something."

"You don't need to do that. I can't believe that Assface thinks he actually has a chance with you after what he did. I can message you in, like, twenty and see where you're at or if you need me to come by sooner."

"Are you sure?" He sounds angry more than anything.

"Yeah. I'll put your pizza in the oven to keep it warm, even though it means my apartment is going to smell like pineapple and olives."

"It really doesn't taste as bad as you think."

"I'll take your word for it." He turns around and heads back to his apartment.

"Thanks, Bishop. I appreciate you doing me this favor."

He pauses and looks over his shoulder. "No worries. I owe you one anyway. A favor for a favor, right?"

"Yeah, right. A favor for a favor."

CHAPTER 17
PAIN-IN-THE-ASS EX

Stevie

Joey shows up less than two minutes after Bishop goes back to his apartment. I hate that Joey has the power to bulldoze himself right back into my life like this. He's like a burr—clingy, prickly, and impossible to get rid of.

"Hey, baby." He tries to come in for a hug, but I put my hands out to stop him.

"Don't call me pet names."

"Sorry. Old habits die hard." He gives me what I think is supposed to be a chagrined smile, but it's about as believable as a magic trick performed by a three-year-old. What did I ever see in this tool?

"Where's my suitcase?" I ask as he slips past me into my apartment. I glance at Bishop's door before I close mine, relieved he's willing to help me out even though it's stupid drama no one really needs.

"Oh shit, sorry. I knew I forgot something." He lets out a low whistle. "Wow. This is a sweet pad. How come we didn't rent a place like this?"

"Because we couldn't afford a place like this."

"Is Rook footing the bill or something?"

"Or something."

He nods. "Cool. Wanna give me the grand tour? I bet the bedrooms in this place are huge. You got a king-size bed?"

"I'm not showing you my bedroom, Joey."

He holds his hands up. "Whoa. Don't get so defensive. I'm just trying to break the ice. I know you're still holding a grudge, but we can get through this."

I run a palm down my face. I'd really like to tell him to go fuck himself, but it will make this whole gala situation that much more difficult. I promise myself that once this is over and I have my suitcase back, I will tell him my grudge is going to last until the end of time, and possibly even beyond that, so moving on would be smart. "Can we deal with this fundraiser-decorating thing?"

"Yeah. Sure. Let's get the work out of the way so we can catch up."

Joey wants to sit on the couch, but I insist it will be easier to do online research at the dining room table. I should know better than to think it's going to thwart him. He pulls a chair right up beside me and keeps slinging his arm over the back of mine, making comments about how nice my hair smells. Which is bullshit, because I haven't washed my hair in days.

I get up to pour us glasses of water. His is lukewarm from the tap— I'm not offering him anything that will make him feel welcome—and I need some space from his breathing down my neck, literally. I don't think it's been more than twenty minutes, but I fire off a text to Bishop, telling him that anytime he's ready, I could use an intervention. I'm not even finished filling my own glass when there's an aggressive knock. I feign surprise and skirt around the counter so I can answer the door. Joey looks totally put out by the interruption.

"Oh! Hi, Bishop! What's up?" I say loudly.

Earlier when he stopped by, he was wearing sweats and a T-shirt. Now he's shirtless, with all his perfectly defined muscles on display. He's wearing a pair of actual shorts, but they look like they're from the eighties. They show off the bruises coloring the inside of his thigh. They're no longer black and blue and purple. They've faded to yellow green around the edges, the center a mottled purplish pink. If I'm not mistaken, there's a slight sheen to his skin. Or maybe it's the lighting.

He arches a brow. "Wow. You should've gone into acting." He brushes by me, using only one crutch, the pizza box in his other hand. "I'm here for my rubdown," he announces. He tosses the pizza box on the counter and makes a show of being surprised by Joey sitting at the table with his mouth hanging open.

"Oh shit. Did I get the time wrong?" Bishop taps his temple. "I had it in my head that you were gonna work me over for dinner."

"Bishop Winslow?" Joey's chair screeches across the floor. He crosses over to where Bishop leans against the counter. Their size difference is almost comical. Joey is maybe five eight or five nine, although he tells everyone he's five eleven. Bishop is mammoth in comparison.

"Joey Smuck. I'm a huge fan." Joey wipes his hands on his jeans and holds one out.

Bishop looks at his hand but doesn't take it. "Your last name is Smuck?"

"Yeah. How do you two know each other?" Joey looks to me and drops his hand. "I didn't think you hung out with your brother's teammates."

"Stevie's my neighbor. She woke me up in the middle of the night when she moved in here." Bishop turns his attention to me. "How long ago was it now?"

He doesn't give me time to respond, which is just as well, because I have no idea where he's going with this.

"Anyway, she was a beautiful fucking mess, and I was an asshole because she was making one hell of a racket. Now she gets to cause me physical pain on a regular basis, since she's helping me rehab. It's endless retribution. Isn't that right, bae?"

I almost choke on my spit with the *bae* comment. I cough a couple of times to clear my throat and choose to ignore the pet name. "Uh, yeah. That about sums it up."

"You're rehabbing an NHL player? Why didn't you say anything?" Joey asks.

"Because it's none of your goddamn business, is it?" Bishop says with a smile, then smacks himself on the forehead. "Oh shit, I'm not supposed to be here for another hour, am I? I totally forgot you had that thing you said you couldn't get out of. I can start with my stretches while you guys are doing whatever you're doing. That's cool, right?"

He struts across my living room and grabs the yoga mat, winking at me as he passes.

"You won't even know I'm here." He unrolls the mat in the middle of the living room so we'll have a perfect view of him from the dining room table.

Joey looks like he wants to argue or help him hold his balls—I'm not sure which is more likely. We settle back in at the table, but I honestly can't concentrate on anything now, and neither can Joey.

Bishop's sudden appearance in my apartment means that Joey now thinks he needs to stake a claim on me. He stretches his arm across the back of my chair and moves in even closer, so I slide mine in the opposite direction.

All the while Bishop is warming up less than twenty feet away. However, he's not doing normal stretches. They're almost obscene, like he's warming up for a *Magic Mike*-style performance. He also keeps groaning, loudly, which is distracting.

Eventually he pushes up from the yoga mat and saunters over, abs flexing, along with every other muscle in his body. "Sorry to interrupt, but can I get your help for a sec, bae?" He's laying it on super thick.

Joey leans in even closer. I can feel his breath on my cheek. He must've eaten something with onions or garlic recently. I elbow him in the ribs, trying to get some space. "Sure."

I start to push my chair back, but Bishop holds up a hand. "You can stay where you are. I need you to work out a knot. You know exactly how to loosen me up."

I can feel how red my cheeks are. It's obvious that Bishop is being intentionally suggestive, and it makes me highly aware that he's been pretty reserved up to this point despite how antagonistic we are with each other.

He knocks Joey's arm out of the way and drags the chair away from the table. Rocking it back on two legs, he then spins it around with me still seated. I'm not sure this is recommended for someone with a groin injury. He slips one hand under his knee to help raise his leg and plants a bare foot on the seat of my chair, sliding his toes under my butt to keep it in place.

His package is at eye level, and the fabric of his shorts is shiny, stretching across the front and making everything even more pronounced.

In my periphery Joey looks like his head is about to pop off. I fight to keep a straight face. "Where are you tight?"

I'm still wearing my gross old sweats and my giant, repulsive sweatshirt that I've had since my first year of college. I've painted in this hoodie. Bishop fingers the material at the sleeve and makes a face. "Are you wearing a T-shirt under this? Can you take this off? You know how sensitive my skin is, and this feels like sandpaper. If you need new hoodies, I can get you some team ones."

"Thanks, but that's not necessary." I can't believe how extra he's being.

We reach for the hem at the same time, but Bishop gets there first. He pulls it up a couple of inches, the fabric sticking to the shirt underneath and exposing my navel. He separates the layers, his warm fingertips grazing bare skin. Electricity crackles through my veins at the contact, and a wave of goose bumps flashes across my skin.

I hold my tank in place while he lifts my hoodie. I have to release my shirt eventually so he can pull the hoodie over my head. He tosses it on the floor. I'm wearing a tank underneath that reveals a significant amount of cleavage. Which is where Bishop's eyes go.

"That's way better," Bishop says to my boobs.

"Glad you're more comfortable." All the snark I mean to channel into that statement comes out as breathy.

"So much more comfortable now that you're not wearing that stupid hoodie." He grabs my hand and presses my fingers against a spot about two inches shy of his trouser sausage. "It's tight right here."

I have to remind myself that this isn't Bishop flirting with me. He's doing me a favor by making it look like there's more going on between us than there really is. "Here?" I put pressure on the area, and he sucks in a breath.

"Yeah. Not too hard, though. It's still sore." He subtly shifts his groin forward, closer to my face.

I keep my eyes on the bruises on the inside of his leg. There's a purpose for this, and it's to make Joey uncomfortable.

As I massage the area, Bishop groans, loudly. "Ahh yeah, right there. Fuuuuck, Stevie, that's it, that's the spot. Jesus Christ, ah shit, *oh Gaaawwwwwwd*, gentle, gentle, yeah, just like that, uuunnnnggggghhhhh."

I wish my hair was down so I could hide behind it and laugh. I tip my head forward and twist my face so it's pretty much pressed against the inside of Bishop's knee. As if he knows what I'm thinking, he tugs at the tie holding my hair up in the horribly messy bun, and it tumbles free, cascading around me in a pale-blue waterfall. It desperately needs to be washed, but at least now I have some cover.

Bishop groans again and grabs the back of the chair, forearms resting lightly on my shoulders as he bows toward me. His stubbly cheek brushes mine, his nose at my ear. "Think I'm making him uncomfortable or horny?"

"Probably both." My lips almost brush the inside of his leg.

The position we're in is intensely intimate. I can smell sex and sweat and possibly baby powder, which is . . . strange. I have the urge to part my lips and find out what his skin tastes like, which is really messed up, since my cheater ex-boyfriend is sitting a few feet away, observing this. But then, maybe that's the point. Bishop knows all about what happened, because I told him, so this intentionally intimate scenario is likely him helping me get even for what I walked in on before I became his neighbor.

His fingers tense against the back of my neck when I accidentally graze his penis. Which is very, very erect. Since we started rehab sessions, I've grown accustomed to his semis. I'm constantly touching him in areas proximal to his peen, and I wear running shorts, sports bras, and occasionally tanks when we have sessions because it gets hot working on a guy his size. Besides, he lives in his underwear, so why should I feel uncomfortable? Thus his reaction isn't unexpected. But the sound that comes out of him—half agony, half desire—sends a shiver down my spine and a zing between my legs. It's impossible for me not to imagine what his sex noises must be like.

"I should probably go." Joey's chair screeches across the hardwood.

My hand is still splayed across the inside of Bishop's thigh. When I start to move it away, he laces our fingers together, keeping it where it is. Bishop stays curled around me. "You sure, man? Stevie's almost got the knot loosened up." His voice is gritty and low.

"It's cool, bro. I know you need to be on the ice. I'll see you at work tomorrow, Stevie." Joey sounds like he's been huffing helium.

"Okay, see you then." My voice is muffled and breathy.

Bishop keeps my hand locked against his thigh and his fingers pressed against the back of my neck until my door clicks shut.

We're both breathing heavily, and my palm is damp against his skin. Generally when we're doing PT, he makes comments about his discomfort, and I suggest he think about dead things while we take a break and he gets himself under control. Occasionally, he might tell me the spot right under his balls needs to be loosened up, which is often the point where I cause him some physical pain and we go back to being mostly professional. But this is different.

Bishop holds the back of my chair with one hand and uses the other to slowly lower his leg to the floor, with my help. I expect him to step back and give us both some much-needed space, but instead he straddles the chair and takes a seat on my legs, arms draped over the back.

"Uh, Bishop?"

"I need a minute," he mumbles and drops his forehead to my shoulder.

He's not resting his full weight on my thighs, but I'm carrying a lot of it right now. His position sort of reminds me of a strip club lap dance—or what I imagine it must be like to have one, since that's not an experience I've had before.

In the past few weeks I've spent a lot of time with my hands near his crotch and manipulating his legs. I've even had them thrown over my shoulder—one at a time, but still, I've had lots of his body parts flush with mine.

What I haven't been is completely surrounded by him. Bishop is a lot of man. A lot of mostly naked man straddling my lap. It's overwhelming to have him this close, in this position. I don't really know what's happening here. Joey is gone, so he doesn't need to be all up in my space anymore, and yet he is.

I gently grip his forearms, and the muscles jump beneath my fingers. "Are you okay?" It comes out a cracked whisper.

Bishop makes a noise; it's more of a grunt than any kind of word I can decipher.

I inhale a slow breath, trying to calm down and frown when the scent coming off his skin registers. I obviously wasn't imagining things. "Why do you smell like baby powder?"

He snickers, warm breath caressing my collarbone. "I rubbed down with baby oil before I came over."

I snort a laugh, which seems to break the odd sexual tension taking up all the space around us and sucking the air out of the room.

Bishop pushes off my lap with a groan and takes a wobbly step back. I grab his hips to help steady him. Since I'm sitting and he's standing, his crotch is once again right in my face, his hard-on extra obvious. When it doesn't seem like he's at risk of falling over, or falling back in my lap, I let him go. He moves out of my personal space, and I feel like I can finally breathe again.

"I think mission 'make Joey uncomfortable enough to leave' was a success, although I have a feeling I'll be fielding a lot of questions tomorrow after that performance." I search for my elastic and find it on the floor. After gathering my hair up, I secure it in a knot on top of my head. "So thanks for that."

"It was one hundred percent my pleasure. That guy is a douche, and an idiot."

"Mmm. I think I might share the *idiot* title for staying with him for an entire year." I move to step around him, wanting more space and less at the same time.

"Hey." Bishop's fingers wrap around my wrist. "Don't do that to yourself. Don't own other people's bad choices and make them yours."

"I should've seen it coming."

"Sometimes we don't see what's right in front of us, though, do we?"

I tip my chin up to meet his gaze. There are a whole lot of unspoken words there. Ones that need to remain that way, since I'm reporting to a team of NHL professionals now. It's a challenge to ignore the chemistry zinging between us, though. I've been doing my best to keep it on lockdown for a lot of reasons, one of which just left my apartment.

Not to mention Bishop is an NHL player who is most definitely going to get media attention when he's back on the ice. It's not something I want to get caught up in.

My phone buzzes on the table, startling us. I glance at the device and catch Pattie's name as it flashes across the screen. I'm sure she wants to know how things went with Joey.

"Should I work you over now?" I motion in the general direction of Bishop's still-bulging crotch.

"Yeah, just go easy on me tonight. That little stunt I pulled was awesome, but now I'm sore."

"I wondered about that."

"Totally worth it, though. I wish you could've seen his face. He looked like he wanted to maim me."

I spend the next forty-five minutes with my hands all over Bishop. He's right about his stunt not being the best idea, based on how much groaning and bitching he does.

I expect him to leave right after, but instead he gets out plates and serves us both cold pizza. Half is the way I like it; the other half has the same meat options but no pineapple or green olives. He also pops the cap on two of the beers he brought over. I'm ridiculously thirsty for some reason, so I drain the first beer quickly and grab a second one.

Bishop stretches out on my couch, commandeers the remote control, and flips channels until he finds Sportsnet. He picks an olive off his slice and flicks it at my plate. "Your disgusting toppings are commingling with mine."

"It's not disgusting. It's delicious." I take a huge bite and moan my delight. It doesn't even matter that it's cold; it's still awesome, and I haven't eaten since lunch. I cover my mouth with my hand. "Yours is boring."

"Three kinds of meat isn't boring."

"It's certainly not adventurous."

"Fruit on a pizza is not adventurous, Stevie. It's gross and wrong."

"Tomatoes are technically a fruit, and they're slathered all over pizza," I point out.

"Yeah, but they're not sweet, they're savory, and they live in the vegetable area of the grocery store, so it's not the same. Would you put peach slices on your pizza? No. You wouldn't, so you shouldn't put things like pineapple on it either. Especially with something as repulsive as green olives."

"Let it all out, Shippy. Tell me how you really feel."

"Do *not* call me that."

"Call you what, *Shippy*?"

He pokes at the corner of his mouth and gives me a dirty look. "Stop."

"Or what?"

"Or I'll smear that pizza all over your face."

"Do that and I'll make sure you regret it tomorrow during our rehab session."

"What're you gonna do, wear a thong and tassels and use my leg for pole dancing?"

"That sounds a lot like a fantasy, *Shippy*."

He makes a grab for my pizza slice, but I'm not the injured one. I roll off the couch and spring to my feet. "So slow, *Shippy*. You need to work on your reaction time."

"I hate that nickname so much, you don't even know."

"Fine, I'll stop . . . if you try my gross pizza."

"No."

I lift a shoulder in a careless shrug. "Have it your way, *Shippy*." Every time I use it, it grows on me a little more. It's really kind of horrible, and it doesn't seem to fit him at all, which is maybe why I like it so much. Also, his irritation is entertaining.

I drop down on the far side of the couch and take another bite of my pizza, making enjoyment noises.

"Seriously?" Bishop arches a brow.

"What's wrong, *Shippy*?"

"Aside from you calling me Shippy five hundred times in the last two minutes, you sound like you're getting off on your pizza."

"It's really good. Just take one bite, and I'll never use that nickname again." I edge closer.

"Fucking fine. One bite. Then no more of this Shippy shit."

"I bet you'll love it and order it in secret all the time." He's stretched out on the couch, legs spread wide, bruises on display. I move closer until my knees touch the side of his thigh and hold the slice in front of his face.

He purses his lips and turns his head, like a kid who doesn't like his dinner. "If I don't like it, I'm spitting it out."

"Nope. You're not a toddler. You have to swallow." I get right into his personal space, kind of like he did with me when he was making Joey uncomfortable.

"I don't even like the way it smells. I'm definitely not going to like the way it tastes."

"If women can stomach jizz, you can swallow a bite of this pizza."

His eyebrows lift. "Does that mean you're a swallower?"

"No point in tasting it twice. Besides, all the salty taste buds are at the front. If I'm already in the middle of a deep throat, it makes more sense to swallow rather than swish all that nasty gelatinous crap over all of my taste buds so I get the bitter, the sour, and the salty."

Bishop's mouth drops open for a second and snaps shut just as quickly. His jaw tics and his eyes darken. "Your ex really is an idiot. Who cheats on a woman who willingly swallows?"

"I'm the idiot for staying with him for as long as I did." I poke him in the lip with the end of the pizza slice. "Take a nice big bite so you get an olive and some pineapple."

"If I barf on you, I'm not apologizing."

"Stop being such a baby and take a bite."

"Fine." He takes a robust bite and almost gets one of my fingers.

His expression is priceless, and if my phone were closer, I would totally snap a pic and add it to his personal contact. He does that thing that reminds me of a cat before it throws up, like he's gagging.

"Swallow it, Shippy."

He narrows his eyes and chews faster, his throat bobs, and he reaches around me for his beer, guzzling what's left in the bottle. "Nasty."

"It's better when it's hot."

"I would rather eat a dirty, sweaty pussy than take another bite of that disgusting combination of toppings." He shoves half his slice of all-meat-and-cheese pizza into his mouth, presumably to cover the olive-pineapple taste he's not so fond of.

"I haven't showered since yesterday, so I have one of those if you feel like dessert." I slap a palm over my mouth. "Oh my God. Pretend I didn't say that."

A slow smirk spreads across Bishop's face. "First you tell me you're a swallower, and then you offer me up your pussy for dessert? When I'm ninety years old and senile, I'll still remember this conversation."

I roll my eyes to hide my embarrassment and the fact that I'm now thinking about what it would be like to have Bishop's face between my thighs. "I was being sarcastic about my filthy lady bits, obviously. The lack of showering was for Joey's benefit and meant as a deterrent." I motion to my messy bun. "It looks like I styled my hair with bacon grease."

Bishop takes me off guard when he wraps his wide, warm palm around the back of my neck and pulls me closer. He drops his head, and I feel his lips at my temple and his nose above my ear.

He inhales deeply. "Smells fruity to me." His rough stubble scrapes against my cheek, and I'm pretty sure it's his lips skimming my throat as he tips my head to the side.

"What're you—" I suck in a breath when I feel the warm wet swipe of his tongue along the underside of my jaw.

"Taste pretty fucking good to me too," he murmurs.

I don't know what's happening here. I can't breathe, or move, or think beyond the feel of Bishop's palm wrapped around the back of my neck and his warm breath on my skin.

This is a bad idea for a lot of reasons. Not the least of which is the fact that we both have to keep our relationship professional. It's a layer of complication that didn't exist before.

I put a palm on the closest part of his body to steady myself. It happens to be his thigh: his very muscular, thick thigh.

"Bishop." The breathy half moan tells us both more than I mean for it to. Despite knowing how much trouble this could cause, my unshowered lady bits are hella excited.

He bites the edge of my jaw and groans. I adjust my palm on his thigh so I don't fall forward, and my fingertips graze the hem of his ridiculously short running shorts. His lips keep moving, teeth nipping as he closes in on my chin.

He mumbles something against my skin, and suddenly his hands are on my hips. A second later I'm straddling his thighs. I am so glad I lost the sweats when we started the rehab session, post-Joey defecting. I grab his shoulders to steady myself and to prevent him from taking the brunt of my weight, but Bishop seems to have other ideas.

He pulls me down so my ass rests on his thighs, despite my protest. He makes a sound that seems a lot like a growl mixed with a grunt and raises his hips at the same time as he pulls me forward.

And I feel him, *all of him*, hard and thick and right damn well *there*. The natural reaction is to roll my hips, because I want to create glorious friction that isn't a result of me and my hands and my trusty vibrator. I have a huge, well-built, incredibly hot, and obviously horny man between my legs. Every thought I had about this being a seriously bad idea evaporates with the first slow, purposeful grind.

Bishop makes a choked sound and bites the edge of my jaw, a lot harder than I anticipate.

I gasp, then groan as I roll my hips again. "God, that feels so good." I run my fingers through his hair, enjoying the satiny slide of the strands as I grip them. My intention is to tip his head back so I can find out what his mouth feels like on mine while we dry fuck each other.

Bishop's fingers flex on my waist, and his next groan is followed by a string of profanities.

I freeze and he drops his head, face pressed against the side of my neck. He growls a low *Fuck* against my skin. As much as I want to indulge in another hip roll—because I am thoroughly enjoying the feel of his cock rubbing on me, even through the layers of cotton and Lycra—I am once again reminded this isn't a great idea.

Bishop lifts his hips a couple of inches, and this time the noise that comes out of him is familiar. If there's one sound I recognize, it's him in pain. "Goddamn mother-humping shit!" His lips part, and I feel the wet swipe of his tongue and the sharp press of his teeth before he sucks my skin, hard.

"Ah!" I fist his hair and shove his face farther into my neck, sort of like what I've seen Lainey do with Kody when he was a baby and decided to use her nipple as a chew toy. It seems to have the desired effect. Bishop releases me from his teeth. I have to pry his fingers loose from my hips.

"No, don't!" He tries to prevent me from clambering out of his lap, but his face is contorted into a grimace of pain.

I wriggle free and scramble to the other side of the couch. As soon as I'm no longer grinding my lady parts on his junk, he cups himself, then slams his head against the couch cushions a couple of times while he continues to groan and swear. "I just want some goddamn friction! Is that too much to ask for?"

"I don't think you're ready for friction." I'm all pitchy and breathless.

He rolls his head toward me, gaze moving over me in a hot, angry sweep. "I managed to whack off in the shower yesterday. It didn't feel awesome, but at least I got a little relief." He jabs an annoyed hand toward the obvious bulge behind his hand. "This is damn well torture." He's still cupping himself protectively—as if he's worried I'm going to spontaneously hump him. He was the one who pulled me into his lap, not the other way around.

"It's probably divine intervention or something." I avert my gaze before I can do something even stupider than trying to make out with him, like offering him a handy or a blow job to take the edge off.

He opens his mouth to respond, but his phone buzzes on the coffee table and his brother's name flashes across the screen. At the same time mine flashes with a new message. Thank God for poorly timed interruptions. I pick up my phone, even though the message is from Joey, which I'm not at all interested in checking. But at least now I'm not staring at Bishop's bulge. I can feel his eyes on me as he reaches for his phone.

"Ah shit," he grumbles.

"Is everything okay?" I side-eye him so I don't have to look directly at him.

"My brother can't find his freaking insulin."

"Is he at home?"

"Yeah." He hits the call button and brings his phone to his ear. I can hear Nolan's muffled voice. "You check the coffee table . . . the fridge . . . the linen closet? Fuck. If I tell you where I keep it, then I'm going to have to find another place to put it so you don't lose it. You what? Jesus, Nolan. How the hell did you find it?" He runs an aggravated hand through his hair. "I'll be right there. We'll be talking about this shit, though. I was in the middle of something." He ends the call. "I gotta go. He found my spare earlier today and now he can't find either kit, and he's been looking for an hour already."

"Oh God, that's not good." I follow him to the door.

"No. It's really not. I wish he'd take this more seriously. One day I'm not going to be here to save his ass."

"You know, you can keep a couple doses here if you need to, just in case."

"That might be a good idea." He steps out into the hall, crutch braced under one arm. "Oh, and this discussion isn't over." He motions between our crotches.

I roll my eyes. "I think it would be better if we chalked that up to hormones and pretend it never happened."

Nolan opens the door before Bishop can argue. He looks from Bishop to me without making eye contact and grimaces. "Sorry for the interruption."

"You should be, asshole. You ruined my night."

"Let me know if you need any help," I offer.

Bishop waves me off, and they disappear into his apartment. I close the door and lean against it, running my fingers along the edge of my jaw where Bishop bit me and down to my neck where he sucked the skin. I rush to the bathroom and flip on the light. The spot is flushed pink, and there are tiny crescents from where his teeth were.

The near kiss is the only thing I can think about when I get into bed. And it follows me into my dreams. I don't need the complications that come with getting involved with Bishop, but I don't know that I'm going to be able to keep my crotch from gravitating to his if I find myself in a situation like that again.

CHAPTER 18

RESISTANCE IS FUTILE

Stevie

Joey corners me the next morning at work and tries to ask me all kind of questions about Bishop and what's going on between us.

"I'm helping him rehab, and I'd appreciate it if you'd keep your big yap shut about that."

Joey crosses his arms and leans against the locker beside mine. A tuft of hair peeks out from under his arm, and I imagine his armpit troll suffocating. "It looks like a hell of a lot more than rehab going on. Does he know we used to date? I get it, Stevie, you need a rebound, but this really isn't a good way to get back at me. Who's going to get hurt in the end?"

It frustrates the hell out of me that he automatically assumes I'm hooking up with Bishop as a means to get over his idiotic ass. "What are you trying to do here, Joey? Give me relationship advice?"

"I don't want you to do something you end up regretting."

I slam my locker shut, wishing his fingers would get caught in it. I remind myself that I'm at work and that his goal is to rile me up and get a reaction. There is no damn way I'm going to give him the satisfaction. "I've already done something I regret. I dated you for a year. I think that's going to stay at the top of my list for a while."

Joey steps to the right when I do, blocking my way out. I want to punch him in the groin. He puts his hands up in mock surrender, or like he's trying to corral me. "Look, I know you can hold a grudge like nobody's business, Stevie, but do you know his reputation? Have you seen the kind of women he dates?"

"I don't hold grudges."

"You're still mad at me for making one little mistake."

"Boning someone who wasn't me on my birthday is not a little mistake."

He ignores that and shoves his phone in my face. Apparently he's been busy stalking Bishop on social media. The hashtag #BishopWinslowSighting is typed into the search bar. "Look at this."

"Why are you checking out Bishop in his underwear?"

"I'm not checking him out!" Joey looks over his shoulder to make sure we're still alone. Unfortunately we are. "There are tons of these pictures, and lots of them are recent. Like within the last couple of months there are at least half a dozen. Do you really want to get involved with a guy like this?"

To a normal person, what Joey is showing me would imply that Bishop is a ladies' man. But I happen to be privy to information regarding the women who are in and out of Bishop's apartment, and I know they're his brother's friends. I even recognize one of the pics as Nolan's most recent sleepover friend from last week. All the photos have been taken in Bishop's apartment, and half of them are blurry, as if they were snapped on the sly. In some Bishop doesn't seem to realize he's being caught on camera, although in a few he's covertly flipping the bird by scratching his chin or his temple with his middle finger.

I can easily explain this, but it's almost better that Joey thinks he's some womanizing douchebag. There's even gratification in his believing it's true. "It's really none of your business, is it?"

"Fine. I'll drop it."

"Look at you, finally getting it after all this time." Once again I try to step around him, but he blocks my way.

"Hold on. We still need to get together to talk about the decorations for the fundraising event. Why don't you come to my place tonight?"

Seriously. There is no way he can be this clueless. "I'm busy."

"You can get your suitcase. I'll even drive you back to your place after. We have to get this done. They're expecting us to know what we're doing and submit a budget proposal by the end of the week."

I sigh, annoyed and defeated. Once this stupid project is over, I'm definitely telling him to fuck himself. "Fine. I'll come over, but only because I want my damn suitcase back and so we can get this planning bullshit out of the way. I have a client in fifteen. I need to go."

"Okay, I'll meet you in the lobby at five." His grin is so smug I want to punch it off his face.

"I have clients until six. I'll meet you at your place."

"It's okay. I can wait."

"Awesome." I leave him in the staff lounge. And grumble my irritation that I'm still stuck dealing with him.

Bishop messages me early in the afternoon to verify that he's coming to my place around seven. I let him know that I might be late because I have to take care of a couple of things. I'm nervous about seeing him after last night and what almost sort of happened. Less than a minute later I get another message from him with a bunch of annoyed-looking emojis, as if I'm doing him some kind of disservice by not being available whenever he wants me.

I send him a slew of GIFs basically telling him to shove his crown up his ass. I figure there is zero point in keeping it from him that I'll be late because I have to get some stuff from Joey's and we still have to deal with the freaking decorations for the gala. Also, he should be warned that I'll likely be in a seriously bad mood, so if he thinks we're going to rehash what happened last night, he is sorely mistaken. I firmly believe denial is the best plan. I leave my phone in my backpack for the remainder of the afternoon, not interested in dealing with Bishop's entitlement, or his thoughts on friction, or Joey and his douchery.

My final appointment of the day ends up canceling, which means I'm done earlier than expected.

"Want to come with me and Jules to the pub? We can grab some apps and a drink?" Pattie threads her arm through mine. I haven't had a chance to talk to her all day, since we've both been fully booked.

"I'd love to, but I have to deal with Joey." We walk down the hall toward the lobby. My mood has been decent until now.

"I thought you did that last night."

"There was an interruption."

Her eyebrows rise. "A neighborly interruption?"

"Yuppers." I stop short as we approach the front desk, which means Pattie also comes to an abrupt halt, since our arms are linked. "What the . . ."

Bishop is leaning on the front desk and talking to the receptionist, Bernice, who looks like her head is about to explode.

"Whoa. Who's the hottie?" Pattie asks.

"That's Bishop."

She lets out a low whistle. "Wow. I'm used to seeing him with a furrowed brow and a lot of hockey gear."

"I'm used to seeing him in his underwear."

"I didn't realize how lucky you were until now. That man is ridiculously hot."

"Yeah." And I was dry humping him last night while he almost cried in pain. I unhook my arm from Pattie's and close the remaining distance, stopping a few feet away. "Uh, hey."

Bernice is midsentence, probably telling Bishop all about her poodle, Duchess, based on the vacant look on his face. At the sound of my voice, his head snaps in my direction. His eyes drop all the way to my shoes and slowly rise to my face. "I'm guessing you didn't get my message."

"I'm guessing not. Pattie, this is Bishop; Bishop, this is my friend and colleague Pattie, who is also a physical therapist."

They shake hands, and to Pattie's credit, she plays it totally cool, but then her brothers play college football, which is almost like having a celebrity in your family.

I rummage around in my backpack in search of my phone. Of course it's at the bottom of the bag, which makes things awkward, especially since I can feel Bishop staring at me while he and Pattie make small talk. "Want to give me the CliffsNotes version?"

"I'm taking you to the douche ex's to get your suitcase."

Pattie choke-coughs on a laugh.

I slap Bishop on the arm and look around for Joey, since he's supposed to drive us to his place. Which was supposed to be *our* place. This should be super fun and awkward all the way around.

"I sent him home already," Bishop says.

I don't even need to look at his face to know he's smirking.

"How are we getting to his place, then? I'm not taking the bus with you." As soon as the words are out of my mouth, I realize how ridiculous they are. Bishop doesn't need to keep travel costs down by taking public transit. Although for a few seconds I imagine what it would be like for him to have to jam his mammoth body into one of those tiny seats.

He holds up a set of keys. "I drove here."

I snatch them out of his hand. "You should *not* be driving."

"I made it here just fine."

I prop a fist on my hip. "Have you even been cleared to drive?"

"I've been cleared for light workouts, so driving seems reasonable, doesn't it?"

"Are you serious with this? One is in no way related to the other. At all. What if you had to react quickly? Or brake hard? You can't even do a hip thrust without crying."

"Untrue. I can do a hip thrust fine, just not with any weight on my thighs."

I can feel my face turning red. I shoot him a warning glare. "No driving until you're cleared, and I want that in writing, not words from your mouth. I won't have you undoing all my hard work. The last thing I need is you reverting back to a super a-hole."

"This is better than daytime soap operas," Pattie says, reminding me that I'm chewing Bishop out in the middle of reception, and he's grinning like I've told him I'm taking him for ice cream.

"You're not helping," I tell her, then give Bishop my attention again. "We should go before people start to recognize you."

"I'm not high profile enough to get recognized around here," Bishop argues.

And, of course, because the universe is on my side and clearly agrees with me, two clients come up to him and ask for autographs and photos. I offer to take the pictures, and I make him pose for at least twenty shots before I finally pass their phones back. I put on a sweatshirt and pull the hood up to hide behind before we leave. I also put on my gigantic aviator-style glasses.

"What're you doing?" Bishop asks.

"Covering myself up in case people recognize you again and want to take more pictures."

He flicks a loose lock of pale-blue hair. "You stand out way more than me."

"Whatever. Let's just go."

Bishop is still on crutches and seems to enjoy shambling along at a snail's pace. "Can you move faster?" I mutter from behind the safety of my hood.

"I thought you didn't want me to reinjure myself."

"You have a groin pull. You're not suddenly a ninety-five-year-old with brittle bones and a double hip replacement."

He tugs on the back of my hood. "If anyone is drawing attention, it's you with this freaking sweatshirt on when it's over seventy degrees and half the girls wandering around here are dressed like they're ready to go to the beach."

"That's because they're college students and it's a prerequisite to dress for weather ten degrees warmer than it actually is. I'm being reasonable with my hoodie."

"Not even a little."

We manage to make it to his car—thank God he doesn't drive something ostentatious and expensive like my brother does—without anyone accosting him. Since I have the keys, I rush around to the driver's side and close myself inside while he fumbles around with his crutches and lowers himself into the passenger seat.

"Thanks for the help."

"You managed to get yourself here just fine."

I haven't driven to what was supposed to be my apartment ever, so I have to program it into Bishop's GPS. I'm anxious about going to Joey's and Bishop being with me. I'm also freaked out about last night, and I'm waiting for him to bring it up, but he doesn't. He sits in the passenger seat, tapping his fingers on the armrest.

"You know what I find interesting?" he finally says.

"I'm sure you're about to enlighten me."

He stretches his arm across the back of my seat and fingers a lock of my hair. I know he's touching it because I can feel his hand resting on my shoulder. Also, he gives it a tug. "That you'll change the color of your hair to something that stands out but hide behind a hood because of the possibility that some random person you don't know is going to recognize me. It doesn't make a whole lot of sense. You know that, right?"

"The two are unrelated."

"Your hair screams 'Look at me.'"

"But no one wants to take pictures of me and get my autograph because of it. All they know is that I have fun hair. They don't know I'm related to Rook, or that I'm . . . working on rehab with you, but if they see me with you or my brother, all of a sudden I stop being the girl with the fun hair and I start being Rook Bowman's sister or that chick who was with Bishop Winslow."

He doesn't say anything in response. Instead he keeps twisting my hair around his finger. I can feel him looking at me still, and it's distracting. Thankfully, we arrive at what was supposed to be my apartment building. I parallel park down the street and try to force myself to get out of the car, but all I can do is sit there, gripping the steering wheel and staring at the building.

"You okay?" Bishop asks after God knows how long. He pulls my hood down and slips his fingers under my hair. His calloused palm curves around the nape of my neck, just like last night. His thumb sweeps back and forth, slow and soothing.

I'm so screwed. I like this guy, and I shouldn't for a lot of reasons, most of which I cited last night in my head. The other reasons, the ones I haven't voiced, are the ones that plague me the most. As much as I believe Bishop's reasons for wanting me to rehab him. What if I'm wrong? It would be a pretty elaborate plan on his part, and it would also put him on par with a sociopath, but I also didn't realize that I was pretty much dating one of those for an entire year until I walked in on him with someone else. And he's not sorry because he hurt me. He's sorry because he got caught.

I also don't want Joey to be right that I'm using Bishop for more than just an opportunity to rehab an NHL player. I would prefer not to turn him into a rebound.

I'm a bit of an emotional mess, if I really think about it. I don't want to drag Bishop into that, but I've already started to get attached to, and depend on, him. I don't say any of those things, though. I might be an emotional mess, but I'm not stupid.

"I haven't been back here since the night I arrived."

"You mean since—"

"I caught Joey screwing someone else."

"On your birthday."

"On my birthday." Shit. I think I might cry. It's dumb. It's been weeks since it happened, but coming here makes it all feel fresh again.

"What's the apartment number? I'll get your suitcase for you."

I finally let go of the steering wheel and look at him. "You can't do that. It's a heavy bag; you'll set yourself back."

"I'll be fine, and you'll stretch me out when we get home."

I rub my temples. "I still have to organize the decorations with him."

"We'll take care of it when we get home too."

"But Joey signed us up to work on this thing together." Avoiding him entirely isn't a great strategy, and it definitely isn't one I can continue to employ forever. But in this case maybe it's better to have Bishop deal with Joey until I'm truly ready to do it on my own.

"And Joey is a dickhead who doesn't deserve to spend five seconds in your presence. Don't worry. We'll get it all sorted out. Nolan works at one of those party warehouses, so he'll have loads of hookups for us."

"That's an odd place to work."

"The hours are flexible, and he's a part-time manager. We might as well take advantage, since he has the connections."

I scrub a hand over my face. "Joey thinks you and I are together."

"Good. Let him think that. Isn't that actually better for you anyway? Won't it get him off your ass?"

"He called you my rebound." Goddamn it. Why can't I keep my stupid mouth shut?

Bishop shifts as much as he can so he's turned toward me. His knees hit the center console, and his thumb keeps sweeping back and forth on that sensitive spot behind my ear. "Does that bother you?"

"Does it bother you?" I fire back, because answering that question is complicated, and the truth makes me feel way too vulnerable.

"Coming from your dickbag ex? Not in the least. That guy is going to say anything he can to get under your skin and into your head." He gives the back of my neck a squeeze. "Let him believe whatever he wants. What's the apartment number?"

"One-two-one-three."

"I'll be back."

He unbuckles his seat belt and gets out of the car. The back door opens, and he nabs a single crutch. Before he hobbles off, he taps on the window, so I roll it down.

"Just to be clear, you *don't* want me to beat the fuck out of this guy?"

"No. You have a groin injury, and that is the opposite of helpful for healing."

"Is that the only reason you don't want me to beat his ass?"

"Mostly, yes. Plus I still have to work with him."

Bishop purses his lips but nods. "Okay. Noted."

I watch him enter the building, trying to understand what the hell is going on between us. I'm so confused. It seems to take an actual eon for him to finally return. I get out of the car so I can help him with my suitcase. Surprisingly, it's still in one piece. I just hope all my things are still in it.

"Is he still alive?" I hoist the suitcase in the trunk.

"He's fine. I mean, his ego might not be in the best shape, but if he's been causing you problems, I don't think he will anymore."

"What did you say to him?"

"That he's a stupid asshole and he doesn't deserve you and he's lucky he ever had you at all. I also told him I'd be helping you take care of whatever this party shit is, because you shouldn't have to deal with him." He closes the trunk. "Oh, and I told him he needs to stop texting you all the time. If you want to talk to him, you'll be the one to reach out.

I also said that was really un-fucking-likely, since I plan to monopolize all of your spare time."

I tip my head back so I can look up at Bishop. God, he's beautiful. Ruggedly stunning. And he showed up at my work today out of the blue. And told off my ex-boyfriend. I'm going to be super lucky if I don't start bawling. "Thank you for doing that for me."

"I did it as much for me as I did it for you. I'm hungry as fuck, are you? Confrontation always makes me want to eat."

And just like that, the urge to cry disappears. I snort a very unbecoming laugh. "Something greasy and definitely not on your preseason diet?"

A grin tips up the corner of his mouth. "It's like you can read my mind. But we're not going for pizza, because I can't deal with the olives-and-pineapple shit."

He tosses his crutch into the back seat and heads for the driver's side.

"Hey, what're you doing?"

"I'm gonna drive."

"No you're not."

"Yes, I am. You're emotional and you look like you're halfway to yelling or crying, or maybe both. Besides, they cleared me to drive today."

"I don't believe you. Who is 'they'? Why didn't you tell me that back at the clinic? Why wait until now?"

He shrugs. "Because I like watching you get all riled up. It makes me happy that you get so pissed off when you think I'm doing something I shouldn't."

"I am shooting laser beams out of my eyes at you. I want proof that you've been cleared."

"That's what I told my team PT, so you should check your email. You can do it on the way to get food. I'm about to get hangry, and if you think I'm an asshole on a good day, wait until I haven't been fed."

While he drives, I pull my phone out of my purse and do as he says. I find the email he's talking about—the one where he's cleared to drive short distances—and grumble about him being forthcoming from now on.

We stop at a burger drive-through, where Bishop orders enough food to feed a family of four, and we eat burgers and slurp shakes in the parking lot.

"Can I ask you something?" Bishop pops one of my fries into his mouth, having already finished all four of his burgers and his own extra-large fries. I'm not even sure he tasted his food.

I shrug. "Sure."

"How did you end up with that douche?"

I swirl a fry in ketchup and think back to when I met Joey. I'd just moved from New York to LA for my master's program. I'd met him on the first day of class, and he asked if I wanted to get a drink. I'd said yes. "I was lonely, and he was there, I guess."

After several long seconds in which the only sound is our chewing, I finally look over at Bishop.

"Wanna add anything else to that, like maybe an actual explanation?" He steals another fry and reaches for my shake, because apparently he's already finished his, as well.

"You can have these." I trade my shake for the fries.

"I'm sorry. I'm probably pushing it, aren't I?"

"It's okay. It's all stuff I think about but don't usually say out loud. Honestly, I don't know why I ended up with him for an entire year. I think maybe it was partly because I didn't want to be alone? That I wanted someone who was . . . mine? When I moved to LA, I had this idea that I'd be spending all this time with my brother Kyle and his wife, Joy, and my nephew Max."

"And that's not how it turned out?"

I chew on the end of my straw. "Nope, not even a little. I felt like an outsider, kind of . . . displaced, I guess. Like I didn't have a real role anymore. Kyle had Joy and Max, and I didn't have anyone."

"That must've been hard."

I nod. "I missed all the things that were familiar. Then my mom sold the farm and moved out to LA, too, which was nice because it meant I had her around again, but she spent a lot of time with my brother's family, which was understandable since it was her first grand-child, but I still felt like something was missing, which was when I met Joey. So in a lot of ways I guess he ended up being a convenient distraction from all the other stuff going on. I think I knew early on that it wasn't a great fit, but for a while it was better than the alternative."

"Which was what?" He slurps my shake, which is now empty as well, based on the loud suction sound.

"Being alone, I guess? Having everyone worry about me? RJ had just reconnected with Lainey, he had a baby, and there I was, out in LA, trying to glom on to my family because I didn't know how to be on my own, and everyone else was busy with their own things. I had school, but . . . I needed . . . something."

Bishop twirls a lock of my hair around his finger. "Or someone?"

"I thought moving to LA would make everything easier."

"Easier how?"

"Not being faced with the memory of my dad every single day and how he was just . . . gone. We were really close, like, super tight. I think my mom selling the house and the farm hit me a lot harder than I expected it to, you know? I couldn't go back to New York during holidays because we didn't have a place to stay anymore, and all the memories of my dad were no longer tangible. I couldn't walk into the living room and see his recliner or remember him falling asleep in it. My mom sold the truck we used to go for drives in because it wouldn't have survived the trip to LA. It was a lot of change in a short span of time, and I think I hadn't really grieved the loss. Or it was a new level of grieving. I don't know."

"It would be like losing him all over again," Bishop says quietly.

"It really was."

"What happened to him?"

"His body just gave up. He took such good care of himself—ate healthy, stayed active, did all the right things to help manage the diabetes—but his body couldn't keep up with him. He went into a coma and never came out."

"I'm sorry, Stevie." He stretches his arm across the back of my seat and slips his hand under my hair, palm curving around the back of my neck. It feels nice, comforting.

"I don't think it was until I moved out to LA that the loss really and truly hit me. Being away from my mom, the farm. I didn't account for the way that would affect me. Joey was nice, and he wanted to spend time with me. He didn't know my brother was a hockey player at first, and I didn't tell him until we'd been dating for a while, because I've learned the hard way that people will use you to suit their purposes. Anyway, I wanted someone to bring to family events so my brothers wouldn't try to pull the whole dad thing on me. He was kind of like a shield, which is a horrible thing to say."

"It's not horrible. He was protection against more pain."

"Yes. Exactly. Like I know my brothers both mean well, especially RJ, but my whole life it's been about him and his career and his life and his success. When our dad died, I think he felt like he needed to step up somehow, but it was a reminder that Dad was gone. I was struggling to cope, so when Joey came into my life, I used him as armor. He was my defense against the loss I couldn't seem to deal with. Everyone thought I was fine because I was with him. He was safe because, while I liked him and was comfortable with him, I wasn't ever in love with him." It isn't until I voice it that I realize it's true. He was a convenient shield.

"I really hope your family appreciates you." Bishop absently rubs the back of my neck; at least I think it's absently.

"In another family my accomplishments might be celebrated more, but it's hard to compete when you have a brother who's a star NHL player. It's not RJ's fault, or my parents', but when you have a kid who shows that much promise and potential, you do whatever you can to help them succeed. I'm proud of RJ, but when you have a light that bright beside you, it sort of forces you into the shadows. Not that I mind the shadows. I prefer them to the spotlight."

"Is that why you avoid games and telling people Rook is your brother?"

"Sort of. I don't want to get used because my brother is who he is. It's happened before, and I'm sure it will happen again."

"How do you mean?"

"Sometimes people would use the fact that I'm his sister to try to get to him. Especially when he went through his bunny phase."

"He was pretty high profile for a while there. I wasn't sure if any of it was taken out of context or not."

"Kind of hard to take a threesome in a hot tub out of context," I say derisively. "He made such bad decisions for a while, and my parents were so angry with him. I was almost . . . glad to see him fall from grace for a while, maybe?"

"Because the media wasn't spinning him as a golden boy?"

I cringe and nod. "It's not that I didn't want him to be successful. I did, I still do, but he had no idea what kind of impact his choices had on me. We grew up in a rural town. The entire high school practically worshipped him. When he started sleeping around with puck bunnies, I was suddenly the most popular and hated girl in the school. For, like, half a second I enjoyed the attention. And then the catty, bitchy behavior came out. Girls can be horrible to each other."

"You're kind of the opposite of my brother. He uses my name to get women into bed with him and doesn't feel bad about sending them packing, because he knows why they're there."

"That would make me feel . . . hollow."

Bishop nods. "It's his way of avoiding getting into an actual relationship. I think he's afraid to settle down with any one person because his health is what it is. Even if he takes great care of himself, he'll still

face challenges, like your dad did. And knowing that he could potentially be leaving behind all these people who need him . . . I think he
doesn't like that possibility. Besides, we didn't have the best role model
with our dad."

"How so?" I'm afraid to look directly at him, for fear he won't
answer. This is the most open he's been with me, although I did pretty
much spill my guts to him.

"He traveled for work often and left my mom to take care of
us. My brother was a lot of work as a kid because of all the appointments, and they needed the health care benefits. I was a lot of work
because, as you know, hockey is time consuming, and my mom was
doing it alone, essentially." Bishop stares out the windshield, and I
wonder if he's caught up in the memories of his childhood. It was a
lot for my parents to run the farm and take RJ to all his practices and
tournaments, and that was with both of them around. I couldn't even
imagine how difficult it would be as a mostly single parent.

"They fought a lot, and eventually their marriage dissolved. My dad
bailed, and before the divorce papers were even signed, he was shacking
up with one of his colleagues who he'd been taking trips with for years.
My mom has never said as much, but I seriously doubt that relationship
started *after* their marriage ended."

I squeeze the hand wrapped around the back of my neck. "I'm
sorry. That must've been hard for all of you."

"My dad wasn't very present in our lives, so the divorce wasn't as big
a deal as it could've been. Not for me and Nolan, anyway. It was almost
expected. But I guess it framed the way I dealt with relationships, which
was to avoid them for the most part. I had one long-term girlfriend back
when I got drafted out of college, but it didn't last."

"Because you have trust issues?" I would if that's how my parents'
marriage ended.

He shrugs. "Not really. It was more that she wasn't as interested in
me as she was the attention being with me got her. I guess sort of the

same thing you worry about with friends using you because of Rook's fame. I'm not really interested in being with someone whose primary concern is whether their social media following is growing on account of our relationship status, you know? Besides, you've met me; I don't have a shining personality that women fall for."

"You've grown on me."

"Like fungus."

I chuckle quietly. "We're quite the messed-up pair."

"Everyone has a demon or two, Stevie. You just gotta learn how to live with them and find other people who think all your good parts outweigh the bad." Bishop gives my neck a squeeze and drops his hand. "You ready to go home?"

"Yeah, I'm ready."

When we get back to the apartment, I fully expect Bishop to come in so we can do his PT and deal with the decorations. But when we reach my door, he pulls me in to him. At first I don't get what's going on, and then I realize Bishop is hugging me.

I'm slow to react, but eventually I wrap my arms around his waist and settle my palms on his broad back, the muscles flexing under the skin. I rest my cheek against the soft cotton of his shirt, listening to his heart thumping steadily. He smells really good, like greasy takeout, but also faintly of cologne.

I realize that this is the first time Bishop has hugged me on purpose. It doesn't escape me that it's also the first time he's really opened up to me about his life and who he is, or that it's also been an emotional day and maybe that's why he's being all . . . affectionate.

Eventually he leans back, and I tip my chin up so I can see his face. His expression is serious and intense, although that's fairly common for him. I'm pretty sure I have burger breath, so I make sure I exhale through my nose.

His gaze moves over my face like a gentle caress. "We need to talk about last night." His arms are wrapped around me, and I'm still shocked by the hug, so it takes me several long seconds to process his words.

I let my palms settle on his forearms. "We can pretend it didn't happen, can't we?"

"Is that what you want?"

I shrug and stare at his Adam's apple. What I want is for him to tip my chin up and press his lips to mine. But all I can think about is what Joey said about him being a rebound, how Bishop dismissed it, how I don't want to use him, and how I should be focused on his rehab and not what dating him would be like.

Bishop releases me but doesn't put any distance between our bodies. "I'm sorry, Stevie. I shouldn't have—"

I shake my head and cut him off before he can finish that sentence. "Things got intense. Let's just forget about it."

He's silent for several long seconds. "Okay. If that's what you want, that's what we'll do."

"Okay." I start to turn toward my apartment door. I want things to stop being awkward between us. The sooner we have a session, the easier it will be to get things to go back to normal.

Bishop wraps his hand around mine, stopping me from keying in my code. "I'm going to call off tonight's session, and we can work on the decoration stuff tomorrow."

"Why tomorrow? Why not now? It's not that late."

"Just because you want to pretend nothing happened last night doesn't mean it didn't, Stevie. It's been an emotional night for you, and if I come in right now, I'll be inclined to deal with things that you don't seem to want to."

"Are you psychoanalyzing me?"

"More myself and the potential outcomes of my actions. I'll go take a hot bath and do some stretches, and tomorrow we can go back to tormenting each other when emotions aren't running as high." He bends, and I feel the warmth of his lips against my crown.

I have to force my hands to stay at my sides and not wrap around his neck. I have to fight not to tip my chin up or take back what I said about pretending last night didn't happen.

Bishop drops his hand, steps back, and winks. "Your hair smells a lot nicer tonight, bae."

I laugh and roll my eyes. "I'll see you tomorrow."

He waits for me to let myself into my apartment. I stand with my eye pressed against the peephole and watch him unlock his door, confused about what happened and worried about the flutter in my chest.

CHAPTER 19

THE EVOLUTION OF FRIENDSHIP

Stevie

"So you're just friends?" Pattie has asked this pretty much every other day since Bishop stopped by the clinic for the first time to pick me up, something he's gotten in the habit of doing over the past couple of weeks.

"We're friends, yeah." I bite the end off a fried pickle. They're oddly delicious, even when they're no longer hot and crispy.

Pattie points a pita triangle covered in hummus at me. "Don't think I didn't see what you did there."

"*We* see what you did there." Jules motions between her and Pattie.

They exchange a look and turn their arched brows on me.

I don't say anything else, because there is really nothing else to say. I'm still rehabbing him, and as I suggested, we pretend that the grind and almost-kiss never happened. But when I'm alone, in bed, it's a whole different story.

"He's supposed to be back on the ice next week, right?" Jules props her chin on her fist.

It's annoying that everyone in the hockey-watching world is aware of Bishop's recovery schedule. "Yup, and I've been asked to keep working with him, since they expect him to need more TLC once he's back in the game." Every time we have a session after his on-ice practices, he's stiff and sore because he pushes himself too hard.

"I bet he's going to need more TLC." Pattie pokes her cheek with her tongue and makes suggestive hand gestures.

"It's not like that."

"You're together all the time. You cut nights out with us short so you can fit in rehab sessions. He picks you up from wherever you are, even if it's across town, and he video calls you when he's away with the team. How is it *not* like that?"

He always wears a ball cap, a hoodie, and sunglasses when he picks me up from anywhere that isn't the clinic. I didn't even have to ask him to do it either. Because he gets me. Once he even wore a fake beard. It drew more attention than if he'd walked in in his damn underwear, since it was a Santa beard. "Sorry to burst your bubble, but we haven't even kissed."

They both freeze with food items halfway to their mouths.

"That is total bullshit," Pattie says.

Jules nods her agreement. "I've seen him kiss you."

"Let me rephrase: we have not exchanged saliva."

"But, but . . . we've all seen him kiss you," Pattie splutters.

They're not wrong about the forehead and temple kisses; those are frequent and almost always when Joey is present. There was only that one time when things got out of hand and our sex parts met through clothing and his mouth was close to being on mine. I shake my head to clear the image of me riding his lap. "On the forehead or the temple, maybe, but not here." I motion to my mouth.

"What about here?" Jules points at her crotch with a pita triangle. A glob of hummus drops into her lap. "Ah crap!" She grabs a napkin and starts dabbing at it under the table. "Man, now it looks like I have a jizz stain on my yoga pants."

"Go to the bathroom and wash it off."

"And miss this conversation about your not-boyfriend boyfriend? No way!"

"First of all, if I'm being kissed, it better be on the face lips before my nether ones; secondly, he is *not* my boyfriend."

"Well, why the hell not?" Pattie tosses her balled-up napkin on the table.

"Because we're just friends."

"But you're *always* together," Jules says.

"Because I'm rehabbing him."

"There has to be more going on."

"Sorry to disappoint, but there isn't."

"Is this because of your brother?" Jules crosses her arms. "Is he the reason you two aren't hooking up?"

"No."

"Then what's it about?"

"The season has started, and he wants back on the ice, so he's focused on rehab, and so am I. He's been working really hard, and it's paying off, obviously. His determination is impressive." And sexy. So, so sexy. It's been incredible to watch him push himself right to the very limit of what's comfortable. I've learned exactly where his line is and how to pull him back from it. It's been gratifying for both of us to see him make such incredible progress over the past few weeks.

At that moment, my least favorite asshole drops into the seat beside me.

Joey doesn't make a move to put his arm around me. I'm not sure exactly what Bishop said when he retrieved my suitcase, but Joey has backed right off. It's been nice.

On the other side of that shiny, happy coin, he's also started openly flirting with women in front of me. It's more of an annoyance than anything. That stupid fundraiser-dinner thing with all the damn athletes is coming up soon, and I know he's going to bring a date. It's not that I care if he brings someone; it's that I'm not interested in making small talk with his next victim. I realize that I haven't wanted to cry about what happened in a while. Looks like I'm making progress too.

"How are you ladies doing today?" He shifts his chair so he's angled toward me.

Pattie and Jules give him frosty smiles and respond at the same time with, "Fine."

He raps on the top of the table and turns his somewhat wary smile on me. "So, uh, looks like everything is covered for decorations, huh?"

Bishop took care of everything the day after we picked up the suitcase and had that talk in his car. Since then he's been making Joey sweat over it. Just this morning he sent an email with an itemized list of what's being delivered. We don't even need to pick anything up. "Looks like it."

"Is there an invoice? We're supposed to pass that on to management. They said to keep it under a grand, and there's a lot of stuff on that list that looks kind of expensive."

"It's a donation." I start packing up my lunch, uninterested in being anywhere near Joey right now.

"Oh, okay. I guess all we have to worry about is setup, then."

"We'll help with that!" Pattie and Jules collect their things as well, and we leave Joey alone in the staff lounge.

We still have another twenty minutes left in our lunch hour, so we take the opportunity to grab coffee from the shop across the street.

"You're bringing Bishop to this thing, right?" Pattie asks.

And we're back to talking about their favorite benched hockey player. "He doesn't want to come to my freaking work event. Plus it'll be all of those athletes who want to be professional hockey players. How much would that suck for him? He'll be mobbed the entire night."

All the people I work with have been cool about it when he drops by, but then they work with athletes who often eventually become professionals, so they know better than to fangirl or fanboy. People will be all over him, and I might indirectly end up in the fringes of his spotlight. I'm not sure how to feel about that.

"I bet he'll want to come anyway." Jules shoots a sly smile at Pattie.

"Yeah, we'll see." I don't plan to ask him. He already did me a huge favor by getting my suitcase for me and helping me with the decorations, so I don't want to put that on him too.

◆ ◆ ◆

Later the same evening, I have Bishop's leg thrown over my shoulder, and I'm almost lying on top of him to get the deepest stretch possible—the dude is flexible—and his leg hair is tickling my cheek.

"I can see down your top," he groans.

"You're the one who bitches about my hoodies irritating your sensitive skin."

"Yeah, but I didn't say anything about not wearing a bra."

"I am wearing a bra." Hanging out with Bishop has grown increasingly confusing recently. He still makes inappropriate comments, and we spend a lot of time together, but unless we're in front of Joey or he's hugging me good night, he never puts his hands on me.

"Not a very good one if I can still see your nipples through the fabric."

I release him from the stretch. "Would you look at that? You managed to hold that for thirty seconds with only a minimal bitchfest about something."

"Well, you were crushing my dick, which is trying to react to your nipples, so I think my bitchfest is warranted. Are we done with the torture for tonight?"

I eye his crotch. "I think we've probably both had enough."

He gets up off the floor with only the smallest of grunts. He glances at the clock. "Shit. The game's starting." He rolls over the back of the couch and stretches out along the length of it. He grabs the remote from the coffee table, turns the TV on, and flips channels until hockey comes on. Minnesota is playing Vegas, and Seattle is facing off against them next week. It will be Bishop's first game back on the ice.

"Make yourself comfortable." I roll up the yoga mat and tuck it away before I head for the kitchen.

"Wanna grab me a beer? There should be a few left in there from the weekend."

"Anything else you want? Should I make you a sandwich? Maybe a fruit and cheese platter?"

"Nah, I'm good. Maybe later."

"Obviously you missed the sarcasm."

He tips his head back and grins widely. "Calm down, I'm kidding."

I return to the living room with a beer for each of us. Bishop moves his long legs enough for me to sit down and then stretches them out over my lap. It's his way of not-so-subtly asking me to massage his thighs postsession.

"That fundraiser-event thing at your work is next Saturday, right?"

"Mmm." I tip my head back and take a swig of my beer, then rest the bottle high up on his thigh, sort of near his junk.

He doesn't react, just tucks one of his arms behind his head, making the muscles flex. "Is that an mmm, yes?"

"It's next Saturday. You'll be coming back from your away series. You're getting regular massages from the team therapist, and your team PT will make you stretch while you're away, right? And you'll use the sauna. I'll email him later this week." His team PT and I correspond directly because it's easier for both of us. Also, I've discovered that Bishop will omit information if he's the one passing it along.

"What time does the thing start?"

"Not until five, but I have to be there early to set up, so we won't have a session until Sunday."

"My flight lands at noon on Saturday. What time do you have to leave to help set up?"

"I plan on getting as much done as I can Friday night, but I don't want to miss the game, so we'll see. Pattie and Jules are going to help me. We'll go in early Saturday morning to finish up, and I'll probably get ready at Pattie's. It depends on timing and stuff."

"You wanna take my ride and make it easier on yourself?"

I pause with my beer half an inch from my mouth. "You're offering to lend me your SUV?"

"You've driven it plenty. You don't have a lead foot, and you can parallel park like a boss. It's just sitting there otherwise, so why not?"

"Uh, I don't know, because guys' cars are like their girlfriends?"

"Mine isn't. And the tailpipe doesn't make a very good hole to stick my dick in, since it's hot but not wet and tight."

I dig my thumb into the muscle above his knee.

"Ahh! Fuck. Stop!" Bishop flails and grabs my hand. He threads his fingers through mine to keep me from doing it again. "That was nasty and unnecessary."

"So were the words coming out of your mouth."

"Whatever. Anyway, back to this work shindig. Is it fully formal or semiformal?"

"Uh, formal, I guess. Suit and tie for guys, nice dress for girls." I'm going shopping with Pattie and Jules early next week.

"Okay. So since I'm landing at noon, I should be home by, like, one, one thirty at the latest. You can swing by and pick me up at, like, two thirty."

"I'm sorry, what?"

"Just sorting out timelines in my head. You can pick me up at two thirty, or whenever is good for you."

I don't bother to hide my annoyance at his freaking entitlement. "I already told you, I can't fit in a PT session that day. I have to get my hair done and do my makeup and maybe even my nails." I'm not big on self-pampering and that kind of thing, but it's a formal event, and Pattie and Jules are excited to get all dressed up and looking pretty, so I figure I might as well do it too.

"I'm not asking you to fit in a PT session, Stevie. I'm coming with you to this shindig."

"Why would you want to come to my work event?"

"Because Douche McFuckhead is going to be there."

"You don't want to do that, Bishop. It's going to be full of amateur athletes. They'll be humping your leg all night."

"And I'll be humping yours, so it should be an exciting night."

"Honestly, it's sweet of you to offer, but you really don't need to come."

"Do you not want me to come?" He's wearing an expression I've never seen before. He almost looks . . . hurt.

"No. I mean, yes, I want you there, but it'll suck for you."

"So it's settled. I'm your date next Saturday." He focuses back on the game, and I focus on trying to control the butterflies in my stomach.

CHAPTER 20

I'LL CHECKMATE YOUR ASS

Bishop

Things I've enjoyed recently: Stevie, rehab with Stevie, me telling Stevie's ex that he's an asshole and an idiot, me watching hockey with Stevie, me going to ice practice with Stevie—girl can skate like a pro—Stevie's hands on me, the smell of Stevie.

Things I have not enjoyed over the past few weeks: fighting off painful, nearly constant semis when I'm with Stevie; whacking off alone in my shower to the image of Stevie in her running shorts; playing away games where I can't see Stevie; dealing with Bowman's constant bitchy attitude when we're training together, which is most days.

Tonight is my first game back on the ice. I talked to Stevie earlier in the day. She went over my postgame regimen and wished me good luck. We have two more away games before we're back in Seattle, which is another four days of phone conversations and video chats. Four more days without Stevie's hands on me. Four days of whacking off in the shower.

On the upside, I don't have to constantly remind myself not to ram my tongue in her mouth and dry hump her. Small mercies, I suppose.

I've been trying to give her the time she needs to get over the douche ex and me the time to recover from the groin injury. The day I took her to get her suitcase was an eye-opener. I realized a number of things that made me reevaluate my strategy. First of all, she wasn't over what that asshole had done to her. That made sense, since she'd been with him for a year and he'd screwed her over only weeks earlier.

Second, her comment about the asshole ex calling me a rebound has made me not want to be a rebound. Plus the whole almost-kiss situation made me highly aware that as into her as I might be, my body was in no condition to do anything about it. While my brother's cock-blocking via his misplaced insulin pissed me off, it also saved me from messing things up completely.

And that was before I took into consideration the whole conversation with Alex about keeping things professional. I don't want it to look like I'm not taking my rehab seriously. So I put the brakes on and backed off. I eased up on the pervy comments, and I spent more time hanging out with her after rehab sessions. Basically, I injected myself into her life in a way I hoped would seem innocuous beyond all the PT.

Now that I'm back on the ice and I won't be relying on her for rehab, I figure I'm safe to start implementing my plan once I'm back in Seattle, which won't be until Saturday.

For now, I need to focus on hockey. I glance at the clock; in about fifteen seconds I'll be hitting the ice for the first time this season. I get to my feet, ready for my shift.

Rook claps me on the shoulder as he passes. "Don't do the splits."

I grunt in response, because it's better than telling him to fuck off, and take my position left of center. I've been practicing with the team the last week or so, but I don't have the same number of hours on the ice with my line, so it feels a lot like the first day of school.

We manage to keep the puck on Vegas's end of the rink, and no one scores while I'm on the ice. It's not a goal or an assist, but at least it's better than letting them score. Since it's my first game, I'm rotated in every other shift. By the beginning of the third period, we're up one goal—scored by Rook, of course.

I hit the ice, hoping I can help add another goal to the scoreboard to give us some padding. Instead, one of the Vegas players gets up in my space and nearly trips me. He ends up in the penalty box, and I'm pulled from my shift early so the team doctor can make sure I'm okay. One of the rookie players takes his turn on the ice while I'm being checked over and gets the assist I was hoping for.

In the end we win, but I'm not thrilled about my performance. I should be happy that I've managed to play an entire game and I don't feel like I'm going to die, but there's a lot on the line for me, and I have weeks of missed ice time with my teammates to make up for.

After the game I take my time in the shower. The bruising on my inner thigh is pretty much gone, apart from a few remaining yellowish spots. I plan to take advantage of the hot tub and the sauna back at the hotel. I'm in the middle of getting dressed postshower when my phone buzzes from inside my bag. I shrug into my dress shirt and fish it out, smiling when Stevie's name lights up the display.

I answer the call and fumble a bit in my excitement as I bring the phone to my ear. Her smoky voice lights my insides up. "I take it you're not in the sauna if you're answering this."

"No 'Good job on the ice tonight'?" I drop down on the bench and button my shirt one-handed.

"You were too aggressive and played too hard. And you almost took a hit because you wouldn't let your teammates intervene when that asshat from Vegas kept getting in your space."

"I had it handled." I love that she's giving me shit from a time zone away. "Didn't you just get off work? How did you have time to watch the game?"

"I planned my schedule around it. And you clearly aren't following your postgame regimen like you're supposed to, since you're talking to me."

"I'll use the sauna and the hot tub at the hotel."

"That'll be hours after the game."

"I took an extra-long shower." I tuck my shirt into my dress pants and rearrange myself, since my body reacts to the sound of Stevie's voice these days. "Want me to call you in the morning? We can video chat while I do stretches and you get ready for work."

"Sure. We can do that, but I want photographic evidence of you in a sauna *tonight*."

My grin widens. "I bet you do. Want me to drop the towel too?"

Stevie snorts. "Are you looking for an excuse to send me a dick pic, Shippy?"

An elbow to my side reminds me that I'm in the locker room, with half my teammates still wandering around. I glance over at Kingston, who's already fully dressed in a crisp black suit with a team tie, hair perfectly styled, and shoes so polished I can see my reflection in them.

I mouth, *What?*

"You know you have that on speakerphone, right?" He inclines his head fractionally, and I look up to find Rook glaring at me from the bench fifteen feet away.

"Shit." I fumble to take it off speakerphone. It's pretty loud in here, but based on his expression, he knows who I'm talking to.

"Everything okay?" Stevie asks.

"Yeah. I should go. I'll send evidence later."

"Have a good night. Go easy on the beers."

I end the call and jam my phone back into my bag, avoiding eye contact with Rook. I don't particularly care what he thinks about me and his sister; what I do care about is the perception that I'm not taking my rehab seriously.

I finish dressing while Kingston group texts with his family. They're all super tight, and he gets a million "so proud of you" emojis and GIFs. My mom sends me a good-luck message when she remembers, and Nolan always tells me to kick ass if he's around when I'm heading to a game, but it's nothing like the constant back-patting that goes on with Kingston and his family.

I'm unsurprised when Rook falls into step with me. "I thought I told you not to screw with my sister."

"I'm not screwing with her."

He narrows his already-narrowed eyes farther. "Everyone within a twenty-foot radius heard that conversation."

"That was an accident." I can see how he might think it was intentional, though.

"Yeah, right. You dick her around or embarrass her publicly, and we're going to have problems, got it?"

There's no point in arguing with him, especially not here, where there are so many witnesses. "Got it."

He loses his glare when he addresses Kingston. "Nice work in net tonight."

"Thanks." King smiles his friendly, white-toothed smile.

Rook throws a final glare at me over his shoulder as he falls into step with another player. Kingston doesn't say anything about Rook, or what happened in the locker room, when we're on the bus with all the ears of our teammates close by.

I want to head straight for the sauna, but we have twenty-four-hour access, and it's a good idea to go to the bar for at least one drink. I order a light beer, and Kingston, being Kingston, orders a glass of milk.

Some of the guys razz him about it, but it doesn't seem to bother him. He takes the ribbing good-naturedly. King is pretty much the opposite of me in almost every regard: he's easygoing, friendly, and soaks up advice like a sponge. It's one of the many reasons I hang out with him as much as I do. I'm not sure what he gets out of this friendship, but I'm glad he tolerates me.

We finish our drinks and head up to our shared room. "You want to come down to the sauna with me?"

Kingston's eyebrows shoot up as he loosens his tie. "Uh, you're not looking for privacy?"

"Why would I need privacy?"

He shrugs. "Just asking based on that conversation you were having in the locker room, on speakerphone."

"That was an accident," I grumble.

Kingston grabs the back of the chair he's standing behind and chews the inside of his lip. "Can I ask you something without you getting all defensive?"

"Probably not."

A hint of a smile appears, and he nods. "Not sure why I bothered asking, since I know you well enough by now to know that's true. What's the deal with you and Stevie?"

"She's rehabbing me."

"Come on, man. Was it really an accident that you had her on speakerphone tonight? You know how that looked to the rest of the team, right?"

I blow out a breath. "Yeah, it was an accident. I swear. Besides, they don't know I'm talking to Rook's sister. Unless Rook has been bitching about it, the only people who know she's working with me are Rook, Coach, my therapists, and you."

"Okay, so it was an accident, but how much longer are you going to be able to keep whatever's going on with the two of you under wraps?"

"Nothing is going on." Yet, anyway.

"Just be careful, Bishop. That's all I'm saying."

"Sure. Yeah." I don't know what I need to be careful about, but I agree anyway.

We change into swim shorts and head down to the pool. The room is empty, as is the sauna and the hot tub. I take a selfie of me in the sauna room—no dropped towel—and another one of the hot tub and send them both to Stevie. I don't expect a response, because it's late and she has to be up early for work, so I leave my phone with the towels and slip into the hot tub.

The aches from getting back on the ice for the first time are starting to set in, as is the muscle stiffness. I have a massage and a PT session tomorrow once we land in Minnesota, but they're never as good as the sessions I have with Stevie.

"Can I ask you something?"

"Sure." Kingston is sprawled out across the other side of the hot tub, head resting on the edge.

"Say you were taking a woman to a formal work function. Would you get her flowers or something?" I've gone on my fair share of dates, had a few relationships, but I've never been one for hearts and flowers or any of that bullshit. I'm thinking I might need to do that with Stevie, though, since she's been screwed over pretty hard.

Kingston is the kind of guy who would show up with flowers and chocolate on a first date, looking to make a good impression. He's also the kind of guy who doesn't sleep with random women for kicks. Even when he was drafted to the NHL and bunnies threw themselves at him, looking to tarnish his golden-boy image, he never got sucked in. Or off, for that matter. But then, he's had the same girlfriend since the end of college. She's out in Tennessee, so they've been long distance, but still, it seems to work for them. His loyalty is probably part of that.

"Is this a date or a favor for a friend?"

"I guess she thinks I'm doing her a favor." At least that was the impression that I got when I offered to go with her.

"Is that actually what you're doing?"

"Yes and no."

"Can you give me a little more to go on?"

"Her ex is going to be there. He's an asshole, and I don't want her to go alone."

Kingston taps on the edge of the pool. "You don't want her to go alone because you're worried he'll be a jerk or he'll try to take advantage of her?"

"Sure, yeah, that's part of the reason."

"Instead of me dragging the information out of you, why don't you lay it down for me?" Kingston uncaps the bottle of water he brought down from the room and drains half of it in two long swallows.

"So, Stevie—"

"Hold up, we're back to Rook's little sister?"

"Who else would I be talking about?"

"I thought you said there isn't anything going on between you, and now you're taking her to some kind of work function? That's not a favor; that's a date. Does Rook know?"

"It's none of his damn business."

"I'm not sure he'll see it that way."

"Well, he doesn't have control over her or what she does, or what I do." I'm agitated now. "She's not going to that thing alone. I don't trust that ex of hers, and I don't want her to end up in a situation she doesn't like."

Kingston tips his head to the side. "Dang."

"What?"

"You like her."

"Well, yeah, I like her." What's not to like? She's gorgeous, there's no bullshit with the PT rehab, and she's funny and feisty; her body is rockin'; and she's fun to be around, super chill, and genuinely selfless.

"Like you actually want to date her, though."

I shrug, because what am I going to say? The answer to that is yes, I want to date her, but the timing needs to be right. "I don't want the ex thinking he has another chance. He's stupid as fuck and can't take a hint."

"You really love complicated situations, don't you?"

"They just tend to find me, is all."

"When's this event you're supposed to take her to?" King asks.

"Saturday."

He frowns. "We get back at noon on Saturday."

"It's in the evening."

"You better hope our flight isn't delayed."

I hadn't considered a delay. The only reason that would happen is if the weather isn't good. "It doesn't start until five. I should have plenty of time to get home and throw a suit on."

Kingston nods and taps restlessly on the edge of the pool. "So would you call this your first date?"

"We hang out all the time."

"'Hang out' meaning what?"

"Other than PT sessions, we watch hockey, eat pizza, stuff like that."

Kingston blinks several times in rapid succession. "That's it?"

"I pick her up from work a lot."

"Have you ever bought her flowers before? Brought her any gifts?"

"I brought her over an aloe plant once. But, like I said, it hasn't been like that." I don't get why he's so hung up on the flowers.

"Again, please try not to take offense, but are you sure you haven't inadvertently put yourself in the friend zone?"

"How do I know if I'm in the friend zone?" I haven't had a lot of friends who are girls. Actually, I don't think I've ever had a friend who's a girl who isn't related to me. And I only have two female cousins, whom I see a couple of times a year at family functions. They're significantly younger than me, so mostly I avoid them.

It's Kingston's turn to blow out a long breath. "If you put your arm around her and she gets all snuggly but doesn't try to take it any further, it could mean you're in the friend zone."

I don't know what my expression must be, but the panic I feel inside quite possibly reaches my face.

Kingston holds up a hand. "Don't freak out yet. I think this is a different kind of situation, and I'm speaking from my own experience."

"You've been friend zoned?"

"Oh yeah. Lots of times. Especially in high school. I was like every girl's best guy friend all of sophomore and junior year. One of the girls I hung out with a lot ended up dating one of my friends. She told me after the fact that she'd been hoping I'd ask her out, but after a certain point I still hadn't done anything about it, so when he made the move, she said yes. Kind of put things into perspective, you know? Most of the time I was more focused on hockey than I was dating, but I solved the friend-zone problem in senior year."

"What happened in senior year?"

"Someone spiked the punch at the winter semiformal, and the liquid courage gave me the balls to kiss my date. I mean, I asked first if it was okay for me to kiss her, and she said yes, which was good, because she told me if I hadn't made a move that night, she was ready to throw in the towel. She thought I wasn't interested and I only said yes to going with her to be nice."

I feel like it should be obvious that I'm interested. A guy doesn't spend endless hours with a gorgeous woman who combines weird pizza toppings for shits and giggles. But then again, I haven't attempted to make a move on her since the almost-kiss and grind. And any conversation I've tried to have with her about it has been shut down. In fact, she wants to pretend it didn't happen. I hadn't considered that this might be because she actually didn't *want* it to happen at all. She seemed just as into it as I was. Or maybe I've been misreading the whole thing. "If I'm in the friend zone, how the hell do I get out?"

"You can only get out of it if you talk to her and tell her where you're at."

"Right. I get that. So just come out and tell her, then?"

"Sure, but you can sort of pave the way with flowers and chocolate or something, unless she isn't into either. After I was drafted and I had extra cash flow, I started sending Jessica to get her nails done before an event, or before I'd fly her out for a visit. Sometimes I'll even have a dress sent to her place, but you'd have to know Stevie's size and measurements for that. Not all women like to be pampered, but generally doing something nice or thoughtful is safe. She needs to know you're thinking about her in a nonplatonic way."

My constant semis and commentary on her nipples should be a pretty solid indicator that I'm not feeling all that platonic toward her, but I can see how stepping up my game would be a good idea. Maybe she thinks the almost-make-out-session was a fluke. Maybe she thinks I've lost interest, or maybe she's lost interest. I hope not. If she wanted to just be friends, I could deal, but I definitely want more.

I'm way past wanting to claim the pussy. I want to claim the whole woman.

CHAPTER 21

STAND UP

Stevie

I'm in the middle of making myself a buffalo-chicken wrap when a knock startles me. Bishop isn't scheduled to be home for two more days, so I check the peephole before I open the door. On the other side is a very pale, very clammy Nolan gripping the jambs.

"Hey, Nolan, everything okay?"

"Uh, really sorry to bother you, but, uh . . . I think I might need to go to urgent care," he mumbles.

I take him by the elbow and guide him to the couch. "Did you misplace your insulin?"

"I checked all of Shippy's usual hiding spots, but he must've put it somewhere different, and I can't get ahold of him to find out where." He runs his shaky hands over his thighs. "I've been looking for over an hour. You have keys to his car, right? If you can drop me off at urgent care, I'll get home on my own."

"I'm not dropping you off and leaving you there on your own." I squeeze his shoulder. "Besides, Bishop left me with a couple of insulin doses for you just in case."

"He did?"

"Yup, just take some deep breaths. I'll be right back." I leave him in the living room and rush to the kitchen, where I open the drawer with Nolan's emergency doses. Bishop left them here weeks ago, right after Nolan interrupted the almost-kiss.

I prepare the needle, having done it for my dad plenty of times, and offer to administer it for him since his hands are so shaky. It takes about fifteen minutes before his color starts to come back and for Nolan's shakes to stop. While we're waiting, I assemble a sandwich, the kind I used to make for my dad when he'd get busy and forget to take his shot.

"Thanks, Stevie, I really appreciate this," Nolan says before he takes a giant bite of his sandwich.

"I know you do. How are you feeling now?"

"Much better," he says through a mouthful of ham, swiss, and bread.

"I'm still going to take you to urgent care after you finish eating," I tell him.

"You don't need to do that. I'm fine." He wipes away some mustard with a napkin.

"Fine or not, we're going to urgent care to make sure. And we're going to find your insulin case before we go and replace the dose we used so I have them on hand." I arch a brow—an invitation to challenge me.

He blows out a breath. "I'll find it eventually."

It's my turn to sigh. "Look, Nolan, I know living with this isn't easy, but it's not going to go away, and brushing this off like it's nothing isn't helpful either. Bishop worries about you a lot, and when you don't take your own health seriously, it stresses him out."

His expression shifts to annoyance. "It's not his problem; it's mine."

"It might be yours to live with, but it affects him too. You're his best friend. Do you know how hard it is for him when he's away and he doesn't know if you're taking your medication, or if you're out until whatever time in the morning? What you're doing and how you treat your body is shortening the time you have here."

"You're making a big deal out of nothing. I'm fine."

"Only because I was here and Bishop left me with doses. What if you couldn't find the dose and you didn't make it to urgent care tonight? What if you'd gone into shock, and that's how he found you when he came home tomorrow night? Your lack of regard for your own health is actually really selfish. Bishop would be absolutely devastated if something happened to you while he was away."

He drops his head, looking ashamed of himself. "I just want to be normal."

"I get it, I really do, but you're a diabetic, and that means you have to treat your body better, and it means that you can't abuse it. My dad took such good care of himself, and we still lost him when he was in his fifties. It sucks that I don't have a dad anymore. Don't leave Bishop without a best friend or a brother because you're reckless with your life." I push up off the couch, worried I'm about to get emotional. "Once you're finished eating, we're going to check your apartment for your insulin, and then we're going to urgent care. No arguments."

"Okay." Nolan finishes his sandwich and doesn't put up a fight when I follow him back to his place. I manage to find his insulin pack—in the fridge. Apparently when he got home from his afternoon shift, he had a snack and took his shot, and that's where the case ended up.

That mystery solved, I drive him to the closest urgent care and wait while the doctor checks him over. He's fine, which is a relief. By the time we're done, it's after ten.

"Sorry if I ruined whatever plans you had this evening," Nolan says once we're back on the penthouse floor, heading for our respective apartments.

"I didn't have any plans." Apart from watching hockey and thinking about his brother.

Nolan pauses with his hand on the door. "Thanks for helping me out tonight. I'd ask you if you want to hang out, but I'm pretty sure Shippy would murder me."

"Why would he murder you for hanging out with me?"

Nolan gives me a quizzical look, then shakes his head and laughs. "Have a good night, Stevie."

He disappears into his apartment without answering my question. He's kind of an odd guy, but then so is his brother.

I haven't heard from Bishop since he messaged this morning to let me know the team's return flight was delayed. I considered calling Lainey to find out when they'd be home, but that could have incited questions I didn't want to answer, and messaging for an update would have seemed slightly desperate, so all I can do now is look at the weather and wait. Apparently there's some stupid storm in the Midwest affecting flights.

It's a quarter after five, and I'm here, at this gala fundraiser, currently dateless. Thanks to Pattie and Jules peer pressuring me out of something simple and black, I'm wearing a dress that conforms to all my curves and shows off a lot more skin than I'm used to beyond workout gear. It's a dark purple to complement my lavender hair, which I dyed again this week in preparation for the event.

I've already been approached three times, by three different guys, two of whom attend the college and are on one team or another, and also by one of their coaches. He looked to be in his midforties, and as flattered as I am, he's old enough to be my father, so that's a hard nope for me. I might have daddy issues, but not those kind.

Joey apparently had a date lined up, but she came down with the flu or food poisoning—the story keeps changing—so he's a lone wolf on the prowl. I hope I don't become his target of choice since Bishop isn't here. So far I've managed to avoid being cornered, but it's only a matter of time before he tracks me down.

"Bishop better not stand me up," I say to Pattie. She and Jules decided to be each other's date because there are a lot of hot guys at these events.

"He's not going to stand you up."

"How do you know?"

"Because he's way into you."

"What if you're wrong?" Ever since he picked up my suitcase and we had that conversation, things have been different. Sure, he's been around more, picking me up all the time and hanging out at my place after sessions, but he doesn't make passes at me like he used to, and he hasn't tried to hump on me at all. It's just been those freaking forehead or temple kisses. Maybe seeing me melt down over Joey made him reevaluate his position. Plus I told him to pretend the almost-kiss-hump-off didn't happen. And I think he's actually taken me seriously, but now it's messing with my head. Which I realize is my fault.

Joey, being the opportunistic asshole he is, picks that very moment to interrupt our conversation. He slings an arm over my shoulder, having approached us from behind so we wouldn't see him coming.

Last night I was here with Pattie and Jules until ten, putting up decorations. We had to watch the game on our cell phones, which was annoying. We came back early this morning to finish up. Joey conveniently "forgot" he was supposed to be part of the setup equation. On principle it frustrates me, but I have to say I was pretty grateful I didn't have to deal with him last night.

He gives me what he thinks is his sexy smile and notches up the smarmy levels by staring at my chest for far too long. The dress dips low in the front. I don't have particularly big boobs—a solid handful—but they're perky enough that I can get away with going braless, which is important in this dress with the plunging neckline—again, Pattie's and Jules's influence.

He lets out a low whistle. "Wow, Stevie, love the dress."

"Super glad it has your seal of approval."

I try to slip out from under his arm, but he tightens his grip on my shoulder, keeping me glued to his side.

I pin him with an unimpressed sneer. "I wouldn't do that unless you're wearing a jockstrap or you're not worried about compromising your ability to procreate."

"Come on, Stevie, I'm just being friendly."

"If by friendly you mean harass-y, then I totally agree."

I'm about to give him a swift elbow to the ribs when a familiar deep voice makes my lady parts perk up, and Joey drops his arm like I'm made of acid and I'm burning the skin off his arm.

"Hey, Pattie, there you are. Have you seen Stevie? My flight was delayed, and I left my phone in Kingston's car, so he had to drive it back over, and my brother wasn't home so I couldn't call—" He eyes Joey with contempt, and his gaze slides past me but quickly darts back. His eyebrows lift, and his mouth drops. "Holy shit. Stevie?"

"Hey." I raise my hand in an awkward wave. I'm not sure how to take his reaction.

Bishop lets out a low whistle, but it's appreciative, not smarmy. "Wow. You look"—he runs his hands down my bare arms, the touch electrifying my skin, and threads his fingers through mine—"fucking delicious."

"I told you the dress was perfect," Pattie says from my right.

I ogle Bishop like he's a chocolate triple-layer fudge cake during period week. He's dressed in a sharp black suit, probably custom tailored, based on the way it hugs every single one of his incredibly cut muscles.

His dark-brown hair is actually styled, rather than being the haphazard mess it typically is when I see him for sessions, as if he's been running his fingers through it incessantly and forcing it to stand up in different directions. Tonight it's parted to the side: a natural Superman wave that makes him look both like a badass and the kind of guy I'd want to take home to meet my mom. That he went to all this trouble for me, especially after traveling all day and having to rush here after a delayed flight, makes my stomach flutter.

"You look delicious too." Obviously my ability to form words and sentences with unique descriptors has disappeared in the wake of his extreme hotness.

Bishop bows his head and grins, looking all shy boy-man instead of badass hockey player. He lifts my hand and presses his lips to my knuckles. The simple, mostly innocent gesture feels wildly intimate, probably because it sends a shock wave of desire firing through me, peaking my nipples and inciting a sweet ache between my thighs. I'm in so much trouble.

And that's before he parts those soft, full lips of his and bites my knuckle. The shock wave becomes a torrent of lust as he steps in closer, the tip of his polished black shoe meeting the tip of my silver heels. He raises my hands, encouraging me to drape them over his shoulders.

One of his palms sweeps slowly along my arm and over my shoulder, following the thin strap of deep-purple satin. The gentle caress of his fingers is a contradiction to the hunger in his eyes, and a storm of excitement swirls low in my belly. His warm palm splays out as it moves down my back—which is bare because this dress is backless—until he reaches the dip in my spine. He pulls me against him, and I'm pretty sure I moan when the fronts of our bodies meet. "Damn well stunning." He bows his head, and I shudder when his lips sweep along my jaw.

"Holy shit," Pattie mumbles from my right.

"Jesus," comes from my left.

Bishop nuzzles into that hypersensitive space at the edge of my jaw, just under my earlobe. He hums against my skin and then ruins the entire, drawn-out reunion when he says, "How jealous of me is that stupid fuckwad right now?"

It's like being doused with a bucket of ice water. Of course that's what this is all about. He's putting on a show to piss off Joey. How naive of me to assume it could be for any other reason. Sure he gets hard over me, but I wander around in tiny shorts and a sports bra, and he hasn't been able to whack off like a regular human male in more than a month.

I put my hands on his chest and step back. I actually have to use force to make it happen, and his facial expression makes me question a lot of things. Like why does he look so damn irritated and confused right now, and do I actually have the right to be angry when he's explicitly told me he's doing me a favor tonight? Why does he have to be so damn convincing in the facade?

Before he has a chance to speak, or ask a question, or make a statement, the thing I expected to happen tonight does. "Holy shit! Bishop Winslow? Man, that game was kick ass last night! You killed it!" Some twenty-year-old who can't grow facial hair thrusts his hand out, forcing Bishop to take it, unless he wants to look like an asshole.

And that's how the next hour goes. Until we sit down for dinner. And even then, the PT team has been broken up, so we're all seated with aspiring professional athletes who command Bishop's attention. And I sit there, like I would if I were with my brother—not that I look at Bishop like I do RJ—quiet and smiling. I offer to take photos so I don't end up in them. I don't introduce him as my date, because the last thing I need is people suddenly becoming interested in me for something other than my PT skills.

Bishop seems to have different ideas, though. The guy to my right plays football, and based on the size of him, he's defense. He peppers me with questions, and his eyes keep dropping to my cleavage. I guess it's not really his fault; it's there and inviting his eyeballs to have a peek.

Every time he leans in to ask me something, Bishop puts his arm across the back of my chair, and I keep elbowing him in the side. When he tries to whisper something in my ear, I jab him in the IT band.

He mutters profanities under his breath and pulls out his phone. Ten seconds later mine buzzes in my purse, but I avoid looking at the message because I'm already halfway to an emotional breakdown, and I'm afraid his text is going to push me over the edge.

I don't know why I'm being such an idiot about this whole thing. I knew he was doing me a favor. I shouldn't be all butt hurt about it, but I want him to be doing this because he wants to be here with me, not because he feels obligated or to make Joey jealous.

They clear the dessert plates, and the DJ cues up the first song. It's like a bad wedding and a high school semiformal mash-up. I excuse myself to the bathroom as Bishop gets mobbed by yet another group of aspiring athletes—both male and female.

On my way out of the room, at least three people stop me to ask how I know Bishop. Agreeing to have him as my date was a bad idea for so many reasons, not the least of which is the attention he draws. I lock myself in a stall for a full five minutes, trying desperately to get my head and emotions under control.

He's close to not needing me anymore for rehab, and that should make me happy on a lot of levels, but it doesn't. Even without the overt sexual advances, it's started to feel like a relationship of sorts. Obviously it was me projecting. He's back on the ice, where he wants to be, and the less he needs my help, the less time he's going to spend taking up space on my couch. This is him repaying the favor.

When I come out of the bathroom, Pattie and Jules are leaning against the sink, waiting for me. "What's going on?" Pattie asks.

I give her a look like I don't know what she's talking about, and really I don't. I have feelings for Bishop, and tonight I realize how big they've become. "I knew bringing Bishop was a bad idea. He's been mobbed the entire evening."

"So you're hiding out in the bathroom?" Jules asks.

I rub my temples. "I'm not hiding. I'm just . . . gathering my thoughts."

"On the toilet." Pattie goes to lean against the wall but thinks better of it. It's a nice bathroom, but still.

"It's a good place to think."

"You should be out there, saving Bishop from the fangirls."

"But then people will know he's my date, and it'll put me in the limelight." I do everything I can to avoid being caught in the social media firestorm that is my brother's life. Bishop isn't quite as high profile, but now that he's back on the ice, that could change. Add a roomful of athletes who know who he is, and he's in high demand.

"He's taking one for the team for you. Don't you think you should take one for him too?" Jules arches a brow.

I blow out a breath and look up at the ceiling. She has a point. He's here to save me from Joey, and I've pretty much left him to the wolves because I can't handle how I feel about him or all the attention he's getting, which makes me a pretty damn bad date. I guess I should return the favor and save him from the fangirls and boys by acting like his actual date.

The second I step back into the event room, I regret it. The DJ has slowed the music from the upbeat, clichéd dance tunes to something slow. The first person I run into is Joey. He takes my hand and pulls me onto the dance floor before I can protest. Or kick him in the balls.

When I don't make a move to put my hands on any part of him, he leans in, lips at my ear. "Our bosses are watching, so let's at least pretend we get along for five minutes. Besides, it looks like your date is preoccupied." Joey moves my hands to his shoulders and tips his head to the right.

I follow his gaze and find Bishop still sitting in the chair at the table. A brunette who is obviously an athlete, based on her muscle tone, and wearing a very revealing, skimpy dress is practically sitting in his lap. If she could hump his leg, I'm sure she would. As it is, her hand is resting on his shoulder, and if I had to guess, by the way she's leaning in, her boob is probably propped up on his forearm.

"Seriously?" I'm gone five minutes, and some woman is trying to publicly hump him.

"Listen, baby, I know it's been a rough start here. I know it's taking you some time to get over it, but I really think you and me can work this out."

I return my attention to Joey. "Have you started smoking crack?"

"What?" His toothy grin falters, and his gaze moves from my rack to my face.

"Or maybe it's meth."

His brow twists into a furrow. "What are you talking about, Stevie?"

"What are *you* talking about, Joey?"

He looks puzzled. I'm pretty sure he's been drinking. I don't know why I'm even entertaining this, or letting him put his hands on me, other than I'm completely shocked by the fact that the guy I'd like to be my boyfriend is currently snuggling with some fangirl puck bunny.

God, I'm confused.

And my brain is even more muddled when all of a sudden Bishop cuts in. One second I'm trying to impale Joey with my nails through layers of suit jacket and shirt, and the next Bishop's elbowing him out of the way.

"That's my date, not yours, but thanks for warming up the floor for me. Now fuck off." Bishop glares at Joey, who looks like he wants to argue for all of half a second before he steps back.

Bishop grips my waist and pulls me against him. I automatically lace my fingers behind his neck. I don't even think about it, or of the intimacy of having the entire front of my body pressed right up against his for the second time tonight.

Bishop's wide, warm palm rests against my lower back. The skin-to-skin contact should be something I'm used to, but normally it's my hand on his bare skin, not the other way around. The electric feeling is back, zinging through me in little pulses of lightning that end up in my vagina.

It would be great if I were less attracted to this man.

Bishop drops his head so his mouth is at my ear. "What the hell is going on?"

His lips brush the shell as he speaks, making my knees weak. It takes me several seconds to realize he sounds pissed and that he's not asking me to take off my clothes on the dance floor. I have to tip my chin up to reach his ear, causing his stubbly cheek to rub against mine. For whatever reason, I imagine how that might feel on the inside of my thigh, so my response comes out all low and breathy. "What do you mean?"

God, he smells good. Like cologne and laundry detergent and that bodywash he uses. It's not fancy. He uses Old Spice, something I can get from any CVS or grocery store. I bet he even stocks up when it's on sale, because he usually has three or four reserve bottles in his linen closet at any given time. Whatever the smell is, combined with the other, less powerful scents and what makes him uniquely him, it's ridiculously appealing.

"You're being weird. And not like pineapples-and-olives-on-pizza weird. Why were you dancing with the douche ex? Why am I here with you if you're going to pretend I don't even exist?"

"That's not . . . I'm not . . ." He's right. I am being weird. I have no idea what's going on—if he's really here out of obligation, or if I've read more into this than I should—so I splutter and fumble for an excuse that makes sense. "He caught me off guard, and you were busy with your puck bunny."

Bishop pulls back, brow furrowed. It's a sexy look on his gorgeous face. "You mean that chick that couldn't take a hint? I told her seven times I had a date. I'm trying out this new thing where I'm not an asshole all the time to everyone. Especially since I'm here with *you*, and I don't want to leave a shit impression with all of these people." He lifts one hand from my back and flails in the general direction of the people on the dance floor. "You were taking forever in the bathroom, and then I see you with your douche ex all fucking cozy. I'm done dancing around this shit, Stevie."

"Dancing around what shit?" My stomach sinks, flips, and does a couple of roundoffs, finishing with a cartwheel.

"This." His hand leaves my back again and motions between our faces. "You and me."

"You and me?" My head is so muddled.

"Yeah. You and me. Us."

Anxiety makes my mouth dry. I lick my lips and swallow thickly. "I don't understand."

"What do you mean you don't understand?" He seems so incredulous, which increases my confusion.

"You said you were doing me a favor by being my date. Isn't this a thank-you for the rehab?"

He arches a brow. "Do I seem like the kind of person who'd attend this kind of event as a favor?"

I lift a shoulder and let it fall. "You're back on the ice a week early."

"So you think this is me being a nice guy, even though I've proven time and time again that I'm generally an asshole?"

"Are you telling me that this isn't you being nice?"

"No."

"No, you're not telling me, or no you're not being nice?" We keep moving, shifting in a slow circle as we talk, and I get a glimpse of a very angry-looking Joey, glaring while I dance-argue with Bishop.

"Jesus Christ," Bishop grumbles. "I'm not being nice."

"Well, if this isn't you being nice or doing me a favor, what exactly are you doing here?"

Joey appears again as we make another tight, stiff circle. I've never been big on slow dancing, and I don't think Bishop is either. A couple of shuffle steps later, Joey disappears, and Bishop's brow furrows deeper. His gaze shifts over my shoulder and back to me. "I'm making sure your ex knows you're off limits for good."

"Isn't that the same as doing me a favor?" I try to put some space between us, because it's hard to think with my breasts pressed against his chest and the feel of his belt buckle hard against my stomach.

"No."

"No?"

"I'm not doing it for you, Stevie. I'm doing it for *me*."

"Why?" My stomach is full of fluttery things.

Instead of answering, he cups my cheek in his palm and drops his head until his mouth is only a breath away from mine. "Why?"

I nod once, and our lips almost brush with the movement.

"Because if anyone should be your boyfriend, it's me, not that shit-for-brains ass clown."

"Oh." I breathe in as he exhales, tasting mint even though his mouth isn't on mine. "Well, that seems like a pretty good reason."

"I thought so." The hand on my lower back slides up, and his fingers wrap around the back of my neck. "Tell me no if you don't want this to happen."

The chemistry between us swells and fills the air, making it crackle with lust.

For weeks now, I've been imagining what it would feel like to kiss him. Like no is even an option. I don't answer with words. Instead I tip my chin up and lick my lips in anticipation. Bishop's gaze bounces from my mouth to my eyes.

He inclines his head, and his lips touch mine. The moment we connect, it feels like a whole bucketful of lust has been poured over my head. I'm submerged in pent-up desire, and the sensation spreads, running through my veins, heating me up. Having Bishop's mouth on mine after all these weeks of touching without the intent of sexual exploration makes me feel like I've been shot up with some kind of drug.

Bishop is a lot of things: sarcastic, assholey, determined, hotheaded, and a mammoth of a man. But his kiss is all the other parts of him I've gotten glimpses of over the past several weeks: sweet, gentle, soft. At first, anyway.

It begins as an easy, warm press. His lips part, and I breathe in his minty exhale on a whimper. The palm resting against the back of my neck flexes, and his thumb smooths up the side of my throat, stopping at the edge of my jaw. "I want in, Stevie."

I part my lips without any further encouragement, because it's been weeks and weeks of underwear battles and rehab sessions and that one almost-kiss and clothed grind. I want more.

We both groan when our tongues slide against each other, wet, warm, and satin soft. Bishop's hand moves from my cheek, palm easing down my back until he reaches the dip in my spine again. A single fingertip slips under the fabric and follows the waistband of my panties. I'm wearing a thong, because this dress is form fitting and I wanted to avoid panty lines. He pulls me tighter against him, and I anchor my fingers in his hair, a silent but screaming request not to stop kissing me.

Thankfully, Bishop is good at reading my nonverbal cues, and he deepens the kiss. Unlike our conversations, it's not a battle: it's a dance of tongues, searching, seeking, retreating, and coming back for more. With each slow, wet caress, the softness of the kiss shifts and becomes more desperate.

I forget that we're in the middle of a dance floor. I forget that we're in a roomful of people, including my bosses, colleagues, and a number of clients: current, potential, and future. At least until the music stops. I catch a murmur of excitement rustle through the room in the two quick beats of silence before a fast, upbeat tune blasts through the speakers.

I uncurl my fingers from his hair and push on his solid chest. It's weak on conviction, since I bite his bottom lip and suck it before I break the kiss. A low sound, something like a growl, rumbles through his chest. He fuses our mouths back together, and I indulge him for a few more seconds before I truly, and grudgingly, disconnect our mouths.

"We're not alone," I whisper.

We're both breathing hard as we lock gazes.

Bishop drags his tongue across his bottom lip. "We should get out of here before I do something embarrassing, then."

CHAPTER 22
BEST BAD DECISION

Bishop

The week of Stevie deprivation combined with her looking too edible for words and all the pent-up sexual frustration seems to have finally come to a head. So my reaction to kissing Stevie, which is to keep kissing her until the world ends or one of us catches on fire from all the friction, seems entirely logical.

"Okay." It's more of a moan than a word.

I'm hella surprised she doesn't put up more of a fight. It's not like Stevie to give in easily. Not for me, anyway. She spins on her heel, lavender hair fanning out in a wave and settling around her shoulders. Before the night is over I'm going to have my nose buried in that hair. It'll be a knotted mess because my hands are going to be in it, and I'll most definitely have it wrapped around my fist at some point.

Jesus, I'm so hard I could dent a car with my dick. Her hips sway mesmerizingly as she glides across the floor, me trailing behind her like some sort of horndog bodyguard and glaring at any guy who dares to look at her as she passes, which incidentally is every guy in the whole damn room.

Stevie stops to say something to Pattie and Jules on the way out of the hall. I step up beside her and place a protective hand at the small of her back. The dress comes down so low I can see those sweet dimples just above her ass. All I want is to get her out of here so we can pick up that kiss where we left off.

Pattie's gaze shifts briefly to me, eyes narrowing and her smile growing conspiratorially with whatever Stevie says to her.

"See you on Monday."

"I'll be in for takedown tomorrow."

"I wouldn't bet on that." Pattie hugs her and drops her voice, whispering something I don't catch. Whatever it is, it makes Stevie blush. I spot Joey on the other side of the room, looking like he wants to either murder me or be me.

I nod to Stevie's friends and thread my fingers through hers, keeping her close as we navigate our way through the crowd. Recognition flares in several sets of eyes as we pass, but I must be wearing a pretty nasty expression because no one approaches me. As we get to my SUV, Stevie rummages around in her bag for the keys, shoulders curled in as she shivers against the biting wind. A light drizzle coats her hair and her skin.

"Didn't you bring a coat?" I unbutton my suit jacket and shrug out of it.

"I left it in my locker. It's fine there until Monday." Stevie produces a set of keys with shaking fingers.

I snatch them from her hand and drape my suit jacket over her shoulders. I consider going in for another kiss, but the rain is picking up and it's chilly out here, so I usher her around to the passenger side and help her in.

Once I'm behind the wheel, I turn the engine over and crank up the heat before I slide my arm across her seat and curl my fingers around the back of her slender neck. We move toward each other like magnets. Our lips meet, and lust crackles around us like static.

She flicks her tongue out to tease my top lip. "I thought maybe that almost-kiss had been an accident."

"It was. I was told to keep it professional while you were rehabbing me."

She pulls back. "By who?"

"My coach. I listened for as long as I could, but the last thing I was going to do was let you come to this event, where your douche ex or one of those wannabe hockey players could make a move, when I should've said screw it and done it weeks ago."

"Oh. Well, I'm glad you decided to screw it." Stevie shifts in her seat, her warm palm landing on my cheek, fingertips brushing along my jaw and curling into the hair at the nape of my neck. Her lips part, welcoming me in again. I want to get inside her, taste every single inch of her. I want the smell of her sex all over my skin and my sheets and in my mouth.

I can't get close enough to make any of that happen with the center console in my way, so eventually I break the kiss. "I need to get naked with you."

"Same." Stevie starts to loosen my tie.

While car sex was fun when I was a teenager, it's definitely not comfortable, or smart, since we're in the middle of a parking lot. I cover her hand with mine and bring her fingers to my lips. "In a bed, preferably."

She blinks a few times and bites her lip. "Right. Yes. Good idea."

We come back together for one more kiss that lasts so long the windows start to fog before we separate and buckle ourselves in.

"We should probably go to my place." Stevie sounds like she's trying to be conversational, but her tone is low and husky. She twists her hands in her lap, then stretches her arm across the seat and slips her fingers into the hair at the nape of my neck.

I'd rather have the smell of her on my sheets, but I don't want to run into my brother on the way to my bedroom. I also don't want Stevie to feel compelled to be quiet because she's worried he's going to hear. His company never is, but this is not even remotely close to the same. "Sure."

The drive home feels like it takes a million years. We make out in the elevator on the way to the penthouse floor and don't stop until Stevie needs to use her fingers for more than fisting my hair and unbuttoning my shirt.

I kiss along the bare expanse of her shoulder as she punches in her access code. She gets it wrong the first time and growls, "This card-code combo is a pain in my ass."

She manages to get it right the second time, and then we're stumbling over each other's feet, crashing through the door in our haste to get inside. Stevie shrugs out of my suit jacket, dropping it in a heap on the floor. She yanks on my tie, pulling my mouth down to hers as she goes to work on unfastening the remaining buttons on my shirt.

I echo her groan and spin her around, pressing her against the door. It's never worked properly, so it clicks shut when her back hits it. I run my hands down her sides, grip two handfuls of ass, and pick her up. Stevie wraps her legs around my waist, the sound of fabric tearing making us both pause.

"Shit. I was going to return this dress," she mumbles into my mouth.

"I can cover the cost." Seeing as I plan to be her boyfriend, I'd like the opportunity to buy her clothes and shit. Especially nice dresses, and panties, and new sports bras, and those athletic shorts I love so much. As hot as Stevie looks all dressed up, I prefer her casual, maybe because that's when she's most likely to have her hands on me.

"You don't need to do that." She tips her chin up, not in defiance but because I'm kissing my way up her neck.

"I'm going to ruin the fuck out of this dress, so I feel it's only fair that I replace it." I grind against her, enjoying the fact that I can

A. lift her up without it causing me pain;

B. get a boner that doesn't hurt like a motherfucker;

C. achieve the friction I've been dying for.

We make out against the door, essentially trying to devour each other through a kiss until the clothed humping isn't cutting it anymore. I carry her down the hall to her bedroom and kick open the door. The space smells like distilled Stevie: something sweet like cake, a hint of her baby powder deodorant, the freshness of clean laundry, and a vaguely floral scent that I'm pretty sure belongs to her shampoo.

The bed isn't at all girly or frilly. The comforter is a geometric gray pattern layered over white, and there aren't seven million throw pillows to contend with.

I don't set her down on the edge of the bed. Instead I keep my grip on her ass with one hand and use the other to help hoist myself up on the mattress, spinning us around until I can lay her down on the pillows.

"You're going to mess your groin up again before we even get to the good stuff with this shit," Stevie chastises, lips moving along the edge of my jaw, teeth nipping gently.

"Don't worry. It's not going to screw with my game."

She shimmies back until her head hits the pillow. "It's not your game I'm worried about." She grabs the front of my shirt, dragging me closer, and parts her legs so I can fit myself between them.

"Then what's the problem?"

"You compromising your ability to fuck me properly." She hooks one leg around my waist and pulls me down on top of her.

I settle into the cradle of her hips, so damn ready to get my hands and mouth all over her and my achy cock inside her. At least the ache is from being hard for the last hour and not because my balls feel like they're trying to detach from my body. "You want to stretch me out before we get started?" I roll my hips, and she arches on a soft moan.

"Not really, no."

I nuzzle into the hollow of her throat, breathing her in. "You can do that after, then."

"I better not have the energy to do anything but sleep after you're done with me."

I push up on my arms so I can meet her hot, needy gaze. "Is that a challenge?"

She grins. "You respond better to challenges than orders, so whatever works for you and gets me the most orgasms."

I laugh and skim her cheek with my knuckles. Porcelain smooth, warm, and perfect. "You're pretty much the only one I'm willing to take orders from. You know that, right?"

She runs her fingers through my hair. "You followed your coaches' orders to keep it professional."

"Not because I wanted to but because I didn't want them to think I wasn't taking my rehab seriously, and I needed the time to heal."

"So you only follow orders when it benefits you. Is that what I'm hearing?"

"Mmm. It'll benefit you too." I kiss along the edge of her jaw. "Don't worry, bae, I won't screw up all the progress we've made while I'm screwing orgasms out of you."

I wait for a reaction, and I'm not disappointed. Stevie snorts and jabs me in the side with one of her manicured fingernails. "Can you not be an asshole for a few minutes?"

Based on how tight my face feels, I must be grinning like an idiot. I school my expression into something more serious and pull back again so I can look at her. "Flipping my asshole switch off, but only for you, and only for an hour."

She arches a brow. "You think you're going to last for an hour?"

"I've spent more than a month thinking about all the things I want to do to you. I plan on dragging this out for hours." I kiss her again before she can issue another snappy comeback, and our conversation turns into the liquid sound of tongues stroking against each other. I can't get enough of her mouth or the feel of her pliant body under mine.

We fumble and tug at each other's clothes, separating our mouths long enough to get my shirt off and Stevie's dress over her head. She's braless, which I probably should have expected, since it was backless. The last time I saw her topless was the morning after she woke me up with all that racket. I didn't have the time or the wherewithal to fully appreciate what I was seeing then.

I cup her breasts, so full and perky and perfect, with her sweet pink nipples peaking in the cool air. I circle them with my thumbs and push them together, nuzzling into the valley on a groan.

"So fucking luscious." I bite the swell, kissing one and then the other, savoring the salty, sweet taste of her skin, before I take a nipple between my lips and suck the tender skin.

Stevie gasps and arches, fingers sliding into my hair and latching on. I trace the pert nipple with my tongue and scrape along the tip with my teeth, smiling against her tit when she issues a low warning and her fingernails dig into my scalp.

"It's payback time, bae."

"Payback for what?" she asks breathlessly.

"For tormenting me for weeks with sports bras and tiny shorts. I had blue balls for a month."

"How is that my fault? And you started it with the boxer briefs that hide nothing!"

"At least you could get yourself off after a session if you wanted." I suck the other nipple roughly, biting hard enough to make her gasp.

"So you're going to punish my nipples because I could make myself come and you couldn't?" Stevie's eyes are on my mouth, close to her nipple but not quite touching.

"Is that what you did? Make yourself come after I went home?"

Her gaze flips up to mine, and her tongue peeks out as she nods.

"How often?" The words are rough like sandpaper. I want this to be the same on both sides, for her to have struggled the same way I have all these weeks, fighting the same attraction.

"Pretty much every night." Her admission is steeped in vulnerability.

"What'd you think about when you were getting yourself off?" I roll her nipple between my fingertips.

She's silent for a few seconds, long enough that I drag my gaze back to hers. Her cheeks are flushed pink, but her tone is full-on sarcasm. "Grocery shopping."

"Oh yeah? What were you shopping for while you were finger fucking yourself?"

"Dick-shaped items, obviously."

"Obviously." I tongue her nipple, swirling around it in slow, lulling sweeps. Just as she starts to soften under me, I suck hard, and she groans my name. "God, I love the way that sounds." I move to the other nipple. "You know what I'm going to love hearing even more?"

Stevie runs her fingers through my hair. "What's that?"

"You begging me to make you come."

She huffs a laugh. "Not likely."

"Mmm. You wanna place bets?" I smile when she tugs roughly on my hair.

"I thought you were turning off your asshole switch for an hour." I think she's supposed to sound annoyed, but instead she's breathless.

"You flip one switch off, and you have to flip another one on to compensate."

"What's this switch called?" She drags her nails along the back of my skull, causing a shot of icy heat to run down my spine.

"Dunno. Whatever the level above asshole is." I settle between her legs, and we make out, me rubbing myself on her while she shifts under me, both of us seeking friction, neither one of us willing to bow to the other.

Stevie manages to wiggle her fingers down the back of my pants, nails biting into my ass, knees pressed against my ribs. My brain feels like it's fritzing out from all the contact, which is crazy, because she's been touching me for more than a month and I've been able to handle it fine, until now.

Her hand is on the move again, and suddenly her warm fingers graze my cock through my boxers.

I groan into her mouth and thrust, trying to get more contact. The weeks of pent-up tension, along with the injury that's prevented me from being able to jerk off like a normal athlete would, means the brief contact already has me more fired up than if I'd watched a six-hour porn marathon on ecstasy.

I tear my mouth from Stevie's and push up on my forearms, trapping her hand in my pants. I pin her with a glare. It doesn't have quite the impact I anticipate.

Stevie smirks. "Should I assume you fucked your hand before you came to stake your claim on me tonight?"

I quirk a brow. "Listen to that dirty mouth."

Her grin widens. "Is that a yes?"

"What do you think?" Of course I managed my situation. I'm not an idiot. However, based on my current physical responses, I'm not sure my preemptive measures are going to make much of a difference.

Stevie tilts her hips down, providing wiggle room for her fingers, which slide farther into my pants. She bites the edge of my jaw. "Do you know what I think?"

"What's that?" I lift my hips so she has more room to explore.

"That no matter how well prepared you think you are, you're still going to lose control a lot faster than you want." My cock jerks as her fingers glide along my shaft over my boxers. "You know what I want?"

"What's that?" I can barely function already.

"Before you fuck my pussy, I want you to fuck my hand." She grips my erection in her warm palm. "And my mouth."

"Christ, Stevie." I'm not going to argue. It's probably a good idea to take the edge off; that way I can spend all the time in the world making her come for me before I get inside her. I slide a hand under her and roll onto my back so she's straddling my thighs.

I take a moment to appreciate how gorgeous she is: long hair cascading over her shoulders in waves, the end of one pale-purple tendril curling to frame her nipple. All that's left are her panties, and they happen to match her hair. Stevie makes quick work of ridding me of my pants.

She doesn't take my boxers off yet, and I know the torment I was promising her is coming my way. Which is fine, because what she plans to dish out now, I'll give back to her twice as good.

Stevie skims the contour of my erection through my boxers with her thumbs, and my cock jerks with the muted contact.

She smirks. "Somebody's excited."

She places a palm in the center of my chest and leans down, hair falling forward to tickle my skin, nipples dragging across my chest, mouth hovering over mine. "I'm gonna make you come now." She sucks my bottom lip and slips her hand inside my boxers, warm palm wrapping around me, skin to skin.

She pushes back up so she can rub her satin-covered sex along my shaft. We make a mutual sound of tortured appreciation. On the next stroke forward, she slides my cock under the crotch of her panties so I'm suddenly dragging over slick bare skin.

"Ah hell, Stevie." My eyes roll up and my erection kicks in her fist as the head glides past her clit.

"Do you like the way that feels?"

I grip her thighs, trying to hold on to my shredded control. "Pretty sure you already know the answer to that question."

"Mmm, I like the way it feels too." She rolls her hips, a sly, slightly evil smile tipping up the corner of her mouth. "Don't come yet if you want my mouth on you."

For once I keep my mouth shut, aware she's tormenting me on purpose, and any asshole snark I dish out is going to be met with more of this slow torture. So instead I enjoy the view as Stevie shifts to kneel between my thighs, naked apart from her pretty panties, which I'm likely going to destroy when I finally get my hands on her the way I want to.

Finally, *fucking finally*, she wraps one hand around my shaft and cups my balls with the other—God bless her for being a multitasker—and bows forward. Her eyes are on me as her tongue peeks out and she drags her wet bottom lip from the base of my shaft to the ridge. She places a barely there kiss at the tip.

Her hair fans out, soft lavender waves cascading over my thighs. She places open-mouth, wet kisses along my shaft. I shudder when she tongues the ridge and groan when the head disappears between her lips. She takes me in a few inches, then pops off, the cool air a shocking contrast to her warm, wet mouth.

"Bishop?" Her voice is like smoke.

I grunt a response, because I'm not sure I'm capable of speaking right now.

"I need your help." She abandons my balls so she can pull her hair over one shoulder. "Can you hold this for me so it's not in the way?" She spins her hair around her wrist. "Please?"

I manage words this time. "Anything for you, bae."

She grins against the head of my erection, and I reach out, unsteady with my excitement as I slide my fingers into her hair and gather it up, twisting it around my own wrist. Once it's out of the way, she takes me back into her mouth.

She only strokes once or twice before she pops off again, tongue sweeping along the ridge, sucking the head and really, just generally teasing the fuck out of me. "Why don't you show me what you like, Shippy?"

I cock a brow, and she grins. This time when she takes me in her mouth, I guide her strokes, lifting my hips, pushing deeper, moving her faster. Her hands splay out on my thighs, bracing her weight so I can control how she moves, which is really more than I can handle.

I warn her when I'm about to come, which takes a lot less time than I would like it to. I loosen my hold on her hair when my hips involuntarily jerk. I feel her throat constrict, my whole body tightening up, fingers flexing again as I come with brutal intensity.

As soon as I regain control of my body, I pull her off my cock, grab her by the waist, and flip her over onto her back. I capture her wet, swollen lips, and despite the fact that her mouth tastes like my cock and my orgasm, I sweep inside. She tries to wrap her legs around my waist and rub up on me again, but I shift so my legs are bracketing hers and drop my ass on her thighs, keeping them tight together and preventing any hope she had of friction. "Oh no you don't. It's my turn, and I have weeks of torture to make up for."

CHAPTER 23

MAGIC PEEN

Stevie

In hindsight it might not have been the best plan to pretend Bishop's dick was an ice cream cone for twenty minutes. Especially after all those weeks of me being near his groin and him not being able to help himself out. I'm banking on the fact that he's going to want to get in me badly enough that he won't feel compelled to torture me for too long.

Bishop bites and sucks his way over my collarbone, groaning as he stops to tongue my nipples before he moves lower, tracing my navel.

His rough palms glide up the inside of my thighs, pushing them apart. Everything below the waist clenches as he drags his tongue across his bottom lip. "I can't wait to tongue fuck an orgasm out of this pussy."

I groan, because really, what can I say to that? Any kind of fuck at this point would be welcome, and I'll gladly ride his face to orgasm land. Also, I didn't really expect the dirty talk or for it to be as much of a turn-on as it is, especially with the way he's looking at me.

He drops his head, eyes still on mine, lips brushing along the waist-band of my panties. At the same time his fingertips follow the edge until he reaches the apex.

He slips his free arm under my thigh, opening me wider and propping himself up on his elbow. "Your panties are damp." He pinches the material over my clit, grazing it. "Soaked, really."

He's not wrong. I've been rubbing his shaft over my clit like it was going to make a genie appear and grant me orgasm wishes. Plus, making him come with my mouth, and the knowledge that eventually he would be filling me up, has me pretty damn excited, but still . . . it's embarrassing to be called out on how aroused I am.

Or maybe it's a hint. I try to close my legs. "I should freshen up first."

His hold on my thigh tightens. "Like hell." He presses his nose against the damp fabric. "You smell like you're ready to be fucked."

"Jesus, Bishop. That mouth of yours is filthy."

His eyes lift to mine in question.

"I like it."

The crinkle at the corner of his eyes tells me he's smiling. "I figured you would." He inhales deeply and turns his head, biting the inside of my thigh.

I wish I'd had the foresight to take my panties off. I want to shove my hands in his hair and grind all over his face. I manage to restrain myself, because I'm highly aware that extra enthusiasm at this point is going to cause me problems. In the form of Bishop dragging this out even more.

He slips a single finger under the edge of my panties. Thank God. I shake with anticipation, like a cunnilingus junkie waiting for a hit of tongue. He moves the fabric over on either side until he's essentially giving me a vagina wedgie—which seems counterproductive.

Bishop hooks his finger under the fabric at the crest of my pelvis and pulls up, causing the satin to tighten and rub against my clit. I suck in a gasping breath, fighting with my hips not to jerk up. And that's before he slips a finger from his free hand under the fabric but lower, so his knuckle pushes against my opening.

I moan quietly as every single muscle in my body tightens, and I accidentally manage a Kegel. Based on his lascivious grin, I'm pretty sure he felt that.

He licks along the juncture of my thigh. Over and over, up one side and down the other. Then he sucks the soft, sensitive skin right beside my covered clit, and I think I'm going to die.

I give in, shoving my hands in his hair and trying to force his mouth to move an inch to the right.

Bishop releases the skin with a suctioned, wet pop. His lips brush against the satin right over my clit with the slow shake of his head. "You got something you want to say, bae?"

"Bishop." I roll my hips, asking for what I want without words.

He chuckles and nuzzles into my panties, licking the wet fabric.

"Oh my God." I turn my head into the pillow and fight a groan.

"All you have to do is ask, and I'll give you what you want."

"I want you to suck my goddamn clit."

That earns me another dark, low chuckle. "I bet you do." He bites the satin over my magic bean and pulls it away with his teeth. "But you need to ask nicely."

"You are such an asshole," I groan.

"I know." His tongue sweeps along the seam of my panties, so damn close.

"Fine. Please, Bishop."

"Please what?"

"Please just fucking eat me."

He groans a low *Yessss* and with one swift jerk yanks my panties to the side, tearing the delicate fabric. "Sorry 'bout that. I'll replace them along with the dress." He hitches my legs over his shoulders, grabs my ass, and lifts my hips so far off the mattress only my shoulders and head still rest there.

There's no more slow lead-up, no build, no teasing. His mouth covers me, and he sucks hard.

It doesn't take long for the suction to have the desired effect, and I come with a violence that reminds me of summer storms. I can't stop shaking, or screaming his name, or coming. My vision is eclipsed by a metaphorical meteor shower.

It doesn't end there either. When my hips are returned to the mattress, he pushes two fingers inside me and flutters fast and hard until I'm trying to wriggle away from him, the sensations overwhelming after such a vicious orgasm.

"Oh fuck no." He shifts around until he's beside me instead of between my thighs and wraps a palm around the back of my neck, fingers still pumping furiously. "You come again. All over my fingers before I give you my cock."

"You really are such an asshole," I groan.

"I know, but at least you have a good reason to put up with me and my shit now."

He uses his palm to press down on my clit with the next finger curl, and I explode. I'm a rag doll in his arms by the time I finally come down from that orgasm.

As soon as I have control over my body, I pull his mouth to mine, and he fits himself between my legs again. He fumbles with the condom, sheathing himself.

"You ready for me now?" Bishop circles sensitive skin.

"So ready."

His elbow rests against my ribs, forearm under my shoulder, thumb stroking gently up the side of my neck, as he positions himself against me and eases inside, inch by slow inch.

Bishop is exactly on the right side of too much—too much man, too much cock, just plain too much. He hovers over me, hips slowly coming to rest against mine. He nuzzles into my neck, exhaling heavily as his lips part. The soft stroke of his tongue follows the nip of his teeth, and he makes a sound somewhere between lust and pain.

"Are you okay?" I run my hands down his back, and his muscles flex under the smooth, damp skin.

He nods against my throat and then kisses his way up my neck.

"We should stop if you think it's going to set you back." I say the words while digging my fingernails into his ass, so they lack some of the conviction I was hoping for.

This time he makes a noise that sounds a lot like a snort and then bites my chin. When his mouth meets mine, he deepens the kiss for a few slow strokes before he pulls back. Those gorgeous, lust-drenched hazel eyes of his meet mine, and a lazy smile tips one corner of his delicious mouth. "My balls could literally be on the verge of exploding right now, and there's still no way in hell I would stop. Not unless you wanted me to, anyway." He rolls his hips. "Do you want me to stop, Stevie?"

"N-no. Just go easy."

"Don't worry, bae, I'll take good care of you." He covers my mouth with his again before I can protest, since that wasn't at all what I meant.

Bishop finds a slow, steady rhythm that hits my magic spot inside with every well-placed, gentle thrust. When I feel like I'm close to another orgasm, I push on his chest. He pulls back, eyes on fire, brow furrowed, lips thinned in a line, since he's hovering midthrust.

"I don't want to stop; I just want to change positions," I assure him.

That smile of his that I adore so much appears. "Always on duty, aren't you?"

"Just looking to change the view."

"I think it has more to do with you wanting to be in control, but however you want to spin it." He pushes up and sits back on his knees, holding on to my hips to maintain the connection.

I prop myself up on my elbows, appreciating the view of this glorious man kneeling between my thighs. He looks down, shifting his hips forward on a low hiss as he watches his erection disappear inside me. He runs his palms up the inside of my thighs, and his thumbs sweep along the juncture as he pulls back out and circles my clit on the next slow thrust.

The purposeful pressure, combined with the slow in and out, sends me over the edge. The world a wash of white and stars and bliss. Again. When I fall back down from the clouds, I find myself chest to chest with Bishop again, only this time I'm sitting in his lap. Just like the first time we almost kissed, but then he was too early into recovery and all the threads of restraint we were holding on to hadn't snapped yet.

"God, I love making you come," Bishop says on a guttural groan.

"You probably owe me at least another thousand orgasms for being such an insufferable ass."

He lifts and lowers me, faster, harder, fingers sliding into my hair, lips locking, teeth clashing, as we fight to keep the kiss from breaking. I come again, limbs wrapped around him, and he follows after me, all his hard edges melting, letting me see a different, vulnerable side of him that isn't in any way related to his injury.

Afterward he pulls me down so I'm sprawled over his chest, and we fall asleep like that, wrapped in each other.

CHAPTER 24

A SPLASH OF COLD WATER

Stevie

I wake up in the morning feeling deliciously sore. I run my hand across the sheets and scoot over in search of Bishop's warm body, but his side of the bed is empty. I crack a lid and check the time. It's well after ten.

The bathroom door is closed; the sound of the toilet flushing comes from the other side. I stretch out, muscles protesting. I could definitely use an epsom salts bath. That could be a fun thing to do with Bishop.

My phone buzzes from my nightstand several times in a row. It's probably Pattie or Jules. I nab the device and frown as the screen lights up with yet another alert. I have more than a hundred unanswered messages on a variety of social media.

"What the hell?" I key in my code and scroll through my text alerts. It seems like every single human being on my contact list has decided they want to get in touch with me this morning. It makes no sense. Until it does.

A new message pops up from Pattie, so I open hers before I even consider looking at the ones from my brother.

I need details.

Where the hell are you?

Please tell me there are lots of orgasms involved and that's why you're not responding.

Holy shit, social media is on fire

Don't read the comments if you look

Actually, don't look at social media

Call me the second you see these messages

A new message pops up as I'm scrolling through.

I can see that you've read these. I'm calling you.

"What the hell is going on?" I ask as soon as I have the phone to my ear.

"Is Bishop still there?"

"Uh, well, yeah. He's in the bathroom right now."

"Did you just wake up?"

"Yeah. Like literally a minute ago."

"Shit. Okay. I think you need to prepare yourself, because you've gone viral."

"Viral how?"

"There's a video."

"What kind of video?" I get this horrible sinking feeling in my stomach, the kind I used to get when RJ started playing professional hockey and he was constantly on some social media site doing unspeakable things with women. No one ever needs to see their older brother, who up until that point I'd idolized, making out with two women at the same time in a hot tub.

"The kind where it looks like you're trying to climb inside each other's mouths."

"Please tell me you're kidding." My stomach is no longer sinking; it's flip-flopping around.

"I can't do that unless you want me to lie to you." I can practically hear Pattie's cringe.

"Shit." Reality sets in, along with panic. "Shit, shit, shit. Is it really bad?"

"Like, is it a bad video?"

"Is a video of people making out in public ever good?" I roll off the bed and pace the room.

This would explain the massive number of messages I have this morning. There were a lot from my brother, so I'm taking that as an omen of the not-good variety. "What site is it on? Can we get it taken down? People can do that, right?"

I'd like to believe viral in the hockey world is a lot different from viral in the general sense of the word, but I'm not sure that would be accurate. Not with this being Seattle's first year with a hockey team.

"The video has been shared fifty-seven thousand times and has more than four hundred thousand likes."

"Oh my God." I think I might actually be sick.

"If it makes you feel better, it's a really hot video."

I consider that for several stupid, long seconds. It shouldn't make me feel better at all, but in the grand scheme of things I guess it's better than looking like a wasted hag. "I wish that helped." My phone buzzes with yet another message from my brother. Obviously he's seen the video—it's the only explanation for the incessant texts.

"What do I search so I can see this video?"

"I'll put a link in your messages, but whatever you do, don't read the comments."

I don't ask if it's that bad again, because clearly it is.

I'm about to put her on speakerphone and check the link she's sent me when the bathroom door swings open. "Wanna sixty-nine before breakfast?" Bishop stands there in all his gorgeous naked glory, his predatory expression and slight smirk dripping slowly from his face as he takes in what is likely my highly panicked expression.

"What's going on?" He takes several steps toward me. He's half-hard, so his peen bobs distractingly.

"I gotta let you go," I tell Pattie.

"Call me later."

"'Kay." I end the call and glance at my phone.

"Stevie? Why do you look like you're about to freak out?"

"There's a video," I croak, scrolling to Pattie's most recent message, including the link to the video. It was uploaded by user J$0124 twelve hours ago and has endless tags and hashtags attached to it. Since Joey's birthday is January 24, I'm going to go ahead and say he's the reason for this unnecessary bullshit.

"What kind of video?"

"Of us kissing, apparently." I hit the play button.

The video starts as I pull Bishop's mouth to mine. His hand hovers close to my cheek for several long seconds before it settles against my skin. It's a tentative, almost romantic kiss at first, until we really get going. Then it's not so sweetly innocent. I'm the one gripping his hair; I angle his head to the side; I push my hips into his.

We are totally dry humping on the dance floor. In front of my colleagues, bosses, and clients. This is really, really bad.

Another message comes in from my brother.

"I can handle this," Bishop says.

"How exactly are you going to handle this?" I wave the phone around in the air, my panic overriding any remaining thread of logic.

I accidentally hit play again, and the sound of us groaning into each other's mouths fills the room. It's so much different when I'm seeing it secondhand through my phone. And infinitely more mortifying. "RJ is going to lose his mind."

"I'll explain the situation."

"Which is what, exactly?" I start pacing, trying to find a way to calm myself down, but the more time I have to let this sink in, the worse the panic gets. The hashtag #puckbunny is attached to the video. It's essentially my worst nightmare come true.

"That we're dating."

"You can't tell him that!"

Bishop crosses his arms, the furrow in his brow deepening along with the downturn of his lips. "Why not?"

I flail and pace some more. "Because . . . because you can't! This looks so bad!" I've been made to look like a puck bunny. And now all the work we did to get Bishop back in the game means nothing because we're eating each other's faces. I made out with him at a work function. It makes me look anything but professional now. And any recommendation he might have given me is useless since everyone saw us playing tonsil hockey.

"Well, the easiest way for it to stop looking bad is if we tell people we're dating."

"But we're not dating."

Bishop pokes at his cheek with his tongue. "Are you still hung up on your douche ex?"

"What? No! Of course not."

"Then why can't we be dating? We spend all our free time together."

"That was for PT." I hear what he's saying, and he's right: it makes the most logical sense. But I can't get out of the spiral of panic that this video incites. I'll be right in the middle of Bishop's limelight now that he's back on the ice. The same limelight I've worked so hard to stay out of. The one that's only ever given me grief the very few times I've been inadvertently caught up in it.

Until now it's been blissfully peaceful. Sure, Bishop would pick me up in public places, but he always wore a hat and sunglasses, and I always had a hoodie to hide behind. At work no one would make a big deal of him coming to the clinic because everyone was used to athletes, and no one wanted to be the uncontrollable fan who loses their mind over someone they might one day have the honor of treating. Plus I work on a university campus, which is the last place anyone would ever expect an NHL player to hang out.

"Last night had fuck all to do with PT," Bishop says.

"You haven't touched a woman in how long? Emotions were running high. You're on testosterone overload, which I totally get. You were doing me a favor, and we took it to the next level." *Stevie, stop talking!* I know I'm spewing the most horrible BS and I need to stop, but I'm freaking out.

Bishop blinks slowly. "I thought we already established that this wasn't a favor. It was me making sure that your dick ex knows that you're not available and he doesn't have a chance with you. Not ever again. That video makes things a lot easier, if you think about it."

"Easier how?" All I can see is the nightmare this is going to be: people asking questions and wanting things from me because I know Bishop and I'm related to RJ. All the time I've spent protecting myself from the spotlight has been for nothing.

"You don't have to hide behind hoodies and sunglasses anymore. I can pick you up whenever and wherever."

I stop pacing and spin to face him. He's still naked. And so am I. He still has a semi, and I'm anxious. "That can't happen, Bishop. We can't be seen in public together."

"Why the hell not?"

Because I've worked too hard *not* to be Rook Bowman's sister just to end up as Bishop Winslow's girlfriend. My phone rings before I can open my mouth to share that, and like an idiot I answer the call.

"I've been trying to get ahold of you all morning! What the hell is going on?" Awesome. Now I get to deal with my angry brother.

"Hi, RJ." I yank the bedsheet free and wrap it around myself, because it feels weird to talk to my brother when I'm not fully dressed.

"Seriously, Stevie? You're making out with Winslow in public now?"

"Relax, RJ, it was just a kiss. It's not like he stole my virtue or anything. That's been gone since junior year of high school."

Bishop makes a noise that sounds a lot like a growl, but my brother continues his angry tirade, forcing me to give him my attention. "I did not need to know that, and it's not the point. Winslow was told to keep his damn hands off you while you were working together, and clearly that's a bunch of bullshit. How long has this been going on?"

This has so much potential backlash: things I hadn't considered in the heat of the moment, like Bishop getting in trouble. So I do the only thing I can think of as triage. "It was me. I kissed Bishop. He came with me to the event as a favor because Joey was going to be there with a date, and I didn't want to go alone. This is on me; it's my mistake."

Bishop opens his mouth to speak, but I give him a warning glare and a headshake.

"Are you still with him?"

"No. I'm alone right now."

"I'm coming over."

"No. You're not. I have shit to do today that doesn't include you reaming me out for making out with someone you don't like. I already told you: I made a mistake. I don't need you to make me feel worse about it. I have to go. I'll call you later." I don't wait for him to answer before I end the call and toss the phone on my bed.

My bed that smells like sex and Bishop.

"Why'd you do that?" Bishop asks quietly.

"To get you off the hook with my brother and your teammates."

"And did you mean that?"

"Mean what?" I rub my temple, exhausted, even though I've only been awake for a handful of minutes.

"That this was a mistake." He motions between us.

"I don't know, Bishop. I just . . . didn't expect all the attention. It's not something I want, and it never has been." I sigh and turn away. "I have to take down decorations today."

"Pattie and Jules said they would deal with that," he reminds me. "Or is this you telling me you want me to leave?"

"I need time to think. I've spent a lot of years avoiding my brother's spotlight, and now I'm in it in a way I never wanted to be. I don't know how to deal with it at all." I can't look directly at him because if I do I'm afraid of what he'll see. That I don't want him to go at all. That I'm scared and confused and I don't want what's supposed to be ours to be everyone else's as well.

"Right. Yeah. I get it. I guess I'll see you when I see you." He bends to pick his clothes up off the floor and heads down the hall without another word. Several seconds later the door clicks, and I crumple in a heap on my bed that smells like last night's decisions.

I think I just broke my own heart.

CHAPTER 25

THAT WENT WAY WRONG

Bishop

How I'd planned to start my morning: inside Stevie.

How my morning actually went: not at all like I'd planned.

I do the walk of shame across the hall naked, holding all my clothes. Thankfully, no one is there to witness it. My brother isn't home, so I don't have to deal with him, which is a good thing because I'm pretty much in the mood for nothing and no one. Talk about a shitty end to the best sex I've had in . . . well . . . ever.

I don't want to wash the smell of Stevie off me, but I realize going to practice smelling like sex after a viral make-out video goes live isn't a great plan, so I jump in the shower and head to the arena. I get stopped by Alex before I can step foot in the locker room. "We need to have a chat."

Obviously he's seen the video. "I can explain."

"I don't want an explanation. I want you to shut your damn mouth and listen." I follow him down the hall, away from the sound of my teammates, to his office. Alex motions me inside and forcefully shuts the door. "Sit down."

I follow the order and keep my mouth shut, unsure how this is going to play out. A flash of inconvenient memory pops up—one of me with my head between Stevie's legs.

"Wipe that smirk off your damn face." He slaps a palm on the desk, startling me.

I sit up straighter. "Sorry."

He drops into the chair behind his desk instead of the club chair beside me, which tells me a lot about his frame of mind. One of the reasons Alex is such a successful coach is that he treats us all as equals. Right now, I'm not his equal at all. I'm the problem, and he's the coach.

"I asked one thing from you, and you couldn't follow through. Do you understand how that video looks?"

"It wasn't a—"

He cuts me off, his voice rising with anger. "You were supposed to keep it professional while you were being rehabbed. That was it. Instead you're all over social media making out with the person who was rehabbing you. It's like a blatant 'Fuck you' to me. To this organization. Is that what you meant to do?"

Until this very moment I hadn't looked at it that way, but I can see how he and everyone else would. Which is a bit of an eye-opener. I try to come up with some kind of defense for my behavior. "I'm back on the ice, though, so technically I did keep it professional while I was being rehabbed."

"That's not the damn point!" He slams his fist on his desk, making the water glass rattle. He takes a few deep breaths and flips his laptop open. Spinning it around, he cues up the video that's gone viral. The one of me making out with Stevie. It seems a lot more graphic and intense on a larger screen. "Do you have any idea how this looks from the other side?"

Like soft-core porn is the first thought that comes to my mind, but I don't think it's what he wants to hear. When I don't answer right away, he barrels on.

"This whole thing makes it look like you're not serious about your rehab at all, or your teammates, for that matter, or my goddamn orders."

"I've been working my ass off."

"Based on this, it looks like you've been doing a hell of a lot more than that." Alex pinches the bridge of his nose. "Rehab with Stevie is done."

"But—"

"There are no buts, Bishop. We laid out the rules, and you shat all over them."

"I did follow your orders until last night."

He gives me a look that tells me he thinks I'm full of shit. "If there was something going on, you should've been forthcoming, but you weren't."

"I would've told you if I'd had the chance, but that wasn't really possible, now, was it?" Although, to be fair, I planned to change things last night, regardless. I should've told Alex about the event either way, but I hadn't considered how it would look, which is really damn bad.

"Are you seriously lipping off to me, Winslow?"

"I'm trying to explain. I worked my ass off with Stevie. We spent a ton of time together over the past two months, and until last night I kept my end of the bargain. I was hands off and focused. She's the reason I'm back on the ice."

"Which means you don't need her for PT anymore. If she actually worked for the team, she'd be out of a damn job for this. I need you to see the team physiotherapist, and then you can head home."

"What about practice?"

"I think you need to do me a favor and give your team captain some time to settle down."

243

"Let me get this straight. I'm being sent home because Rook is in a mood?"

"You're being sent home because I need to set an example. You went against a direct order, and you didn't come to me when you should have. This could've been avoided. PT and then home. Understood?"

"Yes, sir."

I don't ask any more questions because I don't want to make things worse.

I get to play the following night, but I can't say that's a good thing. My head is all over the place, and Rook is pissed at me, which means everyone is tense. Add to that missing out on practice yesterday, and my on-ice performance is less than awesome. I'm also tight as hell from not having Stevie forcing extra PT on me.

To make a shit night even shittier, I haven't seen or heard from Stevie since she sent me home yesterday morning. I don't know what the protocol is. She wants space, so does that mean I should leave her alone entirely? Do I send her flowers? A pizza? Do I knock on her door and ask her if she's ready to talk? Or do I let the dust settle and wait for her to come to me?

It's late by the time I get home from the game. I stand in the middle of the foyer, breathing in the excessively fragrant flowers sitting on the glass-topped table, considering whether I should knock on her door. I don't want to cause myself more problems with my team, and I don't want to push Stevie to talk about this before she's ready, so I leave it alone, even though I don't want to.

The next morning we leave for a short series of away games. We're playing in Nashville, Tennessee. Being in my home state is something I usually get excited for. It means I'll invariably run into old friends from college, but I'm not looking forward to having to explain the viral video.

My go-to defense is generally to avoid commenting when stuff crops up on social media. It's what I've always done with the women who've posted pictures of me after they've slept with my brother. But I've never had anything spread so far or wide this fast, so ultimately I'm avoiding doing anything because I honestly don't know where Stevie and I stand, since she's not talking to me.

I don't want to corroborate what she said to Rook about it being on her, but I also don't want to say we're dating if we're not. It's a fucking mess. Until we have a conversation, I've decided to keep my damn mouth shut. Lord knows when I open it up and say the things I want to, I usually cause an assload of problems for myself.

Kingston and I are sharing a room, as we usually do, but he's been off with me since the viral video happened. He drops his suitcase on the bed, unzips it, and starts putting his stuff away. Kingston functions on routine. He turns on the steamer he always packs so he can rid his clothes of wrinkles before he hangs them in the closet.

I flop down on the other bed and fold an arm behind my head. "How long are you going to be pissed at me for?"

Kingston moves his boxers from his suitcase to the nightstand drawer beside his bed. "I'm not angry."

"Really? 'Cause it kinda seems like you are."

He rolls his head like he's working the kinks out of his neck before he turns to face me. "I'm disappointed."

"About what?"

"How you're dealing with this whole thing."

"You mean the Stevie thing?"

"What other thing is there?" he asks.

"It's not my fault someone posted a video of us kissing."

His lips thin, and he shakes his head. "Maybe not, but you've done nothing to dispel any of the rumors out there, made no statement; you haven't even apologized to Rook."

"What the hell do I have to apologize for?"

"For not thinking your actions through, Bishop. You put his little sister under a spotlight and did nothing to protect her after the fact. You say you're into her and you want to date her, but your lack of action says exactly the opposite, don't you think?"

"Stevie freaked out and told me she needed time to think and she didn't want to be in my limelight, and now she won't talk to me. Then Coach told me that my rehab with Stevie was over and that he better not find out I'm going behind his back. What am I supposed to do?"

"Something is better than nothing. That video has been up for four days, and you've done nothing. You dodge everyone's questions and make no attempt to dissuade people from believing the worst. No one wants to be portrayed the way she is right now."

"So what do I do?"

He rubs the back of his neck. "Stop making her look like a puck bunny and claim her as yours."

"But Coach said—"

"Coach and everyone else on the team thinks you messed around with her to be an asshole. No one actually knows you like this girl, apart from me."

He makes a good point, one I hadn't considered. "What if she doesn't want to be mine?"

"At least you'll have dispelled all the crap rumors floating around out there. You owe her that much, and the rest of your team, don't you think?"

◆ ◆ ◆

We end up winning the game and I manage an assist, which is a damn miracle, considering how frosty my teammates are being. Understandably so, considering the conversation I had with Kingston earlier. In spite of Stevie's lack of communication, I send her a message to let her know that I still think we need to talk. I want to address the video, but I need a little guidance from her as to the direction I should take, because what I want to say is in direct opposition to what she told Rook, and that will inevitably open a whole different can of worms. I'm not opposed to dealing with him. I need to know what stance I'm taking, because the last thing I want is to throw Stevie under the bus, even if I think her bullshitting her brother is pointless.

As done as I am with today, I hit the bar with the rest of the team. As usual, Kingston orders a glass of milk and I grab a beer. A handful of people we went to college with show up, which means one beer turns into several. I keep checking my phone to see if Stevie's responded, but nothing so far.

On my way back from the bathroom I stop at the bar. I should probably stop drinking soon, or tomorrow isn't going to be awesome, but Stevie's lack of communication and my inability to take action are making me antsy.

Someone edges their way between me and another guy waiting at the bar. The perfume is familiar, and I glance over at the woman crowding my personal space.

"Shippy! I thought it was you! Couldn't forget that back-end view if I tried!"

Shit. This is the last thing I need after today. "Penny."

Her lipsticked smile grows wider, likely at my displeased expression. "Don't worry, Shippy, I'm not here to start problems." She flashes her hand in front of my face, diamond ring glinting in the dimly lit bar.

"Congratulations. Who's the lucky guy?" At least I don't have to worry about her hitting on me.

"Chuck Peterson. Owns the real estate company in our hometown. You remember him, right? He's got billboards all over town these days. Biggest agent in the city."

"That's great." Obviously nothing has changed since she and I broke up: always about status, money, and flash.

I order myself a beer and offer to buy her whatever she wants, because it means I'll get rid of her faster. Of course she wants some kind of fancy-ass drink. Her eyes light up and she slaps my chest. "Let's get a selfie! Chuck will be so jealous that he missed seeing you and King!"

She pulls out her phone and hugs my arm, making that weird face all women seem fond of these days. I let her take the stupid pictures— otherwise she's liable to make a scene—and I even try to smile so I don't look like a complete asshole.

Thankfully, the drinks appear, so I toss some money on the bar and get my ass out of there before she can corner me again and make me take more selfies. I head for a table in the corner where Kingston is holed up with friends from college.

I'm about to take a seat when someone grabs me.

"What the hell, man?" Rook seethes.

I look down at his hand wrapped around my arm. "What the hell, what?"

His lip pulls up in a sneer. "You think this is some kind of joke?"

"I don't even know what you're talking about."

"You and the goddamn bunnies. There's a viral video of you and Stevie, and this is how you manage it, by making her look even worse?"

I thumb over my shoulder. "I went to college with these guys."

"And that's supposed to make it better, when you're posing for self- ies with some chick in a bar but you were macking on my damn sister four days ago?"

"You really don't know shit, Rook."

"Like hell I don't. She's a mess over this. Don't you think you've done enough damage? Is there anyone you think about other than your- self?" Rook is all up in my space, just as agitated as me.

"Are you kidding me right now? You're the reason she's not talking to me. You're the goddamn problem, Rook."

"I'm the problem? I should've beat your ass weeks ago."

"Hey, guys, you need to cool it unless you want to end up on suspension." King tries to get us both to take a step back, but we ignore him.

I'm tired of Rook and his bullshit. Tired of people taking the things I want. "You think I give a shit about a suspension right now? Fuck that. You wanna throw down, Bowman, then let's throw down."

His cheek tics. "You'll be in traction by the time I'm done with you, ass clown."

"Pretty sure it's gonna be the other way around." I'm so pissed off right now there's a haze of red clouding my vision. I recognize, somewhere in the back of my head, that my decision-making skills are highly compromised by the unusual quantity of alcohol I've consumed tonight, Rook's asinine accusations, and the fact that Stevie is dodging me.

But I'm sick of bowing for everyone else, of backing down and walking on eggshells. I've followed every rule, toed every fucking line, and I'm done worrying about everyone else and what they want and need.

Rook tips his chin toward the exit. "Let's take this somewhere without eyes."

I clench and release my fists, mirroring his grin. "Sounds good to me."

We leave the bar, with King and a couple of other guys trailing behind us. I'm pretty sure we have the same idea: find a quiet dark alley to kick each other's asses in. We end up by the garbage dumpsters. It's warm here, and the smell of rancid food makes us gag.

"Guys, this is a really bad idea," King says before I let the door slam closed in his face.

He wrenches it open. His expression is one I haven't seen before as he steps out into the alley. His nose wrinkles at the putrid smell, but he crosses his arms and leans against the closed steel door. "I'm here to mediate."

Rook and I both look at him, then focus on each other.

"I told you to keep your hands off my goddamn sister, and you didn't listen," Rook snarls and then settles into what seems like a fighting stance.

"I don't take my orders from you."

"Alex told you to keep it professional."

"It was supposed to be until I was on the ice again, which I am."

"So you thought you'd string her along and use her like one of your stick-chasing bunnies?" He takes a swing at me, which I don't expect. It's cheap and dirty, an uppercut that makes my head snap back and stars explode behind my eyes.

I trip over some garbage and fall on my ass. He takes advantage of my disoriented state and lands on top of me. For half a second I can fully appreciate the lengths he'll go to in order to protect his sister and how much she must mean to him.

"I'm in love with her, you stupid fuck!" I shout. And I'm not just saying it for the shock-and-awe factor. I've been a miserable asshole the last few days without her, worse than usual even. I feel like a tree that's been ripped out by the roots, robbed of vital nourishment.

Rook pauses with his fist raised in the air, his expression shifting to confusion. I use his momentary distraction to my advantage and flip us over so he's on his back on the ground instead of me. My jaw already aches. If he's broken something, I'll be so pissed.

"I love her, and you're the reason she isn't talking to me!"

King pulls me off him.

Rook scrambles back to his feet. "You're the one with a mile-long list of puck-bunny pictures all over social media."

"Those are my brother's conquests, not mine. When have you ever seen me pick up a bunny? Fucking never."

"Bullshit." Rook spits, but I can see him filtering through preseason, trying to come up with a time when I've chatted up a bunny, let alone taken one home with me. I'm as polite as I possibly can be to fans, considering I'm a dick on the best of days.

"You know what's bullshit? The fact that *your* goddamn puck-bunny history is the reason Stevie is freaking out right now. You're the one who's screwing this up for me."

"What the hell are you talking about?"

I should probably stop while I'm ahead here, but I can't seem to keep my mouth from running. It's been days, and I'm done with Stevie avoiding me and Rook being pissed off at me when he's the damn problem. "She lives in your fucking shadow."

His brow furrows. "No, she doesn't."

"Yes. She does. She avoids the attention because she's terrified that all people are going to see is Rook Bowman's baby sister." I hold my arms wide, giving him free rein to go ahead and try to hit me again. "You have no idea how hard it is for her. She thinks that no matter what she does, her identity is always going to be tied up in you, and she thinks if she's my girlfriend, it's going to be the same damn thing."

Rook seems to deflate. He runs a frustrated hand through his hair. "You let that video go up and did nothing about it."

"What the hell was I supposed to do? She shut down on me and won't talk to me; my team thinks I'm an asshole; you're pissed, which the entire team knows, so it's been great for team morale; and Alex took her off my PT because he doesn't like the optics." We're both heaving, me rubbing my jaw and him rubbing his ribs.

"I didn't tell him to do that."

"You didn't have to. I'm the cause of the dissension, as far as he's concerned. Which means I'm messing up the team. I might be an ass-hole, but I care about this team." I pace, rubbing the back of my neck. Even with everyone pissed at me, I've still managed to make a valuable contribution. "This entire time I've been so patient. I didn't push her for anything. I kept it light. She rehabbed me and we hung out. I focused on getting better and gave her time to get over that stupid dickbag who played with her head. And that was your fault, too, by the way."

"How the hell is that my fault?"

"She just wants a brother. She doesn't need you to try to replace your dad. She wanted you to think she was okay, so she found a shield, and he worked until he didn't."

"What?" His brow furrows even more, his confusion shifting to disquiet. "How do you know this?"

"Because she told me. Because while you've been busy with your life and your career and being so sure I was out to screw her over, I've been listening. And waiting for her to be okay enough for me to tell her how I damn well feel about her."

"*You* made Stevie look like a puck bunny," he argues.

"There are pictures of you fucking around with two mostly naked women in a goddamn hot tub still floating around on the internet!" I jab my chest with a finger. "All I did was kiss her."

"That looked like a hell of a lot more than a kiss, and you damn well know it."

Okay. He's got me there. "It would've been better if it hadn't happened in a public place, and if someone hadn't posted it for the entire hockey-watching nation to speculate over, but in my defense I hadn't seen her in almost a week. Emotions were running high." I use the same line she gave me: her excuse for letting it go as far as it did. Which was bullshit. The only reason it didn't happen sooner was because my dick wouldn't work effectively and I was waiting for her to be over the douche ex. Also, Alex's orders figured in at least a little.

He crosses his arm, lip still twitching. "She told me she kissed you, not the other way around."

"She figured you'd overreact, and she didn't want you to try to kill me. Seems like she was right about that."

He rolls his eyes, and then they slide back to me, narrowing. "You were there." It's not a question, and his voice is suddenly low.

I realize I've stepped in the biggest pile of dog shit ever, because I admitted, accidentally, that I was at Stevie's the morning after the video went viral. It doesn't take a rocket scientist to put two and two together.

He's in my personal space between one blink and the next, gripping my shirt. He's maybe an inch or two shorter than me but just as broad. If I have to guess, I'd say it'd be a pretty even fight, or at least it would've been until a few seconds ago. "Did you *sleep* with my sister?"

I raise one hand in surrender and grip the wrist of the hand currently fisting my collar. His hold is tight and close to my throat. Also, he looks about ready to commit murder. "Rook, listen."

"Answer the damn question, Winslow."

I shake my head. "I can't."

"Bullshit! Answer the damn question."

"It's not my place to tell you that. You'll have to talk to Stevie if you want that information."

"You son of a bitch." He spins us around and shoves me against the brick wall.

"Rook, man, take it easy," Kingston says.

I'd forgotten he was here.

Rook barely spares him a glance. "Don't interfere, King. I like you, but you get in the way, and I'll take you down too." He bars his forearm across my throat.

"Calm down, Rook," I grind out.

"Don't tell me to calm down. She's my sister."

"And I'm in love with her."

He exhales angrily, like a bull getting ready to charge. "If the roles were reversed, would you kick your teammate's ass for putting his hands on your sister?"

"I don't have a sister."

"Pretend you do."

I sigh. "I can't. All I have is a brother who name-drops me to bag women."

253

"King, if Winslow slept with your sister, would you punch him out?"

Kingston's eyes dart around like he's looking for someone else with his name to answer. "Uhhh . . ."

"Be honest," Rook snaps.

"I don't use violence to solve my problems," Kingston replies.

Rook twists his head to look at him with one eyebrow raised.

Kingston sighs. "I would probably be inclined to punch him."

"Seriously, King?"

"Sorry." He shrugs. "It's a brotherly duty. Plus, there's the video . . ."

"You suck, man. Don't think I won't remember this when you have woman problems down the line."

"I don't plan to sleep with any of my teammates' sisters, so I should be fine." I swear Kingston is smirking. Asshole.

"I get four shots." Rook unbars my throat and takes a step back, cracking his knuckles with a sinister smile.

"Two, and no face and no groin."

"No way. I deserve at least one face shot."

"You already got in a face shot."

He jumps around like a boxer and shakes out his hands. "That was before I knew you slept with my sister."

"Three shots, all body. No groin or head shots. We don't want evidence anyone can see or a concussion," Kingston interjects.

"Whose side are you on?" I ask.

"I'm not on a side. This is about brotherly justice, and I'm hoping after this you two will finally put the antagonism to rest. We're all pretty damn tired of it, so let's get this done so we can all move on." Kingston makes a get-on-with-it motion.

Rook nods and hops around a bunch more, making a show of clenching and releasing his fists.

"Just take the shot—"

He slams me with an uppercut to the diaphragm, and I stumble back into the wall, heaving.

"That was for the video." He beckons me forward again.

I suck in a few deep breaths, straighten—it hurts a lot—and step away from the wall, bracing for the next shot. He fakes me out a second time and lands a hook to my side. I fall on a bag of garbage, which explodes under me. Thankfully, it seems to be a bunch of paper and plastic.

"You all right, Ship?" Kingston asks.

"Fine. Gimme a sec."

Just as I get back on my feet and Rook returns to his boxer stance, the door slams open, sending Kingston stumbling forward. "What in the ever-loving hell is going on here?" Coach Waters steps out in the alleyway, face contorting with a grimace as he takes in the three of us and the odor registers.

I try to cop a natural lean against a dumpster because my side is killing me. Also, I might vomit soon, thanks to the pain and the putrid smell out here. Meanwhile Rook shoves his hands in his pockets.

"Just having a conversation, Alex," Rook says. It would be somewhat believable if we both weren't breathing heavily. We're also sweaty.

Alex looks to Kingston.

He clasps his hands in front of him. "They're resolving their differences, and I'm mediating to ensure it doesn't get out of hand."

"So you're refereeing?"

"No, sir, just mediating a discussion as an impartial observer who would like to see my teammates get along so we can play the best hockey possible."

"You could probably sell a space heater to someone living in a damn desert," Alex grumbles. He turns to us and sighs. "You two get it all out?"

"Just about, yeah." Rook nods.

"Yup," I add.

"Get your asses up to your rooms. We've got an early morning." Alex holds the door open and ushers us all inside. Kingston leads the way and we follow, with Alex behind us, like a kindergarten teacher making sure his kids don't get out of line. "Jesus, you two smell like you were rolling around in the dumpster," he gripes.

He chaperones us to the elevator, shaking his head as we wait for the doors to open. "You good to get these two upstairs without them murdering each other on the way there?" he asks Kingston.

"Yes, sir. I'll make sure they keep their hands to themselves."

The three of us step inside, and I think Kingston instantly regrets it because Rook and I stink like trash. He jabs the button for our floor, and the doors slide closed.

"I have one hit left." Rook gets back into his fighting stance.

I hold my arms wide. "Have at it."

He goes for the spleen this time, and I stumble back, grabbing hold of the handrail so I don't go down. He can really throw a punch. I cough a few times. "You gonna stand in my way with Stevie?"

"Not if you're what she wants." The doors slide open at his floor, and he takes a step out into the hall, holding his hand over the sensor. "But if you break her heart, I'm going to break you."

"I'd let you."

"Glad we're finally on the same page."

CHAPTER 26

DAD-BRO

Stevie

It's the day the team is scheduled to come home, and I'm up ridiculously early. I've been sleeping like crap since the whole thing with Bishop went down. It got worse after he sent me a *We need to talk* message a few days ago. In my experience, a message like that has never been attached to a positive conversation.

I wander around my apartment for a good half hour before I get antsy and decide I need to do something active to help manage my anxiety. I know the team is supposed to be home early this afternoon, but there are a lot of hours between now and then, and I don't think I can handle hanging around my apartment, waiting for him.

I want to message Bishop, but it's been three days of silence from me since he sent his text, so messaging seems pretty anticlimactic at this point. Also, if I send one now, then I'm going to either check every four seconds to see if he's replied or continue sending messages until he responds, which will make me look desperate. Even if this is accurate, I don't think it's a good strategy.

I realize I've fucked up. Does it suck that there's a viral video of me and Bishop making out? Yup. But that wasn't his fault, and I've spent a week avoiding him instead of dealing with the fallout, because I'm scared. Avoidance seems to be my go-to tactic for handling uncomfortable situations. I need to grow up. Hindsight is such a bitch.

Fortunately, Pattie and Jules have already invited me over for brunch today. It's meant as a distraction from Bishop's impending return. It's still way early for me to go over there, so I take the bus to the clinic, intending to burn off some anxiety. I change into my bathing suit and head to the pool. It doesn't matter what kind of physical activity I engage in these days; it all reminds me of Bishop.

I flip over and start a steady back crawl. When I reach the end of the pool, I somersault underwater and change to a front crawl. After a few laps I come up for air and shriek when I find a pair of hairy-toed feet at the edge of the pool.

"Jesus Christ, Joey! What the hell are you doing, other than being a creepy-ass bastard?"

He ignores the insult and gives me a look I can't quite decipher. "How are you, Stevie?"

"I was fine until you scared the crap out of me with your hobbit toes." Joey's feet have always freaked me out. I swim over to the ladder and pull myself out of the water. I left my towel in the changing room, so I have nothing to wrap around my body apart from my arms, which don't cover much. Thankfully, I'm wearing a full-coverage bathing suit that mashes my boobs down and is purely functional, unlike the bathing suits I wore when Bishop and I had our water-therapy sessions.

I wish I could stop thinking about him.

"Really? You're not upset?"

"About?" I shake my head to get the water out of my ear.

"Oh shit. You haven't seen it yet, have you?" He feigns surprise.

I sigh. I have no interest in falling into another trap set by my douche ex. "Why can't you leave me alone, Joey?"

"Look, Stevie, I know I can't win you back. I get it, but I don't want you to set yourself up to get hurt again. I thought you should be prepared."

"Prepared for what?" I try to step around him, but he blocks my way and holds his phone up in front of my face. I grab it from him, ready to toss it in the pool. At least until I see what's on the screen.

Bishop with a petite brunette tucked in to his side. It could be nothing. But it could be something too. Especially since he's not angrily glaring at the camera. If it is something, I have no one to blame but myself, since I'm the one who said sleeping together was a mistake. I'm such an idiot.

"Looks like I really know how to pick 'em, huh?" I slap the phone against Joey's chest.

When I try to walk away, he grips my wrist. "I'm sorry, Stevie. I just thought you should know."

"Well, I know, so job well done. Can you let me go now?"

"I could take you out for coffee if you want to talk about it? I messed things up with you and me. I might not be able to fix it, but I could be a friend."

I close my eyes and exhale slowly, searching for an ounce of composure. "You betrayed me and you tried to make it my fault."

"I didn't—"

"Shut up. You never apologized for what you did. You were only sorry because I found out. I'll take ownership for my own mistake, which was dating you for a year in the first place. We never belonged together. I should never have agreed to move in with you. I used you, just like you used me, so we're all squared up there." This time when I move around him, he doesn't try to stop me. "Oh, and I know you're the one who uploaded that video last week, so you can drop all this fake concern. We are never going to be anything to each other ever again." It feels good to finally unload all these months of pent-up frustration.

This time when I walk away from him, he doesn't try to follow me.

Twenty minutes later I'm showered and dressed, but instead of feeling better, I feel infinitely worse. All I want to do is drown myself in pints of ice cream. I poke my head out of the change room, checking for signs of Joey, but he's finally taken the hint. I should've done that ages ago. At least I've stood up for myself, and maybe Joey will finally leave me alone, which is all I really wanted in the first place.

I drag myself to the front entrance, phone in hand, as I search social media for the image I saw on Joey's phone, weighed down by emotions I don't know what to do with. That picture was taken three days ago: about the same time Bishop sent me the message that we needed to talk. Here I was prepared to tell him I was in, and he may have very well already been out.

I'm about to message Pattie to tell her I'm on my way over and that I'll need a gallon of ice cream when I notice I have new texts from Lainey. I love my sister-in-law. She's stayed incredibly impartial during this whole thing, and I sincerely appreciate her lack of sides taken.

I check her messages, hoping she'll provide news on when my brother is supposed to be home, because that will also tell me when Bishop will be back.

Lainey: are you home?

Me: at the clinic

Lainey: on a Saturday?????

Me: just went for a swim, needed to burn some energy, heading to Pattie and Jules', what's up?

Lainey: Just seeing what you're up to, message me later!

A video of Kody with a face covered in chocolate pudding telling me he loves me follows. She's been doing daily check-ins all week. I fire back a series of heart-eyes emojis.

I message Pattie and Jules as I head toward their house. I'm halfway there when a car pulls up beside me and slows to match my walking speed. It would be just my luck to be kidnapped today.

I'm about to tell whoever it is to screw off when I realize the car is familiar, and so is the person driving it. "Need a lift?" RJ smiles sheepishly.

"I thought you guys weren't supposed to be home until later this afternoon?" It's not the best greeting, but it's true.

"A storm was rolling in so we flew out early. Lainey told me you were heading over to your friends' place, and I figured I'd try and catch you on the way." He drums his fingers on the steering wheel. "Can we grab a quick coffee or something?"

"Okay. Sure." I get in the car and fire another message to Pattie and Jules to let them know I'm with my brother.

He doesn't have a chance to say much of anything because the coffee shop is less than fifty feet down the road. He pulls into the drive-through, and I opt for an iced frappé thing. It's somewhat close to ice cream.

"I owe you an apology," RJ says once we have our coffees and are parked on the street.

"For what?"

"About the whole thing with Bishop. I was wrong about him."

And of course I burst into tears, because I really thought he was wrong and now I'm not so sure. To his credit, RJ doesn't panic like most guys would. Maybe because he married a woman with an anxiety disorder, and sometimes that anxiety manifests in tears.

"Hey, what's wrong?" He reaches across the seat and gives the back of my neck a squeeze, which actually makes me cry harder because that's exactly what Bishop would do, and I'm pretty sure I screwed that right the hell up.

I can't answer that question because I've turned into a snot-sobbing mess, so I pull up the image that Joey showed me less than half an hour ago and thrust it at RJ. I wail, "I think he's already over it." I'm not sure I'm even remotely intelligible.

"This is what you're upset about?" RJ asks.

"He's posing! He never does that. Ever. He always looks like someone's shit on his breakfast when people try to take pictures of him, but he actually looks not pissed off here, and I've been miserable for the past week!" I say all this between hiccups and sobs. It's pretty extra, even for me.

"I don't know if I would classify that as a smile, and that's someone he knew from college. And she's married."

A tiny seed of hope forms, but I squash it down. "How do you know that?"

He enlarges the picture until I can see the rock on her ring finger. "Me and Bishop had it out right after this. Like immediately after that picture was taken, we basically threatened to kill each other."

"You what?" I look my brother over. There are no signs of injury, but then all I can see is his body from the neck up and the biceps down. "Is he okay?"

"Yeah, he's fine. I mean, I punched him a few times, and he punched me, but we're over it. I was wrong, Stevie, and I'm sorry."

"So he's not over me?"

"No. Not even a little. He's pretty much the opposite of over you." He pulls me into an awkward, uncomfortable hug, thanks to the center console between us. "I should've listened to you. I made it about me when it wasn't, and I interfered when I shouldn't have, but to be fair, you'd just had your heart ripped out, and I really didn't want to see you go through that again."

"I know, and I appreciate you wanting to protect me, but all it really accomplished was me doubting myself even more." The past week has sucked so much. The not knowing and feeling paralyzed by uncertainty.

He releases me and settles back in his seat. "I'm sorry for that. I just . . . I have a lot of guilt for not being able to be there for you and Mom when Dad passed."

"But you were there."

"But I wasn't really." He shakes his head. "I came to the funeral and went through the motions, but I wasn't there in a way that counted for anything. I dealt with it by putting my head down and playing hockey when I should've been reaching out more to make sure you were okay. I wanted to find a way to fill that empty space, and I guess I figured if I could fill it for you, then it might help me too."

It's amazing how a few words can completely alter one's perception. "I don't need you to be anything but my brother, RJ. And I realize I've made our relationship difficult by only accepting the version of you that's easy to handle and doesn't come with screaming fans."

"I get why you don't like it, though." He runs a hand through his hair. "I know I didn't do a very good job of dealing with things when I first started out, and that made it hard for you."

"It wasn't a version of you I knew." Or particularly liked. "But it's different now. I haven't been very fair to you, or Bishop. I haven't really made an attempt to fit into *all* the parts of your life, just the ones I'm familiar and comfortable with, but it means I'm missing out on a lot." I shift so I can sort of face him. "I kept thinking that if I stepped into your spotlight, I'd stop being me and all anyone would see is your little sister, because frankly, it felt like that *a lot* in high school. And then you went through that phase and, well . . . that was awkward." Especially when girls would slip me their number and ask me to pass it to my brother. Or pretend to be my friend so they could get close to him.

"I'm really sorry my choices affected you like that. And it killed me when you wouldn't talk to me back then."

"I was so mad at you for being a super-dirty man-whore. I looked up to you my entire life, and then you became someone I didn't know."

"It cost me a lot, Stevie. Not just my relationship with you and Mom."

"I know, and I don't want to keep dredging up that past and making us wallow in it. I'm just telling you how it impacted me."

"Well, I think we're even, now that there's a video of you making out with one of my teammates."

I cock a brow. "Not quite the same as a threesome in a hot tub, RJ, and you know it."

He makes a face. "Let's never bring up either of those things ever again."

"Deal."

We're both silent for a while before RJ speaks again. "I think when we tried to fix things between us, maybe we swung too far in the opposite direction, especially after Dad passed."

"I can see that. I just want RJ my brother, not this weird dad-bro hybrid. I love that you have my back, even when I make stupid mistakes, but more than anything I want to feel like we're equals, not like I'm the kid sister you need to take care of."

"I can't promise I won't be protective, because that's just me, and if Bishop screws you over, I'll beat his ass, but I'm going to do my best to just be your brother."

"You can't beat his ass."

"I actually have his permission."

"Why would he give you permission to do something like that?"

RJ gives me his "come off it" look. "Because he has it bad for you."

"You really think so?"

"I don't think, I *know*. And can we address the fact that you hooked up with the one guy on my team I hate?"

"It's not a hookup, and you let me move in across the hall from him, so you have no one to blame but yourself."

"I knew I should've moved you into the pool house when I had the chance."

"Hindsight is such a bitch, isn't it?" I consider my lack of foresight with Bishop. "The whole team is back?"

"Yeah. Bishop couldn't get off the plane fast enough."

"So he's probably home now?"

"There's a good chance. You want me to drop you off at the condo?" RJ offers.

I don't want to make Bishop wait any longer than I already have. "I think home would be a good place for me to go."

He turns the car around, and I send a message to Pattie and Jules that I'll have to take a rain check on brunch. It's time to stop burying my head in the sand.

I send Bishop the message I should have days ago.

CHAPTER 27
UNDERWEAR DECLARATIONS

Bishop

Things I should have done *before* leaving for a series of away games:

A. rescheduled my cleaner to come the day before I get home;

B. done my laundry (or had my cleaner do it);

C. changed my goddamn bedsheets;

D. ordered a bunch of shit to prove to Stevie that I'm it for her and she's it for me, and fuck everyone else and what they think;

E. shaved my balls.

Things I did before I left for the series of away games: none of the above.

So as much as I want to knock on Stevie's door and force her to deal with me the second I arrive on the penthouse floor, I have a bunch of shit to take care of.

Nolan is sitting on the couch, watching TV and eating carrots and some kind of dip.

I take in the pigsty that is my apartment. "Nice of you to pick up after yourself while I was gone."

"I'm taking it you still haven't talked to Stevie," he says through a mouthful of chewed-up vegetables.

"Not yet." I pause and pick up the can sitting on the coffee table, ready to give my brother hell because it's barely noon and he's drinking, until I read the label. "Since when do you drink nonalcoholic beer?"

"Uh, since the past week, I guess." Nolan runs his hands over his thighs, almost like he's nervous.

"Did something happen while I was away?" Nolan drinks light beer most of the time, and he always balks at me when I get him a six-pack of the fake-out stuff, since he's really not supposed to drink at all.

"I had an incident a while back." He chews on a nail.

"What kind of incident?"

"I misplaced my insulin, and Stevie helped me out."

"What? When the fuck did that happen?" And why the hell didn't Stevie say anything to me?

"It was during your last away series, before the viral video. I asked her not to say anything because I didn't want you to worry more than you already do. She took me to urgent care, and we had a talk about me taking better care of myself."

I motion between us. "You and I have that fucking talk all the damn time."

He shrugs. "I know. I guess I just never really realized how hard it was on you. Or how selfish I was being until she pointed it out. So

I figured it would be a good idea to take better care of myself so I can keep being a pain in your ass for as long as possible."

I get a tight feeling in my throat. "Right. Okay. Well, that's good. I'm glad."

"Yeah." He nods like a bobblehead.

"I'm always going to be here to make sure you're taken care of," I say, because it's true. "But it sure would be great if you valued your life as much as I do."

He clears his throat. "I know. I get that. I don't want you to feel like you can't live your life because you're afraid of the way I'm living mine. I realize the best way to make it easier is for me to take my diabetes seriously so you don't have to worry as much."

I blink a bunch of times and rub the back of my neck. "That's really good to hear, Nolan."

"I figure you'd need me to be around for dating advice eventually." He grins.

I roll my eyes. "I already told you. I don't need dating advice."

"Oh really? Does that mean you've fixed things with Stevie?"

"Not yet. I'm about to, though, right after I clean this mess up." I motion to myself and head for the hall, pausing to squeeze his shoulder as I pass. It's as sentimental as I'm willing to get with him.

"I love you too, bro!" he calls after me.

"Yeah, yeah," I mutter, but I smile as I drop my duffel on my bed. At least I have one less thing to be concerned about.

The cleanliness of my apartment is not my first priority, since we can talk at Stevie's place, but the personal grooming and gift buying need to happen before the door knocking.

I shower, shave all the important parts, and head back out to buy nice things for the woman I want as my girlfriend, hoping that by the end of the day that's exactly what she'll be. I buy two hundred dollars' worth of chocolate and an equally expensive bouquet of flowers. I'd stop and grab a pizza, because it's kind of our thing, but I'd prefer not to have olive-pineapple breath in case we make out later. Also, my hands are already pretty full.

I step out onto the sidewalk, prepared to return to my apartment and have a long-overdue conversation with Stevie. The sun has disappeared behind the clouds, and it's started to rain. Perfect. I didn't have the foresight to bring an umbrella with me, so there's no way to hide from the rain. I'm waiting at the crosswalk for the light to turn when my phone buzzes. I shift the giant bouquet of flowers and adjust the bag of chocolate that's cutting off the circulation in my forearm so I can fish it out of my pocket.

The screen lights up with an alert that I have a new message from Stevie. *Fucking finally*. I thumb in the code, getting it wrong twice before I slow down and type it in correctly, and Stevie's message finally pops up.

> I'm sorry it's taken me so long to respond. I'm ready to talk whenever you are.

I begin composing a response, asking if she's home and telling her I'll be there soon, when the light changes and people start moving. I trail behind the group because I'm not the best multitasker and I'm trying to avoid getting my eye poked out by an umbrella.

One second I'm holding my phone, about to press send, and the next some lunatic cyclist is weaving between me and an elderly lady. He almost takes her out but swerves at the last second and bumps me instead. My phone goes flying, skittering across the pavement, which would be fine, except a goddamn cab pulls forward and runs it over. Based on the crunch, I'm thinking I need to replace my phone.

I look up at the sky. "Are you serious with this shit?"

Obviously karma is an asshole like me, because the drizzle turns into a downpour.

The little old lady who almost got run over by the cyclist gives me a disapproving look and ambles across the street under the cover of her umbrella. I scoop up my ruined phone. The best plan is to go home and see if Stevie is there before I worry about replacing it. Besides, if the SIM card is still functioning, I'm sure I can slide it into one of the old phones in my kitchen junk drawer.

I'm soaked by the time I get to my apartment. The living room is empty, and there's a note stuck to the door. I don't bother to read it, since I have more pressing things to take care of. I drop everything on the coffee table and shuck off my wet clothes. I'm down to my boxer briefs when there's a knock on the door.

I don't consider my lack of clothing as I throw it open.

Stevie stands in the hallway, lavender hair spilling over her shoulders. She's wearing a sports bra and a pair of those running shorts, her cheeks flushed like she's been running, or something.

"Hi." Her eyes sweep over me, and she shifts from foot to foot.

"Hey." Well, we're off to a great start.

"Did you—"

"I just—"

She bites her lip, that plush bottom lip that I waited weeks to finally nibble on and that I'd really like to nibble on again, but after we talk.

"I thought I heard the elevator a minute ago," she says.

"I got your message, but then my phone was run over by a cab and I couldn't respond, so I came straight home. I was planning to knock on your door."

"But you wanted to get dressed for the occasion first?" One corner of her mouth tips up in an uncertain half smile as she motions to my boxers. They have a bull's-eye over the crotch.

"It's raining and I forgot an umbrella; my clothes got soaked." I want to jam my hands in my pockets, but I don't have any. "Can we talk?"

"I was hoping we could."

270

"Here? Or should we go to your place?" Since I didn't read the note stuck to the door, I'm unsure if my brother is still home or not.

"My place works." Stevie takes a few backward steps toward her apartment, and I follow. It isn't until we're inside her place that I realize I probably should've put on pants, but I'm here now, and I don't want to leave again.

She reaches for a hoodie hanging from a hook at the front door. But I cover her hand with mine. "You don't need to do that."

"So we're going to have our relationship talk half-dressed?"

"Seems like our best conversations take place like this, don't you think?" Am I trying to lighten the mood? Definitely. Deflect? Also a yes.

She doesn't make another move to cover up, though, so maybe she agrees.

"I'm sorry," we say at the same time.

At what is likely my confused expression, she adds, "It wasn't fair of me to stay silent for an entire week."

"You needed time." I give her words from last Sunday back to her. I generally deal with stuff as soon as it happens, but I get that girls are different, and it was a pretty messed-up situation. My not dealing with it wasn't all that helpful either. "And I should've addressed the video or found a way to manage it, but I generally tend to ignore social media stuff, which probably wasn't the smartest move in this case. At least that's what everyone's been telling me." I really wish I had pockets to jam my thumbs in, but my lack of pants makes that impossible. "I'm not really used to everyone giving a shit about my personal life."

"Me either. Usually that's my brother's thing, not mine."

"But I should've done something instead of nothing. I just . . . I didn't know what. And you wouldn't talk to me. So going on record that I wanted you to be my girlfriend but that I wasn't sure if you were still interested seemed pretty weak. Not that this is any better. I have flowers and chocolate for you, which, when I say it out loud, also sounds pretty damn weak too." I run a hand through my hair. "Shit. Maybe I really do need some lessons in dating, like Nolan said. Maybe I should've put myself on the line more? I could've made a video or something declaring my feelings for you." I wish I would've thought to do this sooner. It might've cleared shit up a lot faster.

Stevie bites her lip and peeks up at me from under her lashes. "I don't need you to combat a video with a video, Bishop."

"Okay. I won't do that, then." I'm kind of relieved about that. I hate interviews in general, and I have zero practice making declaration videos. "I wish we could do over the morning after, though, or even when I kissed you. It would've been better if that had been just ours."

"Me too. I mean, I wish I'd reacted differently the morning after too." Stevie twists her fingers together. "I really haven't been fair to you, Bishop."

"Uh, okay?" I fully expected that I would have to get down on my knees and grovel, or at least apologize several times in succession for not dealing with the video or pushing her to talk. Most of the time I'm not invested enough to do the groveling part. This time it's different, though. "Can you expand on that?"

"Come sit with me." She links our fingers and leads me toward the couch. I settle into the corner, and she takes the cushion beside mine, keeping our fingers twined still. "I've spent the past decade hiding who my brother is, not taking into account how his fame affects anyone but me, and by doing that, I forced myself into a box, and all the people I care about along with me, including you."

"I get it, though, why you wouldn't want to put yourself at risk like that. I mean, I have to deal with the press and social media, but I can pay someone to manage that stuff for me, where you can't."

"I appreciate that you understand my position, but I don't want you to make excuses for me." She tips her head to the side. "I actually liked that you were one of my brother's teammates. It meant I didn't have to worry about you wanting to be around me for any other reason than I was helping you. And you hated each other, so for me that was another win, because you weren't with me all the time because you wanted to get in with him. It had nothing to do with RJ at all, and I didn't want to share that with anyone."

"But then I came to that event with you," I supply.

She nods. "I should've expected all the attention, but instead I buried my head in the sand like I always do. I fooled myself into believing it would be like every other night we were together, and that's my fault. I shouldn't have made you hide along with me. If I'd chilled out about it, then maybe the first thing on social media with the two of us wouldn't have been a stupid viral video that everyone freaked out over, including me."

"If I'd made a move before that night, there might not be a viral video." I feel like I need to take some of the blame for this.

"You were trying to follow your coach's orders." Stevie smiles softly and sighs. "So I'm sorry for the way I reacted, for not being able to handle it, and for telling you I needed time to think and then not responding to your message right away, but I had a lot of emotional baggage to unpack."

"And now that you've unpacked it, how do you feel about everything?"

"Like I wish I would've handled things differently in the first place."

"Sort of like how I wish I hadn't been such an asshole when you first moved in." I give her a half smile.

"The boner-killer insult was pretty unforgettable."

"I was in a mood." I lift our clasped hands and press my lips to her knuckle.

"So rare for you."

"The boner-killer comment was bullshit anyway, and you know it." I lean in closer, fingering a lock of pale-lavender hair. "This past week without you was awful. I hated it. I hated not talking to you, not having you up my ass about workouts, not seeing your face, even if it was on a stupid tiny screen."

"I hated all of those things too."

"I can deal with away games as long as I have you when I get back."

"To stretch you out?"

I roll my eyes, which I realize is usually her reaction, not mine. "Can you ever *not* be pithy?"

She cringes. "It might be my defense mechanism."

"Turn it off for a second, 'kay?"

"Sorry." She presses her lips together.

"I want to be the olive to your pineapple." I smooth my thumb along the edge of her jaw, and she tips her head back: an unconscious reaction, I'm sure, but it says everything words can't. For so many reasons we probably shouldn't fit together, but we do.

She laughs. "I told you it would grow on you."

"I'll never openly admit I like it, though." I cup her face in my palms and dip down and brush my lips over hers. "My whole world is better with you in it, Stevie."

"Mine too."

"I want to take you on dates, in public places. I just want to be with you."

She exhales a shuddery breath and whispers, "I want the same."

"I don't want to have to hide how I feel about you anymore."

"Me either."

I grab her by the waist and shift her so she's straddling my lap. There are a million way more romantic ways I could do this, and I consider running across the hall to get the flowers and chocolate, but we're here, and mostly naked, and I'm thinking this is a pretty convenient setup, so the flowers can wait.

"I want to tell you something important."

"Okay." She laces her fingers behind my neck.

"I love you."

Her eyes are soft and a little watery. "I love you too, Shippy."

"I want to hate that nickname, but coming from you it's not so bad."

"It probably helps that I'm mostly undressed and sitting on top of your hard-on."

"Probably."

She presses her lips to mine, and we spend the next two hours showing each other how we feel with actions and not a whole lot of words—except some dirty ones.

CHAPTER 28
DISGUISE NOT NEEDED

Stevie
One week later

"Please tell me you don't go to all this trouble for every game." I'm currently at a spa getting pampered. Spas and pampering have never been my thing. Having someone do my hair, makeup, and nails is excessively indulgent—but it might grow on me.

"Depends on where we are in the season. For playoff games I go all out, but regular season no," Violet says. An aesthetician is currently bent over her hand, affixing a jewel and a tiny Seattle team decal to her nail. I think that would drive me bonkers, but she seems to love it. "Back when Alex was on the ice, I used to get my beaver BeDazzled for special games."

"Your beaver?"

She motions below the waist.

"Seriously?" She's not laughing, so I have to assume she either has a great deadpan or she really has BeDazzled her lady bits.

"Oh yeah, and if you're not too vigorous about the business, it'll last a week or so. They do that here, if you're interested."

She's definitely serious. "Uh, I think I'll pass."

Violet smiles and nods knowingly. "Probably smart since this is your coming-out party, and I'm assuming that boyfriend of yours is going to want to get down and dirty later. Save the beaver-dazzling for a time when he can really appreciate it."

I've decided I really like Violet, despite the fact that most conversations with her leave me blushing.

After three hours at the spa, we head back to Lainey's to get ready. I dyed my hair again last week: a pale aqua that gradually brightens at the tips. This will be my first official game as Bishop's girlfriend, and to say he's excited about it would be one hell of an understatement.

I change into jeans and a hoodie with Bishop's name and number on the back—I'm not giving up comfort just because my hair, nails, and makeup have been done. Lainey wears her jersey, but the back of hers reads **MRS. BOWMAN**, which is super cute.

My brother has a driver named George who's available for events like this, so once we're all dressed and ready, we head to the arena. We don't have to go through the same doors as everyone else, and there's a box reserved for us, although if we want to sit in the prime seats, we can do that too. I decided I should rip the bandage right off, so we're behind the bench, close to the ice.

The urge to hide under my hood is strong, but we settle into our seats, other girlfriends and wives taking up the ones around us. I've met most of these women thanks to Violet's "movie club." In reality, it's mostly an excuse to get together when the guys are away, eating snacks, drinking, and hanging out while we talk through movies, or pausing and rewinding scenes when the heroes are shirtless. So far the theme seems to be superhero movies. Regardless, it's been fun.

As I sit there absorbing the excitement of the fans and taking in this amazing group of women who support and love these men, I realize that I've missed out on a lot over the last few years. "I should've come to a game sooner."

Lainey squeezes my hand. "It's okay that you weren't ready until now. Sometimes we need to take baby steps. I only started sitting behind the bench at the end of last season, so the fact that you're jumping right in with both feet is a good thing. And we can pretend for RJ's sake that he's the reason you're really here." She gives me a wink.

The volume of the crowd rises to a frenzied pitch when Seattle takes the ice. I sit up straighter, clapping and whistling along with everyone else. Bishop skates across the rink, expression serious, which is pretty typical, until RJ elbows him in the side and nods in our direction.

Bishop's gaze follows his, and he scans the arena, and that serious expression turns into a huge grin when he finds me. I can feel my cheeks heat when he winks in my direction, but he doesn't do anything to overtly draw attention my way.

"Oh my God, look at how smitten that boy is. I am so glad I put bets on tonight's game as your coming out," Violet says to me, grinning widely.

"Is that what the hair and nails and stuff was about?" I ask.

"Just trying to be helpful. You know, I called it at the preseason party. I knew Winslow would have a girlfriend in our ranks before long, and here you are." She seems all proud of herself, like she's the reason we're together.

Lainey leans forward so she can address Violet. "Didn't you want me to introduce Stevie to Kingston?"

"Oh my God, seriously?" I snort-laugh. "As if." Kingston is a really nice guy, but I've never met anyone so straightlaced in my entire life. He looks like he should go door to door and canvass people to join his new religion. "Besides, King's had a girlfriend forever."

"That's beside the point. I was trying to get a rise out of Bishop, and it worked: he and RJ got all snippy with each other, and I knew something was going on there." Violet rubs her baby belly and smiles. "And I was right. Maybe I'm part psychic."

"Or maybe you already knew that Stevie and Bishop were neighbors, since you're married to the team coach," Lainey offers.

"It's more fun to pretend I have psychic powers."

Violet's attention shifts to the right, and she waves enthusiastically, blowing a kiss in the direction of the bench.

The team coach, her husband, sends a wink her way as the rest of the team shuffles down the bench. Once Bishop is seated, he turns and makes the "I heart you" gesture, which gets him a ribbing from the teammate next to him and an eye roll from my brother.

My heart is all light and fluttery in my chest, at least until the game starts. I'd forgotten how exciting it can be to watch live hockey. It makes me miss my dad, and I have a moment of sadness over the fact that I've lost out on so many opportunities to see my brother play, mostly because of my own fears, which I'm beginning to see weren't all that logical.

The game is amazing, especially when Bishop scores a goal in the second period, giving them the lead, and RJ scores in the third. Seattle ends up winning the game 4–2. We wait for the crowds to clear before we leave the arena and head to the restaurant to celebrate with the team.

Highlights from the game and interviews play out on TVs above the bar, but the sound is off. Bishop appears on the screen, his serious expression shifting to a smile when he answers one of their questions and winks at the screen. I'll have to watch that later, when we're home.

We're there for a good half hour before the team shows up, and despite the fact that the back room of the restaurant is reserved for them, there are a huge number of fans clamoring for their attention.

Bishop doesn't blatantly ignore the fans, but he's obviously distracted as he scans the crowds, failing to smile for the pictures people keep snapping. He only grins when he spots me from across the room.

Someone is in the middle of saying something to him, and he walks away.

I shake my head, laughing as he bulldozes through people to get to me. When he reaches me, he wraps his arms around my waist and lifts me until my feet no longer touch the ground. "Did you hear me dedicate my first goal of the season to you, bae?" he mumbles in my ear, lips moving to my neck.

"What?"

He sets me back on my feet and runs his fingers through my hair. "When they were interviewing me, I told them my first goal belonged to you."

"You did not."

"I did." His smile falters. "Is that okay?"

I place a reassuring palm on his cheek and smile up at him. "Of course it's okay, but I had nothing to do with that goal. It was all you."

"You being here helped. I want you at all my home games from now on. That's totally reasonable, right?"

"I'll see what I can do." I tug on his tie. "Come here."

When our lips are an inch apart, he tugs my hood up.

"You don't need to do that. I don't mind if people know I'm yours and you're mine."

He grins. "Good to know, but I'm not planning to keep it PG, so I thought we could use a little cover."

He holds the edges of my hoodie and kisses me. I don't care that people are watching or that they're probably taking pictures. We only come up for air because of the catcalls and the shouts to get a room.

"Stop manhandling my sister, Winslow!" RJ claps him on the shoulder.

Bishop tucks me protectively against him. "I was saying hi to my girlfriend."

I push against his chest, and he releases me, his expression reflecting his worry. I put it there, along with my brother's uncertainty, so I do the one thing I can think of to help ease their fear that this is all too much for me. "Lainey, can you take a picture of us?"

"Of course."

I pass her my phone, and my brother shifts away, but I grab him by the sleeve. "I want one with both of my favorite hockey players."

He seems surprised at first, but then his face lights up, and I know that this has been a long time coming and that it's exactly what we need to help bring us closer together, like we used to be.

I push my hood back and run my fingers through my hair to smooth it out, then smile while Lainey snaps pictures of me first with RJ, then sandwiched between them, and finally just me and Bishop. And then I spend the rest of the evening enjoying time with the people I love the most, wondering why the heck it took me so long to realize that who I am doesn't change at all, regardless of who I'm dating or who my brother is.

EPILOGUE

BAE, FOREVER

Stevie
Eight months later

"Bishop? Are you almost ready to go?" I call out as I load food and some random gifts for Kody into a tote bin. His birthday was over two months ago, but I have a hard time not buying something cute if I see it. It's my job as his aunt to spoil the hell out of him. Besides, Bishop was with me when we went party shopping, and the second I see something I like, he always tosses it in the cart. If I try to return it to the shelf, he threatens to make a scene.

The thing I've learned about Bishop in the months since we started dating publicly: he gives zero fucks what people think. It makes me appreciate the lengths he went to when we first started spending time together to make me feel comfortable and unexposed.

"Almost. You need help with that?"

I glance up to find my boyfriend's package at eye level. It's covered by a pair of boxers with the phrase **CHECK OUT MY PACKAGE** stamped on the front in warning-sign-yellow letters.

"Seriously? We're supposed to be at my brother's in half an hour. I told Lainey I'd help her set up. And I have all the balloons." I motion to the ridiculous number of bags and boxes I'm bringing to the team's end-of-year party and then to his mostly naked body.

Lainey would've been more than happy to order everything for this party, but I love decorating and being crafty—as long as I don't have to deal with people like Joey, who incidentally was fired a few months ago for hooking up with several of his clients. The hooking-up part itself is frowned upon in general because of sexual harassment issues. It was made that much worse when the women found out he was sleeping with more than one of them. Even better, they confronted each other and him in the middle of the gym. It was epic. And karmic.

Bishop stands with his hands behind his back, wearing a half smirk. "We've got plenty of time, and I have a gift for you."

I cock a brow. "I love you, Shippy, but your presenting me with your dick as a gift isn't going to fly."

"My dick is not the gift. At least not right now."

"Then why are you still in your underpants?"

"Because I don't want you to wrinkle my clothes when you get all excited about what I got you."

I roll my eyes but give in because I know we're not going anywhere until he gets his way. "Okay, fine. What's the gift?"

"There are two. Pick a hand."

I tap his left shoulder, and he withdraws his hand from behind his back. He uncurls his fist, revealing a key chain that reads **HOME SWEET HOME**. "We got the house."

"What? When? Oh my God!" I launch myself at him, wrapping around him like a koala bear.

He laughs and hugs me back as he deposits me on the closest waist-high surface, which happens to be the counter. "I got the call this morning. We have papers to sign tomorrow, but I wanted to tell you before we got to your brother's so we could share the good news with them."

"This is so awesome!" I cup his face in my hands and kiss him, pulling away before he can deepen it. "RJ's going to be so excited! This is perfect! I can help out with Kody, and we'll be able to have barbecues this summer, and now my mom can visit and stay with us or RJ—whatever is easiest." I kiss him again. "Are you sure you can handle living down the street from my brother? He's probably going to stop by all the time. Possibly unannounced." I attach my lips to his again.

"He'll learn to call in advance if I answer the door naked," Bishop mumbles before I sweep his mouth with my tongue.

A few weeks ago, a house down the street from my brother went up for sale. With the penthouse lease being up at the end of June, Bishop thought it would be a good idea to call the Realtor. It's a big house, bigger than what we need, but it has lots of room to grow and for company in the form of my mom, or Kyle and his family, and Bishop's mom. Nolan recently moved out of the penthouse and into an apartment of his own—with Pattie. They met at a game in the fall and exchanged numbers, and they've been pretty much inseparable since.

I go for the hem of my shirt, ready to celebrate with a quick orgasm, but Bishop disconnects our mouths and covers my hand with his. "Hold that thought. There's still gift number two."

"How are you going to top a house?" My grin falters when he bites his lip and suddenly looks nervous. "Bishop?"

"I love you," he says.

"I love you too."

He nods, like he's finding some resolve, and drops down to his knee. It puts his face level with my crotch.

"Uh, what're you doing?"

"This worked a lot smoother in my head." He grabs the edge of the counter and pushes back up to a stand. Which is when I notice he's clutching a tiny box in his fist.

"What's this?" I grab his hand with both of mine and try to pry it open, but Bishop is a lot stronger than me.

He uncurls it slowly to reveal a velvet jewelry box. My heart stutters, and I meet his gaze with a questioning one of my own. The last time I saw a box like this was when I helped my brother pick out Lainey's engagement ring.

"I know we didn't start off all that hot, and I'm also aware I'm not the easiest guy to deal with and that I can be moody and difficult, and sometimes I stick my foot in my mouth because I don't have a lot of tact, but I'm a way better version of me when I'm with you, Stevie. I love you so fucking much. And I promise I'm going to keep working on loving you like you deserve to be, and if you'll let me, I'm going to try to do that for the rest of my life." He flips the lid open, revealing a gorgeous ring with a pale-pink diamond.

"Are you asking me to marry you?" It's a dumb question—of course he is—but I'm a little floored. Bishop isn't really a hearts and flowers and jewelry kind of guy, although he does try. He likes to buy potted plants over cut flowers if at all possible, since I kill those more slowly. Usually he's more of a pizza and let's buy a house guy. Or at least I thought he was, until now.

"That was kind of the plan, unless you're not ready for that. Then we can forget about the ring and pretend this didn't happen. Maybe the house is enough for now? Should I try again in a year?" His eyes dart around, and he snaps the box shut and hides it behind his back.

"I don't want you to ask in a year." I tug on the arm hiding the ring. "I want you to ask me now."

"Are you sure? 'Cause I can wait if you need me to."

"Positive." I lean in close to his ear and whisper, "If you ask me, I promise I'll say yes."

He kisses me and flips the lid open again. "Marry me? Please?"

"There is absolutely nothing in the world that would make me happier."

He lifts the ring from its cushioned home and slides it on my finger. "Do you like the ring? I didn't want it to be too much, but if you don't like it, we can go back to the store and find something else—"

"It's perfect, Shippy."

"Yeah?"

"Yeah. I love it." I take his face in my hands and bring his mouth to mine. "And you, so much."

"You must, if you're willing to deal with me every day for the rest of your life." I can feel his smile against my lips as he wraps me up in his arms.

"I can't imagine my life without you and your ridiculous underwear in it."

"Good, because me and my underwear are yours forever now."

ACKNOWLEDGMENTS

As always, hubs and kidlet, you're my world. Thank you for supporting my dreams and letting me ignore the laundry and the state of my office more often than I should.

Kimberly, you're a unicorn. Thank you for being as fond of spreadsheets as I am, and for being on my team.

To my team at Montlake: thank you for making this such a fantastic experience, and for giving my hockey boys a fabulous home.

Deb, that retirement village in Florida is calling. I can see us years from now, embarrassing the grandchildren with inappropriate stories. Let's never change.

Leigh, I'm ever grateful that I popped into your messages and never stopped bugging you. Thank you for being a friend.

Mom, Dad, and Mel: I love you. You're incredible cheerleaders, and your support means the world to me.

Sarah and my Hustlers: it's an honor to have you on my side. I am eternally grateful for your love of books and for all your amazing support.

To Jenn, Sarah, Brooke, and my amazing team at SBPR: thank you for helping me bring my word babies into the world. You're a fabulous group of boss women, and I'm proud to work with you.

Gel, Sarah, and Angy: thank you for sharing your gorgeous talent with me. I'm lucky to work with such amazingly creative women.

To my reader group: thank you for always being so excited for new books, for what's coming next, and for coming with me on this wild journey!

Readers, bloggers, and Bookstagrammers: you're such an integral part of this community. Your excitement and enthusiasm for new stories is infectious and inspiring. Thank you for all you do.

My author friends in this community are such an amazing source of inspiration. I am so fortunate to be part of such an influential group of women. Deb, Leigh, Tijan, Kellie, Ruth, Erika, Susi: you inspire me with your passion and dedication and your continued unwavering support. I adore all of you. Marine, Julie, Kathrine, Laurie, and Lou: thank you for being such fabulous friends.

ABOUT THE AUTHOR

Photo © 2018 Sebastian Lohnghorn

New York Times and *USA Today* bestselling author Helena Hunting lives on the outskirts of Toronto with her incredibly tolerant family and two moderately intolerant cats. She writes contemporary romance ranging from new adult angst to romantic comedy.